Dust of the Universe
tales of family

V.S. Kemanis

"The Zephyr" was originally published in slightly different form in *The William & Mary Review*, "My Latvian Aunt" was a *Glimmer Train* Top-25 award winner, and the following stories were originally published in slightly different form in these print collections by the author: *Women I've Known, Stories*: "Conversation with a Biker," "What I'd Like to Say," "Occupational Hazards," and "Schizophrenia Indicated"; *Gray Zone, Stories*: "Like Love," "Lucky," "A Love-Hate Thing," and "At the Crypt."

Dust of the Universe, tales of family
Commended – SPR Book Awards 2014

ISBN-13: 978-0-9965909-2-1
ISBN-10: 0-9965909-2-7

℞ **Opus Nine Books**
•New York•

Praise for story collections by V.S. Kemanis

"Rich in metaphors and intensely provocative descriptive passages, these stories are to be tasted, savored, enjoyed and read over and over again. *Your Pick: Selected Stories* is a powerful tribute to this author's mastery of the art of creating not just a good story, but a story that needs to be read many times to appreciate the full power of its presentation." — *Readers' Favorite*

"Eleven compulsively readable short stories... Anyone who appreciates supple writing and fine storytelling will enjoy every minute spent reading these stories... A good deal of the pleasure in the collection comes from the writing itself. Kemanis knows how to build a story and keep it going." — *Foreword Reviews* on *Love and Crime: Stories*

"[Kemanis is] unarguably gifted...a great talent... There are stories here that I think I will remember forever. They've stayed with me in the weeks since I read them and make me smile even now as I call to mind their wonderfully flawed characters, their gentle humor, their twists and surprises and, without exception, the compassionate insight at their core." — *SP Reviews* on *Dust of the Universe*

"V. S. Kemanis is certainly one of the most intelligent writers I have read, writers of classics included. Her insight into human behavior is truly unusual... These are believable stories and believable characters... Unwaveringly fascinating." — *The Kindle Book Review* on *Everyone But Us*

"Quietly effective... Perfectly paced and brimming with mood and insight into our darker moments... Kemanis pulls off the difficult trick of imbuing the humdrum with a subliminal disquiet." — David Antrobus, author of *Dissolute Kinship*, on *Malocclusion*

Also by V.S. Kemanis

Dana Hargrove Legal Mysteries

Thursday's List
Homicide Chart
Forsaken Oath
Deep Zero
Seven Shadows
Power Blind

Story Collections

Everyone But Us, tales of women
Malocclusion, tales of misdemeanor
Love and Crime: Stories
Your Pick: Selected Stories

Anthology Contributor

The Crooked Road, Volume 3
Me Too: Short Stories
The Best Laid Plans
Autumn Noir

Visit
www.vskemanis.com

For my sisters and brothers,
Aina, Annette, Eva, Egbert, Jason, and Gregors,
with love

CONTENTS

☾ My Latvian Aunt

AUNT MIRDZA DIED in 2004 at the age of seventy-seven. I'd known her only ten years. My father's sixty-fifth birthday party was the occasion of our belated meeting, owing to one of those epiphanies that strike at the threshold to the sunset years—in Papa's case, a sudden regret at having shunned his sister ever since her scandalous marriage to an older man at the DP camp in Würzburg, 1947.

Mirdza and I were coaxed into attending the distant celebration with invitations we knew better not to decline, sent along with plane tickets to L.A., hers from Toronto, mine from New York. There were follow-up phone calls. "Your sister is coming—*and* your Aunt Mirdza." Papa was confident. "I also booked the Stanley Pendleton Trio." A big to-do, March 15, 1994. I went alone, leaving Marcus behind for a few days to get the kids off to preschool and kindergarten.

Years have passed. There's a Baltic look that sets in particularly hard from middle age on, when the eyes sink into the skull, the hair becomes thin and brittle, the face lengthens and yellows, and the jowls dip below chin level.

You'd think that I, being of mixed breed, would have been spared, but certainly, it isn't so. The other day in a health club locker room a young woman, a complete stranger, looked me dead in the eye and started to lilt happily in Swedish. It took a moment to register before I muttered something about, "just across the water," neither in Latvian nor Swedish.

I'd never learned my father's mother tongue. Upon landing in the States in 1950, Papa was so grateful to his new country that, when he married a coed from Bakersfield Junior College and started a family, he found no utility in passing along a language and culture that lay buried in the rubble he'd left behind. This hole in my upbringing dawned on me during college in the mid-1970s, spawning a righteous period of visceral indignation inspired by the newly emerging roots fad. The phase slowly dissipated, replaced with a misty-eyed swell at any mention of Papa's Atlantic passage by steamer. He is now gone, since 2001, my mother long before him, 1992.

The moment I first saw her is untouched in memory. Aunt Mirdza sat on a corner of the couch in Papa's living room, surrounded by aging Americans, most of them several generations removed from their European ancestors. Her identity jumped out in that quiet Latvian way just as Stanley Pendleton was finishing his Bill Evans-style piano solo in "What is There to Say?" My mystery aunt was stamped from the same press as her brother Karlis, the man who'd raised me, her countenance offering a preview of my own, thirty years hence.

Half of that thirty is now gone, time a witness to my face, gently sagging, revealing her in me.

* * *

*June 13-14, 1941, Night of Terror: Soviet Central
Government Deports Anti-Soviet Element, 15,500 Latvians*

"I was at the farm that day."

"How old were you?"

"Fifteen. Our neighbor to the south came over and said all sorts of people were being arrested. My parents and Karlis were in Riga. I wanted to call and warn them not to come, but the phone was cut off, which kind of scared me. Of course, I didn't know the same thing was happening in the city. Later we heard all kinds of horror stories. There were people we knew—the parents were taken and their new baby left behind, alone in the crib. Just shut the door on it. Things like that.

"The other neighbor, the one to the north, was somewhat on the pink side, a Socialist. I figured there's a safe place and his phone will be working, so I jumped on my bike and went over there, but a big truck was standing in the middle of his yard, the military police. I sort of blustered something about coming over for potato seeds or whatnot and rode out of there as fast as possible."

"Russians were deporting a Socialist?"

"Nothing made any sense. They owned their farm, so naturally they couldn't be Communist because they must be rich. If somebody didn't like you they informed against you. I still don't know why we weren't taken. My father was in the Latvian border guard and we owned a 300-acre farm. They took most of our land in 1940 and left only thirty acres, but they didn't take us.

"They were disorganized, and that could be the only reason we didn't end up in Siberia."

Vilnis was her love, a man seventeen years her senior. Mirdza was a few months shy of twenty-one when she told her parents that they might as well approve the marriage because soon enough there would be nothing they could do to prevent it.

This was the story she told, anyway, during the first of my yearly visits to her Toronto apartment. Having met, finally, at sixty-seven and forty, we latched onto all those wasted years as an excuse for silent anger at my father, a subterfuge for the disappointment we might have directed at ourselves. Easily, long ago, we could have arranged a meeting on our own. The grumbling, estranged siblings, Mirdza and Karlis, had never, really, lost touch. They habitually gossiped about one another with mutual acquaintances from DP camp days and occasionally exchanged preprinted Christmas cards, just to confirm the still-beating heart and unchanged address at the other end.

Not very difficult, then, for Mirdza or I to have asked Papa for a phone number or address, but we outwardly denied our choice of scapegoat, dropping hints with nasty little digs over coffee. "Here we sit together. Let's just call him up now, shall we?" Mirdza mused. "Let's not," I answered. Mean. We locked eyes and smiled because, although she'd surrendered to curiosity and swallowed her pride to attend the sixty-fifth, she certainly hadn't forgiven him for the original injury, his arrogant rejection of her lifeblood.

As children, the siblings had never gotten along, well before Vilnis so shockingly robbed the cradle. When asked to explain, Mirdza always gave the same answer, reducing their intractable conflict to a comfortable platitude: "Your father was a city boy and I was a country girl." Their family had an apartment in Riga and a farm thirty-five miles outside the city where Mirdza spent every possible moment, weekends, holidays, and summers, tending the pigs.

June 22, 1941: Nazi Invasion Interrupts
Soviet Deportation of Latvians

"It was only a week or so later. The Germans came in the middle of the night. In the morning there were fifty or more of them settled in the yard."

"Were you terrified?"

"Actually, we were happy. In a few weeks they occupied the whole country. There was no fighting, the Russians just ran, and we didn't have to worry anymore about being arrested. Life went on. The only people who had to worry were the Jews and the Gypsies and anyone reckless enough to resist."

Usually we sat alone at her small kitchen table, but not during that first visit when she began to offer her stories of Vilnis. I had brought my family along—as it turned out, the only time they would accompany me to Toronto. The folly of bringing the children slammed into us the moment we stepped into Mirdza's sparse, '60s-style apartment, decorated with oil paintings and handmade furniture wrought by the hands of her long-deceased, beloved husband. A cord of angst shot up my spine every time a child escaped parental grasp. "Don't touch!" can be said only so many times. No and no again and please come here to be clamped between the knees or tethered to the table leg. Please. My aunt is telling us a story.

This, in between her breaks from us, the trips to the four-by-six cement balcony for a cigarette. She was considerate in this way, in her own home, five floors up.

A black and white, miniscule snapshot of a young couple in '40s-style clothing was pushed toward me across the kitchen table with yellowed index and middle fingers, thready nails. "I said to them, either you can okay it now, or I'll just wait a few months and then there will be nothing you can do about it!" Said with a Canadian "ou" and two, hard little Latvian "t's" at the end. A glimmer of self-congratulation shone from her translucent blue eyes, so pale they verged on milky underneath the folds of slack lids.

That fog about her made me desperate to burn through it, to gather a complete picture of the love match, a chestnut-haired girl of nearly twenty-one and the inky-helmeted man of thirty-eight on their wedding day, standing vertical-legged in their best suits, the girl clutching a small bouquet of hand-picked flowers, no money for anything more. Just beyond the lens perhaps my father, a mere nineteen, looked on with a smirk of disdain. Get over it, Papa. Your parents eventually did.

I was confused about the twenty-one business, wondering if it was just part of her anecdote, a made-up fact for family legend. "Was that German or Latvian law, there in the DP camp?" What a stupid question out of all the great questions that could have been asked and answered when there was still time. This one never was answered, interrupted by six-year-old Trina. "Mommy! I'm going to throw up!" I grabbed Trina for a frantic dash to the tidy little john, where we hovered, luckily, over a false alarm as I silently thanked my little one for sparing the grout between all those inch-square floor tiles in colors of salmon, pearl, and caramel.

When we returned, Marcus was down on a patch of open floor wrestling with little Ryan while I, very embarrassed, apologized with the flushed girl in my lap, her head pushed up into the cozy cave under my chin. Mirdza gave a straight-backed smile and said with a sniff, "We never could have children." Of course I knew she was childless, but there was a certain awkwardness in that confession, delivered without a scrap of sorrow or regret.

It appeared then that she looked upon my children with a scientific, distant curiosity, those specimens of cell and gene descended from her brother. Not once did she touch them or attempt to engage them in conversation during that first visit or the single trip she made to my home, when the children were older and capable of human discourse. Against all reason it bothered me, her lack of grandmotherly ways, though I scolded myself for being so selfish.

On another visit, when we were alone, she explained, "I always thought it was because of the war. We were constantly hungry. Maybe it would surprise you what we thought about?"

Ears open, I awaited further nuance to her confession. The Childlessness of Mirdza and Vilnis.

"Not big juicy pork chops or cakes and cookies and whatnot. It was always bread. I thought and dreamt about bread, the smell and taste of it in my mouth." Her brow knit around the blight of hunger still engraved there. Finally she came to the point. "I lost my period for several years, you see, but I never did ask a doctor about it."

I didn't respond, not knowing quite how. "What a shame," should I have said? The enigma of her, everything about her, was neatly packaged within that rational, matter-of-fact delivery, at once suggesting and denying a cover-up or the possibility of deeper meaning.

"How wonderful!" should I have exclaimed? To be blessed with barrenness, given free rein in sexuality and art and nature in a dizzy time of political exile and personal liberation. To be a young girl defying her family to marry the man she loved, an artist, handyman, and craftsman. To be solitary lovers building a quiet, secluded life on that little farm in a clearing surrounded by woods and bordered by a crystal lake for summer swims in a rugged bit of Ontario. 1948 to 1967.

October 13, 1944: The Soviets Recapture Riga

"The Russians were advancing all summer from the east, pushing the German front toward the Baltic Sea. By October they were practically on our doorstep. We were all staying on the farm, thinking it was safer there. But then the Germans started to dig in."

"Dig in?"

"Making trenches in the garden, ready to fight. Then the shooting started. They were shooting left and right."

"There, on your land?"

"Yeah, in our garden. Nothing to it, I mean, you're so busy doing things you don't have time to be scared. You don't think about the future because you have to pack. We packed all kinds of stupid things. There were no trains naturally, so we drove the horses with two wagon loads.

"There was just one thing that really, really impressed me from the war, not the shooting, not any bombings. The Germans were withdrawing, their tanks and army vehicles taking up the whole highway and the refugees on horseback and in wagons, one after another, on the gravel shoulder. I was driving one of our wagons. There was a boy, maybe seven or eight years old on a huge horse, riding bareback. I don't know whether the horse shied or what happened, but the boy fell off and the horse stepped on his leg. I could hear the bones crunch. And of course he screamed and nobody stopped. You couldn't stop. You couldn't do anything, because the traffic was one by one. I can still see that boy on the horse.

"When we got to Riga we reorganized, made some backpacks from potato sacks and packed whatever we could carry. We gave everything else away, our horses and wagons, our apartment. I don't know who got them. And then we pushed onto a little boat headed for Germany.

"That night a Russian plane went over quite low, sort of limping back home. I was on deck sitting right beside the soldier manning the machine gun, shooting at the plane. And you know, if you have a weapon right there you're not the least bit scared! All that shining ammunition—you can see where it goes and it was fascinating."

One of my inherited treasures is an index-card sized plastic box containing Ektachrome 35mm slides and a teal and black colored plastic viewer that fits snugly in the palm of my hand. Unfold it, insert a slide against the translucent backdrop, press an eye to the crude magnifying glass, and magically they emerge in 3-D, Mirdza and Vilnis, their moments on this earth forever mine.

1952, 1956, 1961, in the woods, the clearing, Mirdza with the pig, Vilnis chopping firewood, slabs of bacon in the smokehouse, their new Ford, summer together on the shore of the lake. Cigarettes between their fingers in almost every picture, relishing the taste of tobacco in the brisk outdoors and in the yellow light of a close, wood-paneled bedroom. Mirdza, propped up against the headboard, is fully clothed in a dull, rust-colored sweater and plaid skirt, hands fisted together in her lap, knuckled around a jutting, burning cigarette as her soft, young, still round face, thirty-one years old, pushes up a shy, contented smile for her lover Vilnis, camera in hand. Just the two of them in that dim room with the single light, and there it is, on the nightstand! The little teak lamp that now graces my living room! "Vilnis G." is etched in cursive on the underside of the base, an imprint he left on all his woodwork and paintings with its assumption that anyone interested enough should already know the last name, Galdiņš.

They would have liked to live entirely from the land but needed to supplement their income. They both contributed. Vilnis was the relentless creator, most of it for Mirdza and himself, but reluctantly for money, designing wood furniture with distinctive hand-cut dovetail joints in woods of different hues, planed so perfectly smooth that the hand still wants to linger, caress, and stroke the living warmth that resides in these children of the soil.

His paintings, singular and disturbing, are composed of veneer shapes under oils in startling colors textured with a putty knife, deliberate, nothing haphazard or impulsive. The viewer, inexorably drawn, is the intended target of his images. Barren trees grope for the sun, a naked sliver of chartreuse moon floats in a dark-night spray of stars, an abandoned city of blue-gray skyscrapers thrusts heavenward. Empty and searching.

Mirdza's apartment was furnished with the smaller pieces of furniture and decorated with half a dozen paintings, each ingeniously hung with a jury-rig of string, paper clips, rug tacks, and double-sided tape. These methods were exposed after her death.

During their Ontario farm years, her monetary contribution was a part-time job she held for more than a decade as records keeper for their rural township. "It was the '50s and of course there were no computers and everything was on paper and done by hand. The real big deal was when we got a microfiche in '58 or '59 and began to store all the documents and certificates this way.

"Still, all the papers had to go through me. Every birth and death in our township."

In the first minutes of the visit when we discussed birth and death records, she asked me, as she usually did, "How are the children?" I responded, as I usually did, with the current list of their strengths and weaknesses in school, extracurricular interests, and recent illnesses. Follow-up questions were few to none. I didn't volunteer extended psychological insights or obsessive motherly gushing. They were my children. It was understood that I loved them boundlessly and achingly, spent my days and nights with them, had given up my career for them. Temporarily. She kept one ear open, would smile distantly and nod at each bit of imparted information.

"Will you be going back to the office one day?"

"Sure, I think so. My brain could use the exercise, and Marcus says," I laughed, "he says I'm really dying to get back. Anyway, the kids won't need me forever."

"Less than you think, perhaps."

I found this odd, almost offensive. "Yes, well…"

"At least, not when they get older," she put in, and my heart, a biased judge, took this as a calculated attempt to soften a blow which had been every bit as calculated.

May 7, 1945: German Unconditional Surrender
Leaves 150,000 Displaced Latvians

"It was only about seven months until the war ended, most of that winter. Luckily, my godmother took us in, somewhere in the middle of Germany. I had a job in a glass blowing factory and Karlis was in school. It snowed so much there were mornings I had to leave the house through the window on skis."

"Through the window!"

"No, really! The snow got that high! It was a tiny village, I can't remember the name. When the Germans surrendered, the Russians took over the town and we had the darndest time convincing the Americans we didn't want to stay. We had just run from the Russians! We had no country.

"That summer the Americans dumped us somewhere in Bavaria on a big farm, about twenty Latvians, mostly well-educated engineers and lawyers and mathematicians and whatnot. They all had to work in the potato fields in the summer heat, and I was the house Negro, the only one who could milk a cow, so there you are! I had it easy.

"And then we heard of the DP camps, so we went to Würzburg. That's where I met Vilnis. That's where we stayed, until 1948."

Each visit with Mirdza, after getting through the domestic small talk, I would leap time to emerge reincarnated as a fly on the cow's flank in 1942, or the tabby mouser on her lap in 1955. As yet unborn were Ry and Trina, my daily joy or leg iron, depending. Marcus was generous about my yearly solo treks, not wanting to repeat that disastrous family visit in 1995, happy to take three or four days off from work to be with the kids, using the excuse that we had no relatives or babysitters at the ready. Our relationship was built on this kind of cooperation, none of it a problem or a source of stress, although the limits were tested when it came to all my trips after Mirdza's death.

By then, the children were thirteen and fifteen, not really in need of a babysitter. But my return to Toronto, again and again, long after my aunt's body had been reduced to ash, might have been seen as a bit off. Marcus pretended not to notice. I see that now. To me, there was no question of the necessity.

Mirdza's friends arranged her funeral. She used to speak of them now and then. There were a few from her childhood in Riga, others she'd known in the DP camp, and newer acquaintances who were members of the Latvian Lutheran Church in Toronto. The most prominent names were Ruta and Osvalds, but there were others, Ilze and Janis and Darta and Imants. I'd never met any of them, an amorphous subset of graying displaced persons labeled "Mirdza's Friends."

Ruta was the one who called me. Her voice, with its pitch and accent so similar to Mirdza's, startled me almost as much as the news. "Mirdza's niece?" she confirmed after she'd asked my name twice. "Your aunt died yesterday, in the hospital." I hadn't known she was in the hospital. "They said it was pneumonia." The endgame to undiagnosed emphysema, I thought, or more likely, a diagnosis known to Mirdza and never mentioned. Her breathing had become progressively labored over the years, and there'd been a previous bout of pneumonia only the year before.

Ruta told me more than enough without the need to ask questions. I listened quietly, allowing my chest slowly to clog. Mirdza and a neighbor in her building were in the habit of checking on one another—something I hadn't known, additional evidence of my dereliction. The neighbor discovered her in bed, limp and feverish, and called an ambulance. She died two days later.

"I stayed with her the whole night through until the end," said Ruta.

The belated, once-yearly niece exhaled a "God bless you" with real gratitude.

"In the last few hours she couldn't talk at all. She was drenched in sweat, her breathing was nearly impossible, a big rattling sound, and she was curled up in a fetal position. I wiped the sweat from her forehead and told her that everything would be all right. Her eyes flew back and forth, searching my face and the room. I don't know what she could see."

"Vilnis, I hope," emerged without thinking.

Ruta paused and I dreaded her response, even worse, her silence for what it would tell me about her thoughts. "Yes," she said finally. "I think you may be right." Ruta would know—she'd been Mirdza's friend since Germany—but her voice was unreadable.

"How did you know where to reach me?" I asked.

"How? But she gave me your number some years ago, after Karlis died. She said to call you if anything happened."

I was dumbstruck.

"Perhaps you didn't know." She'd analyzed my silence. "Mirdza spoke of you often. And your little ones, Ryan and Trina, her great nephew and great niece. She showed me pictures. The school pictures you sent every year."

Yes, I had sent them, hadn't I? Weeks later I would see all the snapshots again, organized by year in a disintegrating, multi-sleeved plastic photo holder in her wallet, some sleeves fat with more than one, the most recent on top. It was then that I cried for the first time.

May 10, 2004: Treasure Hunters Discover
WWII Artifacts in the Baltics

"We buried anything valuable we couldn't carry. Most people did this. We weren't going to give the Russians any more than we had to, and of course we thought we were coming back. Anyway, we were hoping to come back."

I became the harvester of the personal effects, a responsibility willingly relinquished by my sister, who lived a world away in Hawaii. We were the only living relatives, and Mirdza died intestate, a surprise to us. The last time I'd seen her, shortly after her recovery from the previous bout of pneumonia, she'd made one of her dry little jokes that it was time to rewrite her will. She was so organized that this seemed likely.

But there was no will to be found in the apartment, no correspondence from a lawyer or evidence of a safe deposit box. I combed every inch, the desk, the bureau, even the kitchen drawers, warding off the sentry from the Public Guardian's Office, a square block of a man in a plaid sport coat with distrust smeared on his face, dutifully protecting an old lady's meager possessions from theft.

My first shock was to see him instead of Mirdza,

opening her apartment door under my knock, his dangling hand clutching my affidavit and birth certificate, faxed to him the day before. These documents should have been legally enough to convince him of my entitlement, but he clung to doubt with a benign, official sternness, standing briefly in front of each drawer I wished to open before stepping away.

When I reached up to grasp the frame of the chartreuse moon, he stopped me with a suggestion that the paintings and furniture could go to public auction. This was just too much, and I'm afraid I lost it. "These are family treasures!" I choked, teary eyed. He melted then and became a believer in me and perhaps the nicest man ever born, helping to load as much as we could fit into the rented van I had driven up from New York.

A few things I had to let go. Her desk. A hi-fi. Handcrafted bits of Vilnis I couldn't keep. A list was made and a receipt with my signature under the Public Guardian's disclaimer, sealing my liability to any surprise distant relation who might materialize, looking for a chartreuse moon.

Back home, after Marcus helped me find places for the three small pieces of furniture, I took up residence in the basement with my boxes of Mirdza, surrounded by the mental landscape of Vilnis, propped up against the walls. My family didn't see me for days, possibly I didn't eat, much anyway. Nights I spent on the musty couch the kids used for sleepovers, peering into the dark void with tears in my eyes, wondering what I felt about this woman who had spoken so unthinkingly of Jews and Gypsies and house Negroes, who'd inquired politely after my children like a stranger while treasuring the bragging photos in her wallet. This woman who'd been put aside by her own brother yet dearly loved by Vilnis and a nucleus of survivors.

It had hit me hard, the specter of perpetual obscurity, the regret of unasked questions, facts lost forever as I dug through the personal effects, jewelry, scribbles in Latvian, photos and slides, fascinated, angry. Why hadn't she told me about this person or that place? Why hadn't I asked her to describe Vilnis at work, paintbrush in hand, the expression he wore when imagining these bleak land-scapes and lonely heavens?

Hordes of ghosts, the undiscovered works, were scattered throughout Ontario, I was sure of it, never to be found. For twenty years with Mirdza on that little farm by the lake, Vilnis relentlessly created, the first decade in good health, the second in gradual decline. In 1958, an unnoticed cluster of mutant cells invaded his left lung, multiplied, obstructed, were carved away by the scalpel in 1963, and reemerged to multiply again, slowly eroding the mass into black soup.

Six paintings, a coffee table, a side table, a credenza with sliding doors. Smaller wood crafts, a tea tray, a traditional Latvian three-branched candelabra, an office wastebasket, the teak lamp. These were what I had, the desk and hi-fi left behind.

On the day of the funeral, before going to the church, my sister and I had spent an hour with Ruta and Osvalds in their spacious living room, drinking coffee. Centered on a wall under the two-story, cathedral ceiling was an enormous painting, a rectangle perhaps five feet high and three feet wide, its style and subject immediately recognizable. In this one, the barren arms of the trees reached beseechingly toward a pale, cold sun, the branches hollow and dead, like driftwood. The sight of it spurred my incipient confusion, precursor to an insatiable need. Discreetly, I inquired. Yes, they supposed, many more of his paintings must be out in the world, but they couldn't say where.

In my basement retreat, cross-legged on the floor, I inserted one slide after another into the little 3-D viewer and angled it up to the light, searching for clues. Melded into the images of their life together were his paintings and pieces of woodcraft, each of them known and recognized until—sharp inhale, beating heart—a sparkling blue image struck me with the thrill of an archeological find.

Vilnis sat on the couch, a burning cigarette clamped between thumb and two fingers in a masculine custom of old, looking cool and masterful as if to say, "This is my work." The large painting filled much of the wall behind him, caught with a sheen from the light of the flash bulb. A happy scene! He had painted six elongated V-shapes suggesting birds, each one rounded on top like the upper edge of a woman's evening gown. Individual yet social, they flew at angles in a careful hodgepodge, the most prominent among them painted in pure white, the others in graduated shades through a spectrum of blues— powder, periwinkle, cornflower, azure, iceberg—against a royal sky, indigo sun at center. Simple, this, the only truly happy image.

Letters and e-mails were written, photos enclosed

and attached, phone calls made. My actions were automatic, necessary, unassailable. The inquiries concerned an artist by the name of Vilnis Galdiņš and his creations, the intricate wood crafts and oil paintings of naked trees, lonely heavens, abandoned cities, and most important, the happy birds. I'd found a new focus to my search for more of her, my Latvian aunt.

Time and again, Marcus said, "Go." I drove, I flew, I drove again. Gallery owners, artists, curators, art aficionados, all looked at my photos with interest before lifting their eyes to gaze at me blankly. A million and one cups of tea were sipped with my aunt's friends as they treated me to stories of war, exile, renewal, admiration for Mirdza's strength and her husband's artistry, but offering scant insight into their private lives which had remained locked up and inaccessible even to their closest, longest allies.

Among these people I made but a single discovery, a small painting of the familiar trees hanging in the dining room of a modest home inhabited by a skin-and-bones old woman, her accent stronger than the rest, her voice slurred with stroke. Lidija she was called, perhaps—I thought she said—a cousin of Vilnis. They shared the same last name.

Back home from this trip I asked Marcus, "Why are you letting me do this?" Mirdza had been gone eight months.

Never in his life had he experienced an ethnic urge, the pull of ancestry. An "American mutt" is what he called himself if anyone asked. His eyes bore deeply into mine with tragedy, benevolence, resignation. I hid from them, turning my head to press a cheek into the soft material covering his muscled shoulder like a cloth habit, awaiting the sermon I deserved, a tug of the rein.

My priest said nothing, a strong, silent pillar of support to my madness as thoughts raced in my head, a vision of Lidija's face, her eyes, the droning playback of her words, the puzzling congeries. A shudder had gone through her, almost a shake of the head, signaling a barely suppressed recognition as I showed her the photograph I had made from the slide so that I could keep the precious original locked up at home. The happy birds.

"Do you know this painting?"

"Yes, maybe," she said while giving off another kind of look. How did I see it? The deception hidden in her ninety-year-old eyes. There was a secret she wanted to tell but knew she shouldn't. "Mukenzking house" it sounded like, but then she refused to say anything more about the "Mukenzking" family.

A click of connection. I broke away from Marcus and ran down to the dungeon where, amidst the scraps and scribbles was the one I sought, its significance previously unknown and ignored for its seeming irrelevance to anything Latvian. On an index card in Mirdza's hand was written "Mackenzie King House," an address, a phone number and another name, Francesca Veil-Cugina. Immediately I was on the phone with her, this Francesca, the woman who must know.

"My goodness!" she exclaimed. "Mirdza never said she had a niece! And you know, we only just heard! Poor thing. She stopped coming and we wondered what had happened but couldn't reach her or anyone else for the longest time."

"She was a friend of yours?"

"No, but yes, certainly we were friendly. A wonderful person she was. Her goddaughter V. lives here, and well, how about that! Here I am, talking to another V.!"

"I didn't know—"

"She's been so distraught, you can imagine. First, not knowing, and then, when she learned the news."

"May I speak with her please?"

"To V.?" Something caught in her throat. "I'm afraid she can't come to the phone."

I turned to see Marcus at the bottom of the stairs. Wilting slowly, he had the dejected look of a man left behind, his eyes a mirror for the intrigue that gleamed in mine. Even then, I knew that this story would be written, that the names would be changed to protect the living and the dead alike, that the goddaughter's name would have to be V., like Kafka.

"It's all right," I said to him, my hand trembling over the mouthpiece, but already I was plotting, my suitcase packed, my mind on the next plane, in the air, stepping onto the Canadian soil I had left only a week before, driving my rental car through Toronto, its streets by now so familiar, and into the outskirts on a street that was new to me. The long number in the address took me to the very end toward which I hurled at a dangerous speed, up a slight incline, leaving other houses behind, arriving at the threshold of a driveway identified by a drab brown plaque with its announcement in white lettering, "Mackenzie King House." Entering the drive, I snaked in among the trees and shrubs to find the sprawling apartment building hidden from the road, something that looked oddly like an elementary school.

There was a front desk where a doorman sat, looking more like a watchman in charge of the inner door, apparently locked.

I stated my name and asked, "Would you please ring the apartment of Francesca Veil-Cugina? If she's not in, I'll speak to V.—I'm sorry, I don't know her last name."

The servant gave a doubtful look but complied, using a phone at the desk to make the call, and soon a little woman emerged, her features of Mediterranean origin, a smile open and warm. I was greeted and ushered inside with a buzz, the watchman's hand under the desk.

The portal closed behind us with an irreversible sucking noise, giving rise to a suffocating claustrophobia as we traversed a long hallway. Francesca prattled on through the shock of new details coming into relief: a food stain on the upper sleeve of her pastel-print smock, the squish of rubber-soled shoes on linoleum, a man at the far end of the hall gently tugging on the hand of a childlike woman and the animal sound coming from her throat, echoing toward us.

"V. will be so excited to see you! She desperately misses your aunt. Mirdza always made sure she was well taken care of, you know." The tunnel narrowed, walls squeezing in. "Of course, I didn't know V. until she came here; she was in another home when she was young. I understand her parents died when she was just a baby."

"Who were the parents?"

"I could look that up for you. I believe the birth certificate is in the file."

A matter for the township records keeper, I could have thought. But by then we'd arrived at the door, all my assumptions shed like items of soiled clothing along the length of the corridor behind us, leaving me naked, quivering, and vulnerable, wanting but unable to run. Francesca knocked, flashed a card key, and pushed the door open a sliver, calling ahead in a soft, bright voice, "V.? You have a visitor!"

A low, rumbling human hum escaped the crack, and Francesca pushed the door wide to reveal, with a sudden burst, the glory of blue adorning the wall straight ahead of us, so close, on the opposite side of the small room. "The birds!" flew off my tongue in awe before I noticed her sitting—rocking—on the fully-made twin bed against the wall to our right.

"Birds!" she mimicked with an aimless swing of her head toward the painting and back to me, a momentary display of the wide-set, almond eyes. She stood and dropped her vacant gaze to the floor while shifting her weight from one foot to the other and back again in an endless, comforting, flat-footed rhythm, then laughed and raised her head, unashamed of the drop of spittle glistening on her chin.

There's a Baltic look that sets in particularly hard from middle age on. She displayed it in mild distortion, this V., a woman my age. Her face wore the mark of her parentage in a strange alchemic brew of juxtaposed images born from my little 3-D viewer, altered by an errant gene, and transformed by fifty years of time-lapsed photography to become the incarnation standing before me.

I knew her instantly.

And, in the next instant, I knew just as surely that, to honor the secrets of the dead, I would not say a word.

☾ Like Love

"OUR WIVES ARE cheating on us," the man said.

Harold, telephone to ear, tried to visualize a face. He'd failed to catch the name but recognized the voice as belonging to a man he'd met, very briefly and for the first time, about a month ago at a City Ballet fundraiser. The only image coming to mind was a perversely stiff handlebar mustache, waxed at the ends into tight curlicues, something that would cause any soft-skinned creature, woman or child, to cringe whenever the man pressed in for a kiss.

"Are you still there?" the man asked. "Did you hear what I said? This is a serious matter."

"Yes, sure, well. You say they're cheating."

"Cheating on *us*. To be more explicit, they're having sex." Cheating usually did mean sex, Harold knew, and he also supposed he knew what the man meant. Still, the words only grazed the top level of his mind, not fully penetrating as he wrestled with the visual image he needed, a more complete picture of this man, and now, of his wife. "Who are they having sex with?" asked Harold absently. "Or should I say, with whom?" concerned that

26

"whom" might have a plural form he'd forgotten.

The man gave a snorting laugh which became, all too quickly for Harold, a derisive guffaw. "With each other, of course."

"Of course," said Harold, now catching a glimpse of the wife and husband together, wondering how he could have remembered the man first, or rather his handlebar, without simultaneously envisioning the wife. The two of them had stood six inches apart while sipping champagne at the black-tie affair, exuding such a feeling of over-bearing largeness. Not large-magnanimous, but large-overweight and tall—and loud—the wife oozing over the edges of a slick, compressive gown, like the spongy raw dough in one of those pop-open canisters.

Harold, I want you to meet someone. Claire had engineered the meeting from opposite sides of the room, Harold allowing his wife to drag him, reluctantly, into this couple's presence, where he suffered their tactless airs while glancing wistfully around the banquet hall.

Harold must have fallen silent again, for the man said, "You have *nothing* to say about this? They're having an affair, I'm telling you. With each other."

"Um-hmm."

"Two women, two middle-aged women with grown children, doing God knows *what* together. You have no opinion on this? Two *middle-aged* women. You know what they look like. My God! Secret meetings, luncheon dates, and rendezvous. I know they've done it in my bed, probably yours too. Can you imagine? I've just found out, but I'm sure they've been at it for months."

"What did you say your name was?"

"My name?" He fairly yelled before expelling a noise of exasperation, a burst of air pushed from his lungs. Harold almost felt the hot breath coming through the telephone receiver, bringing to mind another image of this man. How could he have forgotten until now? That cigar, an expensive one no doubt, but still a cigar, sticking out the corner of the mouth, nesting under that thick canopy. It remained unlit, but still, it gave off such an offensive odor of tobacco that Harold had been shocked. The gall—threatening to smoke a cigar at a benefit dinner! Any refined or courteous person would never engage in such behavior, but perhaps the unwritten rules didn't apply to the likes of this man, one of the wealthy benefactors.

Harold couldn't remember the man's occupation, or lack of one. In either case, he certainly possessed a sizable fortune, something far beyond Harold's means, which had strained considerably under the weight of his unlikely contributory position of "Patron"—an obligation assumed strictly out of respect and support for his daughter Ronnie, a demi-soloist with the ballet company.

"My *name*, for God's sake!" the man jabbed. "Our wives have been seeing each other for *months* now!"

The oblique insult to Harold's memory knocked something loose, sending the wife's name floating up from a dark curl of brain, where it had been stored along with other information he was in the habit of ignoring. "Your wife. Dolly?"

"Yes. Dorothy."

"And, forgive me, I *am* quite bad with names. You are…?"

"Stanley Bridgeman. *E.* Stanley Bridgeman." The "E" emphasized and set off, like the gold lettering Harold imagined on the man's desk and wall placards.

"Ah, yes, and—that's right! Your son dances with City Ballet? Freddy?"

"Frederick. E. Frederick Bridgeman."

"Forgive me. My daughter has spoken of him as Freddy." Harold could see the entire family now, the son's prominent upper lip like the father's, *sans* handlebar. "You know my daughter, Veronica? She danced in *Pas de Quatre* last year. Did such a beautiful job, and she's only eighteen. Your Freddy, Frederick, is about the same age? Or a little older?"

Another exasperated burst of air. "I can't believe this! I've just told you our wives have a sexual relationship and you have no opinion on it. No reaction at all. You'd rather talk about the ballet while they flee to the Isle of Lesbos to live in a den of hedonism and selfish pleasure. Is it proof you want? You don't think I *know* this? Big red "C's" are scribbled all over Dorothy's calendar, and it's "Claire" this and "Claire" that all the time, and the credit card bills—have you checked your credit card bill lately? Spas and luncheons at hotels. My God, do you have any idea what happened here the other day? In my bed, on *my* side of the bed, a pair of pink panties! I'm sure you'd recognize them because they certainly weren't Dorothy's. 'Here,' I said! 'Here, what's this?' She took those panties in her hand and looked at them so carefully, as if this were such a mystery. Finally, she said, 'Oh. Those must be Claire's!'"

Harold imagined it, Dolly—such a large woman with

a big red mouth and too much perfume—holding a dainty pair of pink panties in her gorilla hand. Yes, Harold remembered those hands now, one on the champagne glass, the other waving fake, plasticky painted nails through the air, the fingers big and long and distended like an ape's. This woman was having "sex" with his own petite Claire. Reportedly.

"Well, I can't say that I've checked Claire's panty drawer lately—"

"My God, you're blind to this!"

"—and I find everything you're saying very interesting, but my opinion, if you really need it, is simply this. I'm not sure what your wife is up to, but I can say that the thought of my wife and yours together, in the manner you suggest, is absolutely absurd."

"Blind!"

"But I must say, I credit you with a lively imagination, and—" *And what?* "Thank you for the call."

At least the man had the sense to call Harold at his office. Possibly he'd searched the wife's address book, which likely contained only the cell and home numbers next to Claire's name. Too risky to phone Claire's fool of a spouse at home, he would have thought, and it was easy enough to look up Professor Harold Murkle at the university. As luck would have it, Harold had been alone in his office, between meetings with students, when the call came. Now, long after the unexpected conversation had ended, Harold was unable to quiet the man's voice.

What a marriage those two must have! Awakening slowly to the implications of the call, Harold couldn't get over his growing sense of pity for the man. Obviously that Stanley Bridgeman, with his "E." and all, was a kook or an alarmist, a man suffering from some deep insecurity with regard to his wife's affections. And what a strange manifestation of his fear—an obsession with homosexual liaisons! Why not suspect a "Charles" or "Christopher" as the big, red "C," a man who enjoyed seeing Dolly's abundant rear squeezed into microscopic pink panties?

E. Stanley, what an imagination you have! Maybe a midlife crisis of some kind or a misplaced anxiety. That was it—Dolly, the victim of Stanley's misguided homophobia. Wasn't the son a ballet dancer? A natural subject of parental concern about sexual orientation. Not that Harold subscribed to that view, and he'd certainly keep an open mind if Ronnie ever took up with a male dancer, but perhaps it was enough in E. Stanley's case to provide a basis for suspicion. No wonder the man's imagination had cross-circuited with all his worries about Freddy—his namesake, E. Frederick—that boy with the long upper lip and close-set eyes. Rather effeminate looking, as Harold recalled.

These thoughts worked on Harold's countenance, leaving a trail of grimaces, frowns, and grins as he finished up office hours, three meetings with students. These three were indistinguishable from any other students he might have seen at this time of the semester last year or ten years ago, each one concerned about his or her grade on the midterm exam in Art History 101A. One student, a pugnacious boy (about the same age as that E. Frederick), negotiated hard like a used car salesman: "This is definitely a B, not a C. If you change it to a B, I'll give you an extra credit paper this week."

Virtually anyone if not Professor Murkle, a recognized expert in the field of Impressionism, could see that the boy's exam merited nothing higher than a C. No, the Professor wasn't about to besmirch his reputation for tough but fair grading on this one. "Can you explain then, just explain" (the boy's face pouting with adolescent belligerence) "what exactly is the difference between my exam and a B exam? Just *what* exactly?"

Harold looked at that face, knowing what he knew and knowing what the boy didn't, certain that an explanation would be futile. Never would this student understand the refinement of opinion and subtlety of insight that were required for a "good" answer—yes, "B" meant something better than average—to the exam question: "Identify two highly acclaimed Monet landscapes; for each, discuss the actualization of technique and emotional effect."

Of course, Harold could have gone into the issue in depth. An explanation for his grading decision existed, fully supported by a yardstick of standards embedded in his consciousness from years of training and a sensitive intuitive cognition of artistic media. Subjectivity was involved; no way to get around it. He wasn't teaching something exact and objective like calculus or biology. But how could a mere boy ever accept that his subjective opinions were immature and inadequate? Why should Harold attempt an explanation of the underlying reasons for his opinion which, among men of his own stature and learning, was indisputable?

And so, he told the boy: "Go look at Monet's work

again, steep yourself in it completely, compare the paintings to the descriptions in your essay and then come back and convince me, if you can, that you've given me more than just an average paper. Your words must attempt to rise to the level of that mastery in the work. You've given me a superficial mimicking of textbook phrases. It shows some knowledge, an average understanding, no more. Go back and try harder next time. That's all I can say."

Harold managed an encouraging smile, for he didn't harbor any malicious feelings for the boy, didn't really wish him to fail. And the student actually went away looking as though he'd been dealt a fair deal. At least he was gone without another word, almost the same way that E. Stanley had suddenly fallen quiet at the end of their conversation an hour earlier, in immediate response to Harold's unyielding and facially rational expression of opinion.

No, you didn't convince me, E. Stanley. Go back and try again. You didn't convince me.

And that's what Harold kept reminding himself all the way home.

As usual when Claire wasn't busy with a special exhibit, she was waiting at home for Harold, ready to pour wine in the den while dinner cooked in the oven. Red tonight—a clue about the meal to come. He was in the habit of one (small) glass before the meal and one during, just enough to aid the digestion and loosen the conversation.

Not that their conversation needed help, nothing like

the artificial assistance required by those Bridgemans, who'd looked quite rosy-cheeked and damp on the brow at the benefit dinner last month. Obviously, that pair needed the lubrication of intoxicants to aid their faltering lines of communication and assuage their unease with one another.

But Harold and Claire were alike in so many ways, from interests to temperament, that even their moments of silence—and there were quite a few of them, now that Harold thought of it—were comforting and anxiety free. If anything, the sole tension between them, slight as it was, emerged from their varying fields of interest and expertise in the art world: Harold, the impressionists, Claire, the post-modernists.

They were quiet people but enjoyed a gentle communication that came with their special understanding and appreciation of art, its emotive force working subtly on the passions. Yes, that was Claire—a quietly passionate woman, delicate, intelligent, and tasteful. Nothing at all like that garish, fleshy, painted ape.

Harold watched Claire as she filled each wineglass exactly three-quarters full, a tiny smile gracing her lips. Nothing devious in her face. It contained no secrets, no hint of a hidden, double life. Her expression told everything: a serene enjoyment of simple delights and complete satisfaction with her life. And with Harold? He imagined her on the bed lying beneath him, eyes closed, that same smile turning the corners of her mouth at the start of their intimate exchange, its breadth and depth growing with the swell of her pleasure.

You know what they look like. Yes, Harold *did* know,

and he liked what he saw, suspecting as well that he was supposed to, at some point during middle age, become disinterested in his wife's naked body, discretely turning away when she walked through the bedroom in bra and panties, making love only when urgency required in the pitch dark while fantasizing about younger flesh. These kinds of feelings were supposed to happen at some point, weren't they?

But Harold thoroughly enjoyed every glimpse of Claire's nakedness, as thoroughly as if they were both still twenty-five. At times she even accused him, with that little smile of hers, of following her into the closet when he knew she was about to change clothes, and of wandering into the bathroom while she was soaking in the tub. He never denied the accusations but responded with a smile of his own.

No doubt that E. Stanley had never experienced anything so delicious as a lifelong carnal interest in his wife. In all likelihood, the Bridgemans hadn't enjoyed sexual relations for months or years now, providing the source of E. Stanley's fears. But Harold and Claire were still quite active; why, they probably surpassed the national weekly average, whatever that might be, for healthy fifty-two-year-olds. Statistics must be out there, somewhere, and Harold decided, even as he sought to remember the day of his last intercourse with Claire, to do a little research in a library or bookstore, when he had the time.

"Enjoying your life of leisure?" he asked, taking the glass of cabernet from his wife. Immediately, he feared that his question might sound like an accusation when, really, he was quite pleased that Claire's position as assistant curator at the Modern afforded her large stretches of time to devote to family and personal interests. She worked long, hard hours only when a special exhibit came through, and the last one, a Botero collection, ended over a month ago.

Claire didn't seem to notice Harold's self-doubt. "Completely," she replied. "I played tennis this morning, doubles with Nanette, Denise, and Dolly."

"Tennis with Dolly?" Harold conjured an image of a tennis-skirted Mrs. Bridgeman.

"Yes, she has a court right in her backyard, lucky girl. And later in the afternoon, I dropped in on Ronnie. I still can't get used to the idea she's gone."

Harold remarked the melancholy note. Was this it? A hole in Claire's life? Something in need of a plug? "Yes, hard to believe she's gone," he said and looked at her, hoping to catch her eye and connect. "Our baby," he tried. "Still so young."

"Hmm. Hard to believe." Claire, her face still touched with serenity, looked beyond her husband's gaze. "But the apartment was the right thing, no question about it. She practically lives at the studio, and now she can just roll out of bed, grab her bag of toe shoes, and be there in five minutes."

"Yes, more convenient for everyone." Convenient? Claire reacted, and Harold saw it there, momentarily, her disappointment at his insensitivity. Since when were decisions about children based on convenience? This was their little girl, Veronica, suddenly gone after eighteen years. And now Harold had a new thought: not just a child, but a female presence was missing from Claire's life. He took a fortifying sip before speaking. "It seems this one is going harder for you—harder for us—than David."

"Well," she looked at him briefly, "the second and last child, I suppose."

"But for women, for mothers that is—not that I buy into pop psychology—separation from the son is supposed to be the most trying."

"It's been four years since he left, after all."

"True."

"Time changes things." Their eyes met, and he saw the time that had passed between them. "And now," she said, still looking at him, "with Ronnie gone, the house is *completely* empty."

Harold froze, watching Claire through the pulse in his eyes, which made a throbbing frame for her face, alternately gray, then grayer. Pressure rose in his temples, and he looked down at the glass in his hand, noticing with surprise that he'd nearly drained it. "I miss her too," he said truthfully, knowing he hadn't as much as Claire.

They lapsed into a prolonged silence before speaking again, choosing mundane topics. During their meal together, the pressure in Harold's temples grew. He rarely suffered from headaches and was puzzled at this one. Claire seemed the same as always, the touch of sadness he'd detected earlier easily replaced with her gentle smile. How could he possibly mention that nonsense with Bridgeman? It might have been good for a laugh between them, but Harold feared the laughter would hurt his throbbing head, threatening to burst at the temples.

After dinner, he helped Claire with the dishes, then announced he was going to bed. Claire mistook his behavior for something else, and moments later, slipped into bed beside him, wearing her sheerest nightgown. Harold barely noticed the gauzy peach apparition through slits of swollen eyes, coming fully awake only when Claire nestled her head into his chest, her hair brushing his chin.

She wanted him, wanted a man—her husband—not a plump female friend. Her gesture, something that should have been heartening, only increased the pain in Harold's temples. He stroked his wife's soft crown, sending more pressure into his own. The room spun around them. Don't you wish, E. Stanley? Don't you wish that "E." stood for Edmond or Ellington instead of Eunuch? Dorothy doesn't want you the way my Claire wants me.

But he felt only pain, not arousal, and he could think of nothing else but his headache. "I'm sorry, Claire. I'm afraid I just don't feel very well tonight."

She lifted her head to look into his eyes, concern in her own. "You're sick?" She touched his forehead like she used to touch Ronnie's and David's, school mornings during flu season.

"Quite a headache is all."

"Hmm." She laid her head on his chest again but in a different way, holding back some of its weight for herself. "Maybe you should take a day off. Stay home tomorrow."

"Let's see how I feel…"

"I don't have much planned. I can call Dolly in the morning and cancel—"

"Dolly?"

"I invited her to lunch is all. Our house. But we can do it another time."

"Don't. Please don't cancel anything on my account."

In the morning, without specific, conscious recollection of the Dolly luncheon, Harold's headache remained intolerable. It was all he could manage to pick up the phone and call his secretary. Appointments and office hours would be cancelled, a sign put on the lecture hall door for his afternoon class. Measures to which other professors resorted occasionally—but not Professor Murkle, not in the fifteen years of his tenure and eight years of assistant professorship before that. All for a headache! An embarrassing absence but necessary just the same.

He was sickened all the more at the idea of facing college sophomores. He remembered the conversations he'd had with students the day before, the words he'd used to justify the grades he'd given. Glib, superficial, and pat. No better than the students' essays, their sentences and paragraphs developed with a marketing plan in mind, what would sell for an A or a B. Where was the depth of insight, the evidence of his wisdom and age? Where resided the reasons behind his judgment and opinion? Buried, resistant to articulation, as good as nonexistent.

After Harold had laid the telephone receiver down, Claire gently asked whether he was finished so that she could call her lunch date and cancel.

The wife's name went unspoken but resounded in Harold's throbbing head. He would not avoid this; he would see and judge for himself. "No," he stated firmly in a whisper to minimize his pain. "I'll stay out of your way," he added, knowing that he would not.

"Oh, it's not that," said Claire. "It's not a matter of *you* bothering *us*. It's the other way around. Dolly tends to be quite—how to put it? Demonstrative. Not a relaxing sort to have around when you've got a headache. She doesn't tiptoe."

But Harold's insistence was clear despite his near silence, and Claire knew his inflexibility well enough not to protest further. She wasn't to make a phone call, wasn't to change a single thing or even mention to Dolly, beforehand, that her husband was home sick. Dolly had been invited and was still invited and would come, despite Harold's condition.

Precisely at noon, the doorbell rang long and loud under the firm pressure of an insistent finger, sending Harold bolt upright from the bed into a revolving room. He was fully dressed and as immaculate as he could manage under the circumstances, still nothing he could do about the bloodshot eyes and his need to squint against artificial light.

As if the bell were less than noticeable (Harold couldn't remember when it had sounded so piercing), Claire yelled out from the kitchen, "Dolly's here!" before going to the front door. All morning, rich aromas of special foods had come creeping, invading Harold's sick room, and now he couldn't help noticing another new thing, an unusually exuberant quality in Claire's voice.

"I'm coming," said Harold, tottering into the hallway. There was Claire, emerging from the kitchen, on her way to answer the door. She turned back, cheeks flushed, and looked at him. "Harold! You should be resting."

"I'll just say hello. Don't want to be rude."

Claire gave a slightly disparaging look—was there something underneath, a secret to cover?—before moving into the entryway and laying her thumb on the latch. Slowly, she opened the door to reveal, squeezed into the framework, the plentiful figure of Dolly, topped with a beaming face and a lipstick-free smile. Harold had difficulty reconciling this Dolly with the image he'd been carrying. She wore a simple dress providing sufficient coverage, and her hair was free floating, clipped back at the sides, unlike the stiff-sprayed off-the-neck hairdo she'd worn at the benefit dinner.

"Darling!" exclaimed Dolly, shifting a large, pendulous handbag on her shoulder before extending the long fingers of her right hand. Claire accepted the hand and closed in for a European sort of kiss-kiss on the cheeks before Dolly looked up, noticing Harold lurking behind in the hallway. She seemed surprised, not rattled. "Professor! How nice to see you again!" She walked past Claire for a polite handshake with the husband. "No classes today? A school vacation day? So many odd little holidays now that I can't keep them straight!"

"No holiday," he said. "Just a day to rest."

"Harold is suffering from a monstrous headache," said Claire, her eyes bouncing between her husband and her guest.

"You poor man!" Dolly reached again for Harold's hand, this time to deliver a motherly, healing squeeze. Her hand was bigger than Harold's but without the apish feel he'd anticipated. He glanced down as she withdrew it. The fake painted nails were gone, and her natural ones were trimmed smoothly into short, squat ovals. "How is it feeling now?" she asked. Harold felt comfortably enclosed, like a cool pat of butter worked deep into the center of an oven-warmed dinner roll. Dolly's large mouth, with lips soft and pink, might have opened wide to admit him.

"Getting better," he lied, discovering in the same moment that his lie had become the truth.

"You might just go off and take a rest, if you like," Claire suggested.

"By all means! Don't stand on ceremony for me!" said Dolly, giving Harold a double-eyed wink and Claire a gentle squeeze on the shoulder.

"Well, thank you, but I'm fine enough to have some lunch, if you don't mind. I didn't eat breakfast..."

"No, you didn't," agreed Claire.

"And something smells very good."

"My goodness, something *does* smell wonderful. Just heavenly! Claire, you always go to such lengths—we don't deserve it, do we Harold?"

"Oh, but you do," said Claire, looking at Dolly. Harold remembered that look, and an image suddenly came to mind from the first day of the Botero exhibit, nearly three months ago: Claire at the museum, gaping in awe at a painting of a rotund woman. How long now? *I'm sure they've been at it for months.* He turned to Dolly, surprised to see a North American facsimile of a Botero painting in the flesh, a ripe plum of a woman exuding the lush fullness of life. Someone who gave of herself and filled the emptiness in others.

He stared, frankly stared, unable to rip his eyes from her, no longer seeing that abhorrent mental image but a warm-blooded woman, drawing him in. Perhaps he saw and felt what Claire did, and perhaps he should have felt uncomfortable for himself, or for Claire, or for his marriage, but oddly, he felt only fascination and wonder along with a medicinal tranquility, as if the aspirin he'd taken had been laced with something stronger.

"Everyone's so hungry, we might as well sit down," Claire announced. Dolly gave Harold the look of a conspirator about to enjoy a taboo delight. He became embarrassed and looked away. They followed Claire, who set out for the dining room, bypassing the kitchen table. A deliberate choice, Harold knew, sensing that the reason had nothing to do with the formality of the dining room but a need to indulge in space. Dolly required it and had the capacity to fill out a room to its four corners. Harold accepted this now without question or offense.

For an awkward five minutes Harold sat alone, feeling useless and ignored, while Claire and Dolly made several trips between kitchen and dining room, laying the table, bringing the food, drinks, and condiments. Their conversation flowed incessantly along with their movement, most of the talk coming from Dolly's mouth, most of the physical contact initiated by her. Dolly was in the habit of touching, just about anywhere it seemed, Claire's arm or hand or shoulder.

Harold's eyes followed them. Each time they left the room he leaned sideways in his chair to see as much as he could before they disappeared completely into the kitchen. There was a touch at the small of Claire's back. Constant chatter, liquid and easy. The words didn't matter. Harold didn't hear the words but was swept into their comfortable intimacy.

A closeness between his wife and this woman had developed somehow, right under his nose these last few months. What kind of intimacy was this? He'd seen other women acting this way together, touching and talking. Half the female sex must be in bed together, is that it, Bridgeman? When did a touch mean something more? Did the eyes give it away? Dolly's eyes were shining, gleaming with powerful emotion, a *joie de vivre*, or maybe love. Could it be lust? What about the excitement in Claire's eyes? Something quieter, but full of possibility.

Still, everything seemed too open. Wouldn't a cheating spouse try to hide that look, try to avoid touching her lover in front of her husband? Not if she lacked a sense of treachery, guilt, or deceit. Women, creatures of love, accustomed to the tactile sense, were allowed to kiss and hug. After all, what more could this giant teddy bear really do to Claire in bed? More than kiss and hug, perhaps, but all those other things?

All of a sudden the women were sitting down and ready to stay, Claire at the head of the table with Dolly and Harold on either side. Dolly stared at Harold across the table with wide, inquisitive eyes. "Is that how you see it, Professor? You two must have such wonderful discussions about this! I'm so honored to be in the company of renowned experts!"

He looked at her, bewildered. Fuzziness had replaced the sharp, jagged pain of his headache, making an impressionist's blur of Dolly's round face. "Pardon me?" he said, aware of bustling activity around them. Claire, not waiting to ask what they wanted, busily filled their plates with several kinds of food.

"Where do you draw the line between subjective and objective criteria? I've always been so fascinated with this question! How can the experts agree on the greatness of certain works of art when it seems like such a subjective decision? Are we not individuals, after all, with different tastes and sensibilities?"

Harold sat, stunned, while Dolly twisted a liberal forkful of linguini, opened wide, and fully enclosed the pasta ball within her succulent mouth, clamping lips tightly around the neck of the fork to aid its shiny-clean withdrawal. She breathed in deeply while chewing with rolling, big cheeks, looking at him expectantly, certain of her entitlement to a profound response.

"A difficult question, yes," managed Harold. To buy time, he bit into a mushroom-filled puff pastry and chewed slowly.

Dolly, at length, swallowed and suddenly looked flustered. "How insensitive, taxing you with all these questions when you're suffering a headache! Please forgive me."

"No, no, not at all. I'm feeling quite better. Maybe it's the food."

"Yes, the food. Claire, you've outdone yourself! This is superb." Claire, quietly chewing, beamed her response. "Harold, you're a lucky man, eating like this every day." And as if to prove her point, Dolly inserted another large roll of pasta into her mouth, letting a stray sun-dried tomato dangle, then drop from the edge of her bottom lip onto her plate.

"Well, perhaps not every day," said Claire.

"No. But, yes," said Harold, thinking that his wife's cooking appeared and smelled different today, but actually tasted very familiar. These were some of Claire's favorite dishes. How many times had he forgotten to compliment her? "I *am* very lucky, indeed." He looked at Claire, and she, for the first time that day, returned his gaze and lingered.

Without actually willing it, his eyes filled with love and appreciation, feelings he couldn't very well hide despite the confusion of his thoughts. Her eyes widened and contracted, as if to catch and hold his love, brightening her gaze and communicating something in return. Her own love for him? Reassurance? Recognition of their inviolable union? She seemed oblivious to the presence of that woman sitting next to her, that Dorothy Bridgeman. Dolly. Who's Dolly?

No more than three seconds elapsed, but for those three seconds Harold erased those interfering Bridgemans and felt completely alone with Claire, fully confident of her love and fidelity—a firm, intuitive belief, no more—until their privacy suffered an intrusion from the, however so briefly, forgotten guest.

"Oh, Claire, something has come up and we *must* change our tennis date for next week." Dolly stuffed a mushroom pastry into her mouth before diving under the table for her handbag. Chewing, she heaved the bag up onto her lap, and without looking, dug deeply inside until she found what she needed: a fat, well-worn, leather appointment book with a thick red marking pen stuck in the middle. She placed the book on a bare spot of table, and it fell open where the pen had bent the pages, exposing the current week of dates. Harold couldn't help noticing two big red "C's," one on the current date and the other yesterday, undoubtedly the doubles tennis match.

Dolly flipped to next week. "Wednesday is just no good for me, darling." She passionately inked over a big red "C" with her pen, leaving a dark wet spot, blood red, soaking through to the other side. "Is Friday possible?"

"If it's one of our early ones, yes." So, there'd been early ones, and therefore some late ones as well. "About ten?"

"Perfect!" Dolly nodded her approval and marked a new "C," closed the book, and set it on the table beside her plate.

Harold's fog continued, unabated. *Secret meetings, dates, and rendezvous.* But this one was hardly secret, and those big, blotchy C's, bright red or not, meant nothing at all next to the near certainty of Harold's three seconds with Claire. And hadn't the headache vanished entirely? He chewed and thought, his internal tumult slowly working its way upward as Dolly and Claire resumed their chatter, a blur of unintelligible sound.

Suddenly, he sat up taller and spoke, cutting Dolly off in mid-sentence. "Getting back to your questions, Dolly…"

She looked at him in surprise.

"About art, that is. I've been thinking lately, more than you might know, about the very issues you raised."

"Oh?" Dolly beamed, like a bright student. The women waited, Dolly filling the moment with another forkful and another spontaneous touch, resting her fingertips atop Claire's hand on the table. Harold saw the touch and tried, this time, not to compare it with something else, not to analyze, describe, judge, or explain it. He longed to know, simply, what it was, just like he'd always known things, assuming the reasons could be found—just like he'd always known Claire and had taken her love and fidelity for granted.

"These questions come up frequently in class, and I do my best to explain." He felt his lie and looked away from Dolly to regain his composure. When he turned back to speak, his eyes shifted from Dolly's intent expression to Claire's serene smile, to the food on his plate, the walls, the ceiling. "Actually, I've set down a number of criteria in a treatise I wrote, what, eight years ago..."

"Twelve," suggested Claire.

"Yes, twelve, entitled *Impressionism: The Masters*, which discusses all those objective qualities in a work that contribute to its greatness, like innovation in technique and perspective, novel or relevant subject matter, the consonance of style, subject, and mood, nuances in shading, original combinations of color..." Harold babbled uneasily, feeling all his so-called objective criteria drifting away from him like ripples in a stream. "These are the intellectual justifications for our opinions. But there's one thing," and his eyes finally came to rest on Dolly's, "that's harder to put into words. And it's something just as important, but it's completely subjective. Maybe we're all enough alike in basic ways that we come to agree on the greatness of a certain work of art just because it touches us all in the same way—hits the same emotional key."

Dolly gulped her most recent mouthful, removed her hand from Claire's, and lifted the napkin from her lap to dab at greasy lips, sighing deeply. "Artistic greatness, like love," she said, squelching a dainty burp behind her napkin.

Harold and Claire looked at her quizzically.

"You just *know* when it's there."

She allowed the words to hang among them before gesturing, in a pious way, opening her hands palms upward, one toward Harold, the other toward Claire, while they kept their eyes fast on hers through a moment of unifying silence.

At length, Harold and Claire pulled their eyes away to behold each other at the altar. He touched her hand, much the way Dolly had, while searching for another intimate three seconds, hoping to go beyond, to show his wife the depth of his commitment to her. "You're right," he acknowledged Dolly, keeping his eyes on Claire. "I could say it's Claire's smile or her intelligence or her cooking or her gentleness. But, none of that really explains it. I just knew when it was there, and I still know it."

Claire flushed but looked pleased all the same. She said nothing, but he didn't expect it from her, not in front of Dolly. Instead, he searched his wife's face and found the certainty he needed, the light of love and feeling in her eyes. The fog lifted.

Smiling, he shifted his gaze to discover Dolly,

fighting tears. "If only Stanley would say something like that!" She sniffed. "We all know it for ourselves, don't we, but wouldn't it be nice the other way around? Wouldn't it be nice just to know when love is returned? But it's all such a matter of faith."

"Oh, but he *does* love you," said Harold, thinking of E. Stanley's fretful admonition. Why would the man be so worried if he didn't love his Dorothy? And what a shame that she didn't know it, hadn't yet experienced the bliss of complete faith the way Harold had, only seconds ago, Dolly herself an indirect cause of it. He saw her perplexed look and added: "I mean to say, I'm certain that he must feel very deeply for you. At the benefit dinner last month, it was so evident."

"You're very kind! My husband has been so preoccupied lately, but that's nothing to concern you." With tears threatening to spill, Dolly became very busy, dabbing at wet eyes with her napkin while scooping up her appointment book with the other hand and diving for her purse. She rummaged around under the table, apparently pushing the book into her handbag.

An "Oh!" and suddenly she was up again, dry eyed and cheerful. She leaned toward Claire, touched her arm, and whispered loudly, "Remind me later, dear. You left something at my house. I have it in my purse."

Harold's ears perked up. The pink panties? Evidence of sex, or a hasty change after tennis? Claire only smiled pleasantly, while Dolly's attention returned to her plate, the tasty remnants soaked up and consumed with a bit of bread. Harold looked on, feeling intuitively certain of an innocent explanation, more than ever aware of his inability to claim certainty.

He gazed at his beautiful wife, the woman he loved and had known for half his life, realizing that today, just today, he'd discovered how much he didn't know about her, how much he wanted to learn! Did she feel as strongly about him? *All such a matter of faith.* He'd seen the love in her eyes, had faith in that much.

And the rest would come, they would grow closer and stronger. He would have faith in that.

☾ *The Zephyr*

THE OTHER CHILDREN had nearly finished their Jesus TV sets when I joined the Bible class that summer. They'd run out of black paint by the time I was ready to decorate mine, and the best Miss Nancy could offer was yellow crepe paper leftover from Easter.

I slapped it on the outside of the box as best I could, applying little globs of paste with the dried-out brush in the middle of the jar cap. Just like the others, my set had white rounds of construction paper for the knobs, and I drew numbers on them for the channels and the volume, but still, my yellow TV ended up looking so different.

It was June 1962, and we were staying six or eight weeks in Reno, however long it took, "pretending to be residents." Bible school was one of my mother's attempts to break up the long, hot, blank spaces of time. The church in Reno wasn't anything like ours in California, just another strange thing to get used to. I didn't know it then, but we wouldn't be returning to our regular church anyway, once all the business of divorce and marriage had been accomplished.

The Zephyr Motel, on the far outskirts of Reno, was

our temporary home. I hadn't a notion what a zephyr was, and a chill went up my spine from the ominous sound of it. *Zephyr*. I told Mom I wanted to stay the whole summer without mentioning that, really, I refused to go back to a place that wasn't home anymore but a different house with strange, extra children and a new father.

The others, my siblings and soon-to-be stepsiblings, took turns one by one visiting Mom and me in our two-room bungalow with kitchenette. The two kids (me and the child of the week) slept on the twin beds in the bedroom and Mom slept on the foldout couch in the living room/dining room/kitchenette.

A couple of times the outgoing father, the one I was more used to, came and took me to a restaurant and asked a lot of questions about things like my favorite subject in school and how the weather had been in Reno. I would turn my head to the side when he kissed my cheek goodbye, and the next morning, I'd find a present on the end of my bed, a paint-by-numbers or a Nancy Drew. If the other bed held a stepsibling, there'd be no present on that one.

There wasn't much for an eight-year-old girl to do at The Zephyr. None of my brothers or sisters could understand why I stayed, but I didn't want to go back, suspecting it would be worse to be scared in a new place than bored in a less-than-new place. My mother and the new father, Bill, would put heads together and whisper, stealing looks in my direction, whenever he came to pick up the departing child and deliver the latest arrival.

"You can just call him Bill," she'd said. He was

"Daddy" to the new kids, who called her Betty because she wasn't exactly taking the place of their dead mom.

"Call me Bill," he'd agreed, saying all those same kinds of things about not trying to replace my father and not coming between us. Maybe he didn't understand that my daddy was on the way to becoming just a present on the end of the bed.

I would spy, watching their moving lips and their shining, smitten eyes that would somehow lurch free of each other to cast a knowing gaze upon me. They'd contrived a justification for my recalcitrance: time for quiet little Debbie to bond, one-on-one, with the old sibs, Allison and Teddy, and to become better acquainted, one-on-one, with the new ones, Trudy and William.

Not in the mood to cooperate, I preferred to sit alone in the poorly lit bedroom with curtains drawn, reading my Nancy Drews or methodically filling in the squares of my outgoing father's graph paper with colored pencils while the current sibling-of-the-week sought company outside, latching onto any available kid looking for action in the parking lot or by the pool. Sooner or later, I would be shooed outside to "go and play."

My brothers and sisters didn't go with me to the Bible school. They always seemed to find something normal to do, and besides, I was the only one who could attend twice a week consistently for six or eight weeks or however long it took to get the divorce papers signed. From my first day, I saw what had to be done. The other students were already on week three, and I had to catch up.

Busy with all that cutting, coloring, and pasting, I had

no time to talk to anyone except the pretty and young Miss Nancy. At most other schools you had to say Mrs. Morris or Mrs. So-and-So, but she let us call her Miss Nancy. She prepared the cardboard box for me by cutting out the large hole in front for the "screen" and four small holes, top and bottom on either side, to insert two bamboo sticks. The ends of a long scroll of Jesus pictures were wrapped around the sticks, which could be turned to view the pictures one at a time like still frames of a motion picture on the screen.

There was Jesus blessing a pile of bread loaves and fish, Jesus touching the forehead of a kneeling blind man, Jesus with blood dripping down his cheek from the thorns. About a dozen of them, with a little caption at the bottom of each.

After four intense sessions, Miss Nancy told me, sadly, it was time to move on, although I'd finished only three pictures, all colored neatly and uniformly inside the boundaries and outlined with an extra-dark layer of the same color, traced on top of the purplish mimeographed lines. Miss Nancy helped me roll it onto the two sticks, saying she was "so sorry" we had to "finish up our projects now," but once I got "home," she was sure my mother would help me to unwind the scroll so I could color the rest.

On the way back to The Zephyr that day, I held the precious set, lumpy and puckered, on my seatbeltless lap in the front seat of the Rambler. My older sister Allison sat in the back seat, singing Pat Boone's "Love Letters in the Sand." My mother looked sideways at my TV, one eye on the road.

"That's very pretty."

I doubted she actually noticed how well I'd colored between the lines because her glance was so fleeting before she looked back at the road, dreamily, with a little smile on her lips and wild, shining eyes full of her new man. That look reminded me of Miss Nancy's eyes when she spoke of Jesus, even though Miss Nancy seemed so much younger and prettier, the shine a bit softer. I dropped my gaze to the box with a throat feeling suddenly just as lumpy, lips just as puckered. The only sound was Allison's raspy, pretend love-sick voice crooning above the engine noise about how her broken heart aches.

"I like that yellow paper on it," Mom tried again. I hunched over the set, peeking up at her. The ardent gleam had vanished, replaced with restless boredom. "You glued it on real nice and even." I'd said nothing to her about the black paint or the crepe paper or the paste jar. Or about Miss Nancy standing next to me with her perfume smell, helpful and patient, saying things like, "We should be able to get enough paste out of this jar, don't you think?"

My eyes stung like I'd opened them in the deep end, diving for caps. Now there were wet splotches to pucker the crepe even more.

I didn't think she'd seen me and thought this would be the end of it, and for a while there was nothing but Pat Boone, when all of a sudden she slapped the steering wheel with the palm of her hand and heaved a sigh: "Ah!" I jumped in my seat and began to shiver.

*　　*　　*

The next day, Sharmane was at the pool without her little brother, Buster. I was happy that Buster wasn't there to throw his army men at us but expected the worst from Sharmane's tongue, since Buster always provided such a convenient target for it.

I didn't know how she spelled her name, but it sounded like a "shark" with the mane of a horse instead of a "k." I'd been shooed outside after many minutes of rolling the pictures, one by one, past the screen, too afraid to dismantle the TV or to ask for my mother's help so that I could finish coloring it.

Allison was already at the pool with Sharmane. They were almost the same age but not at all alike, my sister just ten and going into fifth grade, Sharmane nearly eleven and going into sixth. The only thing they had in common was a copious amount of peeling skin, Sharmane's many layers deep and brown, Allison's newly acquired and raw underneath.

Allison was short and plump for her age with a thick waist and no hint of the figure to come in her one-piece-with-skirt bathing suit. My suit matched my sister's except for the different color: purple flowers instead of orange. We weren't allowed to get two-pieces like the one Sharmane wore in blue gingham. She strutted around the concrete so tall and proud with two little lumps pressing out the front of the top half.

There were no trees by the pool, no plants, no umbrellas, no cabanas, no tall drinks, no floats. Just cracked cement and glare, a metal picnic table with attached benches that wobbled and scorched your behind if you sat down without the protection of a wet towel.

The only source of refreshment was a Coke machine next to the front office, a few searing steps from the pool across the parking lot. The machine ate your nickels and clamped its rusty jaws about the necks of the frosty bottles, not letting go no matter how hard you tugged.

I'd given up early on, not wanting to step inside that office again to ask Mrs. Tillman (Sharmane and Buster's mom) for my nickel back. I'd come to believe that the machine didn't like me and me alone because the ground was littered with bottle caps under the opener. We would collect them, toss them into the pool, and dive for them when Mrs. Tillman wasn't looking. Some had cork inside and would float. Others would sink.

"If she doesn't see us doing it she can't kill us," declared Sharmane with the authority of one who knew her mother well. But secretly I hoped Mrs. Tillman would watch Sharmane from her window and come out from time to time like my mom did, because there was no lifeguard around. Most other kids didn't seem to worry about things like that.

If I'd never seen Mrs. Tillman's face, I would have thought she was the nicest mother imaginable, letting her daughter wear a two-piece and go around in curlers—in public—all summer. Tight to Sharmane's head were rows of little pink sponge rollers from the Clairol home permanent wave box, lined up just like the picture on the instruction page. She was going to keep them in all summer so she wouldn't have to curl her hair again for the rest of the school year. The experiment included many hours by the pool, swimming, saturating her hair with chlorine, and baking in the sun for a stiff, chemical set. On account of Sharmane's experiment, and because our hair was short, we got away with not wearing swim caps.

When I got to the pool, she and Allison were diving for bottle caps. "You again," said Sharmane, spying me when she surfaced. "You never come out here, do you?"

Even I could hear the contradiction, but something about Sharmane's contradictions just drew you in. She swam to the edge.

"Not much," I admitted.

"What you been doing in there?" She stared up at me from the water, her body making a crucifix with her chest pressed against the side and arms stretched right and left along the edge. A handful of caps lay in front of her on the cement. Allison came up alongside, deposited her caps on the edge, and propped herself identically, in imitation. "I bet you eat a lot in there." Sharmane eyed my waist critically.

Allison gave a little complicit laugh, but then seemed to remember her own waistline hidden underwater. She glanced down and looked up at me, guiltily.

"Not any more than you," I said, surprised to be so bold.

"Not so much," agreed Allison quietly, in the midst of torn loyalties.

"How do you think I keep this figure?" Sharmane appraised the lumps one at a time while lifting an index finger to scratch, absently, along a line of scalp between rollers. There may have been blood on her cheek. "What do you think I eat?"

"Yeah, what?" added Allison, although she should

have been asking Sharmane, not me.

"I don't know."

"Just three slices of Wonder Bread a day. Breakfast, lunch, dinner. I wouldn't touch all those TV dinners you eat. That's the fattest kind of food."

I stared at her, wondering if she'd been through our garbage. In California we ate other things, but here, or maybe it was just now, our mother was different. I could already see myself, tonight, sitting in front of Dick Van Dyke, or maybe the Jesus TV, eating from a tin. I looked at Allison, who was smirking and fidgeting at the same time. Of course, she had told her.

"What about your roughage?" I asked, but Allison interrupted with a loud voice, "Debbie made a Jesus TV set!"

"Jesus *what? Jesus H. Christ!*"

Allison's eyes widened at this, and she gaped in awe while Sharmane lifted her eyebrows and skated a blasé glance between us. "That's what my mom always says when she's about to kill us. *Jesus H. Christ!*" A strand of hair had escaped a curler and was plastered to her cheek, a rivulet of blood.

"What's the 'H' for?" asked Allison.

"Hell and High Water." Sharmane's eyes became glittery, the way they always did when she was impressed with herself.

Allison's mouth dropped open, the contradictions drawing her in and turning her own eyes to shine, while I grew angry just to hear these words alongside the Lord's name.

Caught up in her own smartness, Sharmane seemed

to forget entirely about TV sets. "I bet you don't leave any food for that skinny brother who was here last week. He doesn't even look like your brother."

I almost said he wasn't, but Allison jumped in with, "He is *too!*" as if to convince herself.

My feet were burning, and I walked down to the shallow end. Sharmane yelled at my back, "He better not be coming back."

I didn't answer, but I hoped she was right because we had nothing to talk about, even though William was my age. Allison and Trudy were both in fifth and could end up being twins, but William and I would never be twins, I just knew it.

"Buster said he was so weird, just like a girl, he didn't even like to play army men. He didn't even like to be called Billy or Bill. We had to say *William* because he was a Junior or something and didn't want a name just like your dad's. Hey, why do you call your dad 'Bill' anyway? That is soooo weird!"

I could have asked her why she didn't have any dad at all because there didn't seem to be one, and we had two, even if each one might amount to only half a dad.

Sharmane didn't wait for an answer but launched into a low-voiced father imitation: "I'm your daddy, *William*. You have to eat something, *William*. Here, *William*, have a TV dinner. Oh no, sorry, you can't have it. Debbie needs two!"

She laughed crazily, pinched her nose and slid underwater. Bubbles surfaced while Allison and I waited and watched, long enough for me to remember the time I ate William's leftovers off his plate. And it was only the second time we'd had dinner with the new kids.

When she emerged, the blood was washed clean.

On Allison's last night, we did what we always did.

Now I lay me down to sleep...

Allison and I were kneeling next to my bed, Mom in between, our heads drooped over prayer hands. The electric fan in the corner whirred and made a steady, rhythmic clang with each round of the crooked blade.

I pray the Lord my soul to keep...

We wouldn't have done this if a step were here instead of Allison.

And if I die before I wake...

I peeked at Mom sideways, trying to find the shine. Miss Nancy's eyes would have shone.

I pray the Lord my soul to take.

Trudy would have lectured like a science teacher on evolution. That's why we only did this without the other two. But tomorrow, Trudy would be coming to replace Allison, and then we would see.

Amen.

Lights out, tucks and kisses in darkness edged with flashing red. *The Zephyr Motel. Vacancy.* Everything seemed to flash in Reno once you got into town, past all the desert. Step out the door and look away from the pool behind the bungalow and there was nothing but whiteness and glare, a fine kind of pebbly dirt-sand, shimmering and waving into the distance. A long road to town. Beyond that, at night, we could see the throbbing, orange-red glow of a nuclear holocaust on the horizon.

I lay in bed, awake, sweating under the single sheet in

my summer PJs. My heart was beating to come out of my chest, as if tomorrow were the first day of school. There were two kinds of nights, the kind when I was sure I would die if I closed my eyes, and the other kind when I almost wished I would die just to get it over with. Miserable as I was, these thoughts would give me a terrifying kind of excitement.

This night, though, was a little different: I was sure that if my eyes would only gleam like Miss Nancy's when I said my prayers, I wouldn't have to worry about any of these things. She had the kind of shining eyes that made you feel comfortable, not scared.

"Z," I whispered, and put my finger up to trace it in the air, following the image behind the translucent curtain. "E-P-H…" I traced.

"Shut up!" complained Allison.

"Y-R…"

"The zephyr's gonna get you if you don't shut up!"

"What's a zephyr?"

"You don't wanna know."

"Some kind of animal?"

"You *really* don't wanna know!"

I shut up then and let Allison get away with being changed, just like everyone and everything else. The arm under my tracing finger dropped to the bed, and my chin pushed my lower lip into buck teeth, trying to control the quivering, but it just wouldn't stop and tears rolled down into my ears.

Even Allison was different. Last year, I could have said something to her and she would have listened and then talked to me, all night if I needed it, just to make me feel better. But now there was Sharmane, and also Trudy, to change her, and Trudy and Allison would end up just like twins, leaving me behind.

I cried myself into a terrible, choking excitement, almost unable to breathe, and was suddenly so tired I fell into sure death, praying for the Lord to take me. Toward morning, as the flashing Zephyr faded into dawn, it pursued me, colossal and fiery red. I struggled to open my eyes and gagged on the knot in my throat, closed tight against the sound of my screams.

The next day, I found myself at the pool, alone with Buster. We were never alone together, and I wondered how I'd gotten there, thought back, and couldn't remember the steps that had taken me outside. I'd been rolling the pictures past the screen, and then, before I knew it, I was at the pool without Allison, just me and Buster. Allison might have been somewhere with Sharmane, I didn't know, and I may have been angry about that, or about the fact that she hadn't been in her bed when I awoke from my dream, or the fact that she would be leaving later that day.

At first, Buster was lying on his stomach, a towel underneath and an army man in each hand, shooting at ants spilling out of a crack in the cement. His ballooned cheeks were pushing loud explosions from his mouth. I put my towel on the metal bench of the picnic table and sat and watched him. His face was one big run-together freckle with a few white spots. He didn't look at me while he relished his continuous eruptions of flying spit. When Teddy got here, I thought, the two of them would have a great time because Teddy was the same age and loved army men. So far it had been William for a week, then Allison, and now, later today, Trudy.

After Buster got tired of his game, he jumped into the shallow end. He was only six and a half, but he was allowed in the pool by himself, as long as it was the shallow end. This seemed terribly wrong, even though Mrs. Tillman had come out to the pool with her kids a week ago and declared that Buster was a "water rat" who learned to swim when he was two. "Just throw him in and he floats," she said. She was wearing curlers that day too, and when you looked at Sharmane standing next to her mom, you'd think she'd been born with those things on her head.

Later that same day, Bill had come to deliver Allison, and we were all standing by the door of our bungalow when we heard a commotion by the office. Mrs. Tillman, with the curlers still in her head, was clutching Buster under the armpit and dragging him away from the Coke machine, yelling, "I'll tan your hide!" and giving him a whack right there for the world to see before she got him inside. We heard a good amount of screaming then, and Bill shook his head and professed that he didn't believe in "tanning."

Feeling strange to be alone with Buster, I was about to go back inside, but when he jumped into the pool, I realized I couldn't. He wasn't just wading in the shallow end. He was swimming like the steamboat in Huck Finn with big circling arms and splashing kicks, sometimes coming too close to the "4 FT" mark, and I knew he wasn't four feet. I sat clutching the edges of the bench, my hands on top of the towel next to my thighs, and kept my eyes glued on him, even though I had to pee and the sun was burning my back. He kept swimming back and forth, 3 FT, 4 FT, 3 again, and anything could happen to him.

Something would happen to Buster if I left. So I stayed.

Trudy was silent in the back seat on my way to Bible school. She'd said only one thing before she got in the car, after Mom had answered her question about where we were going.

"*Bible* school," she'd said. Just like that, and that's all.

I would rather have heard Pat Boone than the silence Trudy was making.

But I ran into the classroom with relief, leaving them behind. For two hours I'd be with Miss Nancy.

Her eyes were shining a welcome, and we sang our favorite song. *Jesus loves me this I know, for the Bible tells me so.* Nights, when my roommate was asleep, I'd sing this song softly to myself, working on the gleam in my eyes, trying to feel what it ought to feel like, in the dark.

But toward the end of class, something unexpected happened. Mom and Trudy would be coming soon, and for no reason I could think of, a sick feeling pushed up into my throat and tears streamed from my eyes. Miss Nancy took me aside and put her arm around my shoulder and pulled me so close that her perfume was still on my skin when I got back to The Zephyr.

She asked me gently, over and over, what was wrong. I wouldn't say, because it seemed, really, that nothing should be wrong except that all I wanted right then was for her to hold me. Finally I said, just to say something, that I'd had a bad dream.

"Oh, Debbie!" She stroked my shoulder and arm. "Don't worry. Bad dreams are there only to remind us to come closer to the Lord." She put her face very close to mine so I couldn't avoid her big, eye-gleaming smile. "Have faith in the Lord."

More sobs erupted and my shoulders shook. I'd let Miss Nancy down because I wasn't close enough to the Lord.

"Have faith, Debbie. Jesus loves you."

I wanted to ask Miss Nancy if *she* loved me, and if she had any children or if she might want just one more, but I could manage only to look up at her through bleary eyes, hoping she could read the question there.

That afternoon, Trudy and I played jacks in the bungalow. The only part of the floor good for jacks was the little section of beige linoleum next to the oven in the living room/dining room/kitchenette. The part where my mother slept had a bumpy sort of carpet the texture and color of oatmeal cookie dough with dirt spots that could have been the raisins.

While we played, Mom slouched down on the sleeper, all put away into a couch, with her feet propped on the coffee table, pretending to read a magazine. Most of the time she would turn her little smile with Bill in it toward the window, where she would dreamily gaze with her shining eyes that turned dead again when she looked back at the magazine and gave its pages a restless rustle.

There on the linoleum, Trudy and I could fit our two bodies, sitting crossed-legged or on one hip with legs bent under, a little space in between us for the jacks. We couldn't toss the jacks too hard, or one of them might go under the oven, and then you'd have to stick your fingers underneath in the grease and crumbs from other people. Luckily the ball was just a bit too big to be able to roll under.

Trudy was an expert at jacks, almost always making it up to ten-sies, even if one of her jacks got stuck in the tiny triangle missing from a corner of one of the linoleum squares. Allison usually only managed seven-sies, and I was lucky to make five-sies.

"I don't know how you can stand that girl," she said to me. We had just been at the pool with Sharmane, whose tongue had been worse than ever until Trudy got the better of her. Trudy was just as self-assured as Sharmane, but a whole lot quicker, smarter, and kinder.

"What kind of name is *that?*" Sharmane had asked Trudy.

"It's short for Gertrude."

"*Ger-troooood!*" Sharmane let loose her crazy laugh.

Trudy didn't flinch. "I'm named after my grandmother, a famous suffragette and union leader."

Well, Sharmane had nothing to say to that.

"I don't really like her too much," I answered Trudy over jacks.

"Then you have to come back to the new house. We built a tree fort."

I didn't answer but sat mesmerized by Trudy's skill, nailing eight-sies and talking at the same time.

"Grandma taught us how to make chocolate chip cookies." It was their Grandma, the one who stayed with the kids left behind when Bill came up to Reno. "And my uncle came and took us out to the Big Slide and we had Neapolitan ice cream. I swapped my strawberry for William's chocolate."

For a while now, I'd suspected fun goings-on at the new house as I wallowed in the pleasurable pain of my self-imposed exile. I forgot about the jacks and stared past them into the lines and intersections of the squares of linoleum, following a line straight down the length of three squares, then back up for two and, at one down from the top, across for two. A crucifix. Three down, two across.

But someone was talking. "It's your turn," said Trudy in a loud voice. My finger was on the floor, tracing the line. I looked up and saw Mom staring over from the couch, no longer dreamy, and I understood that Trudy had been saying it, over and over, louder and louder.

That night, just as I expected, there was no kneeling by the bed. Once during the first week, when William was in the bathtub, Mom and I had knelt and said our prayers, but this night Trudy didn't need to take a bath and was ready for bed. Mom stayed a little longer than usual, sitting on my bed, stroking my hair, while I looked out the window and followed the outline of The Zephyr, wishing she'd go away.

Now there was no one to go to, not even Miss Nancy, because in Mom's lingering hand I felt that Miss Nancy had told her something about me when she'd called Mom back inside. "You forgot something, Mrs.

Hilliard," she'd called out, using our old name. Mom said I would be keeping it, but she would be taking Bill's, and we would end up with different names but the same family. After stroking my head for a very long time, Mom went over to Trudy's bed and leaned over stiffly and kissed her on the cheek and said, "Good night, dear," sounding like the saleslady at the five-and-dime.

When the lights went out, I wasn't going to sleep, or for sure they would find out whatever was inside my head, or I would die, one or the other. Maybe Trudy had felt the same way when she was my age, just after her mother died. I wanted to ask her this, and about the sickness and death that people only hinted at before looking off into the distance. Trudy would tell us little things about her mother, what she wore, what she said, but never about the sickness and death part, and so, how could I possibly ask her about it?

The cardboard box on the dresser had become an empty, black square in the red-tinged darkness. Still, it stared back. Trudy might have been asleep by then, but I no longer had the urge to sing "Jesus Loves Me," and I used every muscle in my face to hold my eyelids open in the dark.

My plan failed, because the Zephyr chased me again at dawn. I screamed and screamed, the sound trapped inside under the knot in my throat.

Trudy spent her week besting Sharmane, and Teddy spent his being twins with Buster, and then it was William's turn again but he didn't want to come, so Allison came instead. I sat near the window of my room, in safety with the lights out behind the gauzy fabric of the curtain, watching their indistinct figures in the sunlight around the front door of the bungalow: Mom, Bill, Allison, Allison's little suitcase, Teddy, Teddy's little suitcase.

The place was so small and the Reno air so dry and empty that I could hear them. Mom was saying she thought I should go back. "But then I'll be alone!" screeched Allison. "Maybe it's best to leave her be," said Bill, while Teddy kept picking up his suitcase by the handle and dropping it to see if it would fall over. Later, at the new house, Teddy would unpack that little suitcase, or Bill would do it for him, so the next person could use it. William would have to come whether he liked it or not, because it would be unfair to make Trudy come again so soon. With Allison, it didn't matter. She was my sister.

"She's just afraid of the zephyr," said Allison.

Mom and Bill looked at each other and said, "The *what?*"

"Trudy told me. She says it in her sleep."

A shockwave turned their voices into blur and expanded their bodies grotesquely behind the gauze. Bill loomed bigger than the rest but seemed much smaller than I remembered, his legs skinny below the khaki shorts. He touched my mother's arm lightly and they leaned together in a whisper. I blinked and Bill was gone. I blinked again and turned around to see him, standing in the doorway to my room.

My heart jumped and my breath went out of me until all I could see were the particles of dust in the air, dancing in the filtered light. Bill didn't exist, I didn't exist, we might have been no more than two specks of dust, dancing with the others.

Without knowing it, I stood and followed him, walking through the dust, out the door of my room into the living room/dining room/kitchenette, out the front door, past Mom, Allison and Teddy, into the front seat of his station wagon. We drove along the gray line surrounded by a vast, white shimmer while Bill spoke words I couldn't understand in the way you might hear an announcer on a transistor radio far down the beach, under the sound of the waves. The announcer had a comforting, familiar voice, unchanging and constant, there to be ignored until the noise of other voices died down.

That moment happened when we were standing in the middle of a big, bright room in front of a little table with an enormous book lying open upon it. All around were bookshelves and tables and chairs with a scattered handful of people, silently reading, and I knew we were in a library, although it looked different than the one back home. Bill put his hand under the bulk of pages on the right side of the book and lifted them up and over to the left, then leafed through a few more, stopped and ran his index finger down the length of the page. I was standing at his elbow, just tall enough to see where he pointed.

"Here, read this," he said in a voice so quiet it could barely be heard, but at last I understood him because of that whisper, and the quiet all around, and the firmness of the tip of his index finger pressing down at its destination.

I did as he asked, immediately recognizing the dreaded word: "zephyr." He saw my difficulty with the rest and used the index finger of his left hand to cover a long section in italics, using his right index finger to underline the words he wanted me to read: "a gentle breeze from the west."

We may have stood there a minute or an hour, long enough for the words to cause tears in my eyes. "Come," he said, and I allowed him to take my hand and lead me out into the sun. The skin of his hand was warm, dry, and scratchy, a good feeling.

He took me to an ice cream shop, and when I still hadn't spoken after both he and the waitress asked what flavor I might like, he ordered Neapolitan for me. I said, "Thank you," when it came.

I was feeling better than I had in weeks, comfortable enough to allow an excited circulation of questions in my head with the buzzing possibility of their being asked and answered. There were the obvious ones, like why the motel had been named The Zephyr when there wasn't any wind in Reno, and whether Bill's family had ever tried chocolate chip ice cream instead of Neapolitan, but still I couldn't bring the words to my mouth and I let him talk to me about the new house and William and Trudy. I tried hard to eat the strawberry part too but took only one bite and left the rest in the bowl, thinking of Trudy.

Suddenly, he became very serious and said this: "You know, Debbie, after William and Trudy's mother died, I was very, very sad for a long time. And it made all the people around me sad too. So, one day, I realized it would be better for everyone if I was happy, and I decided to work on it. It takes some work. I knew that I would always love and remember William and Trudy's mom, but I could also love other people and be happy with a new family. And I'm so glad that you're going to be a part of that new family."

He smiled then, and his eyes were shining in that comfortable way, because he was seeing me and not just himself.

When we got back to The Zephyr, Teddy and his little suitcase got into the car with Bill, and Allison unpacked her little suitcase, and I stayed planted after all. I was feeling better, but not better enough to change things immediately, and I couldn't very well leave Allison alone, even if she had Sharmane. Just before Bill left, he looked at me over the top of the station wagon and winked. Allison and Mom and I stood waving a long time as they drove out of the parking lot and down the long gray ribbon, until all we could see was a speck of a car, even though there was no possibility they could still see us. Next week that would be me in the front seat.

Later, all three of us were at the pool when Sharmane came out, looking different somehow. Maybe it was because my mom was there, but Sharmane didn't immediately come up to us with her glittery look and a fast comment, and Allison didn't make the big puppy eyes as usual. We were splashing and smiling a lot more than we ever had that summer. Mom, sitting on the picnic bench, was dividing her time between laughing at our antics and reading her magazine. But on this day, she was really seeing, really reading.

Sharmane didn't jump in the water right away and was standing so quietly that I stopped splashing and took a good look at her, tall against the sun, gazing down into the pool at the deep end. She seemed to be waiting there, deciding what to do, and it was then that I saw blue through the holes. Funny that her head looked almost the same, but now there was only air inside each of the rolled shapes instead of a pink curler. And something else. Her face was round and soft, released from the tightened ends of the rollers.

After we'd stopped splashing and said nothing for a long time, Allison suddenly yelled, "Jump!" Sharmane didn't respond, didn't look at us, but kept gazing down into the water. She was working on something. *It takes some work*, Bill had said. "Jump!" yelled Allison again, and soon I joined in, and our screams escalated into a frenzied chorus of "Jump, jump, jump!"

There was a split second when anything could have happened. Sharmane had that power to leave you doubting but at the same time believing in the impossible.

And then she jumped.

Allison and I waited, watching the bubbles surface. Mom waited, I could feel her waiting at my back. The waiting lasted a very long time.

Sharmane surfaced a very different animal, shoulder-length hair plastered flat to her head, a genuine smile spreading from ear to ear. She looked all around, met us each in turn, and let out one of her crazy laughs, but there was fun and company in it this time.

Much later, after her hair had dried, it seemed to fly softly from her head, lifted by the gentle breeze.

☾ *Tidal Waters*

THAT GIRL, CARLY DEFNER, was trouble from the start.
Completely ignored the message (delivered by Pamela's
daughter Rebecca) to pack light for their long weekend at
the shore. The first thing Pamela saw as they turned into
the driveway was Carly's mother (Stacey? Sandy?)
bumping down the front steps of the Defner home with
multiple bags in tow—a large suitcase on wheels, a duffel
over the shoulder, a chunky cosmetic box shoved under
the arm—enough for a sendoff to boarding school.

On the bottom step, the mother pushed around the
daughter as she blithely lounged in the sun, awaiting her
escape with the McClennons. To be sure, Becca could be
just as lazy, but Pamela *never* would have allowed her own
fourteen-year-old to exhibit such disrespect! *That* was the
difference.

Gary inched the minivan up to the house as he eyed
Mrs. Defner's load. Pamela sensed his dismay in the slight
tensing and contraction of his shoulders—the dread of
yet another luggage-arranging ordeal.

In the far back seat, the twins were immersed in their
own world, rewinding their tape recorder to replay

favorite parts of the trip thus far, a narration of the sights along the seven-block drive from the McClennons' to the Defners': *"Oooo, gross, don't look now* [Matt]; *Yowza!* [Steve]; *Tubby T. in her bathing suit!* [Matt]." A neighbor girl had made the mistake of entering her front yard as the McClennons drove by, opening herself to the aspersions of Pamela's pre-pubescent Neanderthals.

Now, as Gary came to a stop mid-driveway at the Defners, the boys took no interest in their new surroundings. Becca, in the middle-back seat between twins and parents, sat up and removed her ear buds. She didn't make a move for the door just yet, waiting, apparently, for her parents to make fools of themselves.

Pamela was the first to jump out with a chipper, "Hi Carly!" in her usual effort to span the gap. Gary approached Mrs. Defner to lend a hand. Becca finally tumbled out of the sliding side door to greet her friend with a sleepy grin and rolling eyes—a disavowal—behind her mother's back. Gary, tall and solid, easily hoisted Carly's luggage and bounded off to the back of the minivan.

Pamela greeted Mrs. Defner. The response was tepid, a wan smile, and now, hands free, an awkward tug on the frayed bottoms of cutoff jeans wedged into the crotch above ample thighs. Her feet were bare and her knees dirty and callused as if she'd been at work in the garden— odd, since only a few skeletal bushes could be seen in the front yard. After another tug, she crossed her arms over a cotton peasant blouse. Not inappropriate for a hot summer morning, but neither was it something Pamela would ever wear.

Stacey. That was the woman's name, wasn't it? Her voice came to mind, stored in Pam's head from their first meeting, seven or eight months ago.

Pamela glanced at her watch. The morning was almost gone. "So much for a day at the beach! At this rate we won't get there 'til three or four." She pulled a bit of paper from the pocket of her Capris. "Here's the number. Feel free to call any time!"

Taking it, Mrs. Defner nodded at the scrap and raised her tired eyes while Pamela manufactured a smile and glanced away, seeking a new topic of conversation or a hoped-for glimpse of the unknown Mr. Defner. She chattered into the awkward pause: "We'll be back sometime Monday night. It depends on the traffic, but at least we'll be avoiding Sunday when everyone is coming home from the beach."

Mrs. Defner untucked a hand from her chest and waved it in the air. "Whenever is fine. Go on and have a good time."

"It usually works out well when Becca has a friend along. The twins always have each other, you know, and Becca feels left out." But all of this had been said on the phone, and their eyes started to wander. At the back of the van, Gary had pulled out all the bags and was mentally computing the dimensions as he massaged the back of his neck. "I'll just go see if Gary needs help," said Pam. Mrs. Defner nodded and gave another wave of the hand.

"Impossible," Gary muttered, hefting the largest suitcase and wedging it into the back storage space. "Have the boys pull the seat forward."

"They don't have any room as it is."

"Well, there's no other way. Boys!" Gary leaned in and grabbed the top of the back seat. "Pull this seat up! No, there, under the seat, push the lever..."

The twins voiced strident objections as they shortened their space, jamming their knees up against the middle seat—"Becca's gotta move up too!"—compressing their jumble of board games, playing cards, tape recorder, Frisbee, pillows, football, tortilla chips, baseball and mitts into a trash-compactor rectangle on the floor between the back and middle seats. "Should have gotten the damn luggage rack!" Gary said to the open air. He wasn't one to lose his cool completely, but the undertone of annoyance set Pamela on edge.

"I'll get Becca to pull up the middle seat," she said, and wandered off up the side of the van, continued around front, and peeked down the other side. She turned and approached the house, paused at the front steps, leaned sideways and allowed her eyes to follow the driveway to the detached garage in back. A dusty window in the garage door was cracked diagonally from corner to corner.

The girls and Mrs. Defner were gone.

She would just move the seat herself. She turned to go back, took a step, and halted. The parched concrete was blinding. Should she go inside?

The house sat baking in the sun, nothing inviting about its plain façade or the blocky, gray cement front steps, a metal handrail loose and rusted. She didn't touch it as she climbed the four steps, knocked, waited, and rang the bell, a little illuminated circle. No one came immediately, nor after a while, how long she couldn't say but it seemed too long. She thumbed the latch and opened the door.

Inside, the hallway was dark. Around the corner of an open doorway lurked an imprecise living room in filtered gray, curtains drawn. A small house, only one level, but the remaining rooms existed beyond view behind closed doors, down unknown passages. The smell of yesterday's dinner clung to the walls. Something fried. An image came to mind: Stacey prone on a lumpy couch in a dark room, a cold wet rag pressed to her forehead— *Go away*—only the lips moving.

From a distance floated traces of life, a murmuring. "Hello? Girls?" The sound of Pamela's own voice surprised her. "We're about to leave!" She hesitated, on the verge of calling out for "Mrs. Defner" or "Stacey," not wanting to appear too formal but afraid of being wrong. At the far end of the hall a door opened. Out stepped Becca, then Carly, holding a canvas drawstring bag, heavy, stuffed with possessions.

"Carly forgot something," Becca announced in a voice that didn't belong to Pamela's child.

"Okay, come on. Let's get going. Carly, where's your mother?"

"That's okay," she said with a surprising smile, big white teeth bursting through the surliness. "I already said goodbye."

"All right then." But Pamela remained fixed while the girls pushed around her and out the front door. A moment passed in silence before she was out again in the bright sunshine, wondering at her sudden need for a deep breath of that hot, humid air.

* * *

Children change one year to the next, a challenge Pamela had always enjoyed until lately, when she'd started to worry about slipping behind. In the past she'd always managed to catch up with the kids before her ignorance or unpreparedness could do serious damage, but this year, little errors in perception had set her off balance.

Case in point. During the early planning stages of the shore trip, she was still grounded in the past when she told Becca, most cheerily: "How great it'll be to see Meg again!" The lifelong best friend had been their regular guest on summer trips. But Meg was attending a different high school now, and Becca had made a new friend at the beginning of freshman year: Carly, with that limp sheet of hair obscuring one eye and four piercings in the single exposed ear (one through that hard knob of cartilage in the middle), suggesting frightening possibilities.

Not that Pamela could finger anything specific. The moroseness, she assumed, was an affectation masking the positive qualities buried within, waiting for a random impetus to propel them upward. Like that sunny, unexpected smile. So many children looked and acted exactly like Carly, hiding their strengths under the false trappings of style. Pamela just wanted something different for her own child. She didn't know what it was. Alertness, eagerness. To be awake.

From the start, Gary voiced no objection to the invitation, and maybe he was right. Let their daughter experiment with new friendships. Pam understood the logic and tried to internalize it. If we object, she'll resist us. Besides, this is our chance to learn more about Carly.

We've taught Becca solid values. She has the right instincts. We'll learn to trust her. We've got to learn to trust her.

A reasonable argument, but it couldn't seem to vanquish a throbbing, visceral plea: What had become of their daughter? Where had she gone—that sweet and lovely girl of ten or eleven?

On the way to the shore, the girls carried on their intense whispering with heads together under a merged canopy of falling hair. The back and middle-back seats had been moved forward, while Pamela and Gary maintained their legroom in front, compacting the back into a pile of objects and people, blocking windows, making driving that much more difficult. "Who wants the bananas on their lap?" The twins got a kick out of that one, Pamela's voice recorded for all eternity, rewound and replayed a hundred times while the plastic container of fruit made the rounds from lap to lap.

Pamela tried to ignore them and help Gary navigate. She wanted to focus on him. She'd intended this—an important side purpose of the trip—boys and girls paired up and occupied, allowing Pam and Gary more time together.

An hour underway, she relaxed enough to throw him a big smile.

"Off at last!" he responded with a smile of his own. A grueling year and they both deserved a rest. The shiny newness of parenthood had long worn off, and they'd entered the next phase of middle-aged parents of middle-childhood children with their shifting palate of interests and hormonal surges. Pam looked forward to the day, hopefully soon, when she and Gary could take a vacation away from the kids, and everything would be civilized and grown up, maybe even honeymoon-ish, once again.

"When do you think we can do this alone? Next summer?"

"Hmm... They'll be ten and fifteen. That's old enough to leave them on their own, isn't it?" A paper airplane sliced the air from the back seat over the girls' heads, hitting the rearview mirror and falling into Gary's lap. His hand slipped, the car swerved.

Pamela turned. "Steven!"

"It was Matt! I didn't—"

"You'll cause an accident!" Bending sideways to Gary's ear: "Becca would never be able to control them." Her eyes instinctively went to the rearview and met Becca's, staring back. Heard everything, of course. All that secretiveness—a favorite ruse of omniscient teen-agers. Becca's eyes slid down and away as she leaned into her friend for another private consultation. There was laughter, the self-conscious teenage girl kind, but still, the exclusion pricked and stung. Turning halfway around, Pamela lamely asked, "What's so funny?"

"Nothing," replied Becca with darting eyes.

Always the story. Pam surrendered to the futility and turned back to face the unfolding highway ahead, glancing just once more in the mirror, searching for her daughter. But their eyes didn't meet again for the rest of the trip.

Because there were so many of them, and judging the girls old enough, she'd arranged for adjoining rooms at the Villa Del Mar. The boys were on the fold-out couch in the "living room" of Gary and Pam's suite, and the girls had a separate room next door.

The Villa was an aging but homey restored mansion the McClennons visited every summer. They'd stayed in just about every room and were accustomed to the musty smell, the frayed edges of carpet on the stairs, and the noisy hum of the soda machine on the second-floor landing. The owners, Fred and Estelle Walters, had done little over the years to correct the ravages of time and sea air, but the Villa's distinctive details were part of its familiarity and the McClennons wouldn't have it any other way.

When they arrived, Pamela went into the office to register, leaving Gary behind to supervise the unloading. Fred was at the desk, his worn-driftwood face a comfortable welcome.

"Just four nights this year?"

"Afraid so."

"If you want a few extra nights, I have the space. Only need to ask!"

"Don't think it's possible. We have such a busy summer planned," Pamela explained. She looked into his ocean blue eyes and saw the hard times. "The boys have diving team most of the summer, and we're visiting my folks in August. No time left!"

"Well, glad you could make it these few days. Always good to have you."

When Pam returned, Gary had managed to enlist the help of every child, including Carly, and they trudged up three flights to the top floor with their designated loads.

In the first moments, the kids dropped everything and tore through the rooms, making comparisons, finding fault in each other's accommodations. The suite afforded the boys less privacy, but it had a kitchenette with a half-size refrigerator, a cupboard full of plastic dinnerware, a microwave and range top. To Matthew and Steven, food was more important than almost anything else. The girls' room was very small and lacked a kitchenette but had a balcony with a view of the beach, offering the chance to gaze out and inspect the other young people down below. It held the promise of gossip into the wee hours under the stars on warm summer nights.

Pamela helped the girls set up, unwilling to leave them alone immediately. She unzipped Becca's suitcase and removed her case of bathroom items. "That's okay, Mom," said Becca. Carly was leaning against the bathroom doorjamb, surveying the main room with her uncovered eye. She screwed her face into a wrinkled pout. "This place smells." Pamela was reminded of the stale grease odor in the Defner home but said nothing. She walked past Carly into the bathroom, where she placed Becca's things, lotion, acne cream, cleanser, makeup remover, toothpaste, toothbrush—"That's okay, Mom"—floss, shaving cream, razors, neatly on the left side of the sink. "Maybe you want to put your cosmetics here, Carly," she suggested, pointing to the right side, but by then, the girls were no longer hovering near the open bathroom door.

Pamela entered the main room, heard voices, parted the curtains, and saw the girls jutting over the edge of the balcony, elbows propped on the railing. Out beyond stretched a wide expanse of sandy beach sprinkled with umbrellas and bright rectangles of towels, tanned bodies, the green-blue Atlantic vanishing into an indistinct horizon. The sun was behind them, midway down from noon.

Pamela stepped onto the balcony. "Oh! Doesn't it look beautiful! Let's get down to the beach, girls!"

Becca turned her face halfway over her shoulder. "That's okay, Mom. We'll stay here."

"Well, first we'll have to have a meeting," she declared, fearing a sudden disintegration of order. "I'll get Gary and the boys."

Not waiting for a response, she turned and went back to the suite where the boys had already rummaged through the food bags and were making peanut butter sandwiches on the kitchenette counter. She called through the closed bedroom door, "Gary, you in there?"

"Yeah."

"Let's get everyone together. We have to plan the rest of the day."

"Don't need any plans. Let's just go down to the beach."

"I wanna go to the pool!" gurgled Matt around peanut butter.

"But the girls. They're over there alone. We have to set some rules."

"They'll come with us."

"What makes you think they'll come with us?"

The door flew open and out stepped Gary, a tall projection, brimming with life.

"I'm going with Mom and Dad to the beach,"

declared Steven.

"What about the pool?"

"You boys, definitely, are coming with us."

Now *that* was a rule. An ironclad rule, no thinking, no negotiating allowed. "The boys stay with us, no question," agreed Pamela. "But the girls said they want to stay in their room—"

"On such a beautiful day? We've got three or four hours of beach time."

"That's not fair, they get to do what they want. We're staying here too—"

"No! I wanna go to the beach with Mom and Dad."

"You boys are going with us, that's it. You're not roaming around on your own."

"But you're letting Becca do whatever she wants to!"

"No, we're not!" said Pamela. "Gary, let's go talk to the girls. Stay here, boys."

Back in the hallway, Pam jiggled the doorknob to the girls' room. Somehow, during her short absence, the door had been locked. "Becca?" She knocked. "Rebecca McClennon, please open up!" She willed her voice into a pleasant singsong. Shortness rarely worked.

The door opened on Becca's sullen face, and the parents walked right in. "Where's Carly, dear?" asked Pamela.

Becca shrugged and turned her head, vaguely motioning. The full-length curtains ballooned under a sea breeze, exposing an empty balcony. The bathroom door was closed, the room semi-dark.

Pamela accepted Becca's answer, didn't want to push it. For a long moment, they stood in a sheltering bubble of silence, its deceptive protection gradually surrendering to outside intruders: crashing surf, distant laughter, squeals of playing children, clanking kitchenware, an angry male voice. Pamela was taken by a swell of discordant emotion, aching love and a dread of inevitable mistake—the slipping edge of control—etching a permanent impression of this place and moment as she stood eye-to-eye with her fourteen-year-old. Becca was already a grown woman in some ways yet so unbearably, heartbreakingly unaware, refusing to look her mother in the eye.

"We're going to the beach now and would like you and Carly to come along."

"We'll just stay here, okay? It's too late to go."

"It's only four," Gary said. "We've got at least three hours left."

Pamela turned to him. "When do you want dinner? You want to go to Giovanni's?"

"Sure, but let's go late. Maybe eight or nine."

"Nine's too late," said Becca.

"Eight, then. Listen up." Gary's signal that he'd taken control. At times Pam resented this, but at the moment, she felt instant relief. "You can stay here, or you can come out to the beach later and find us. You'll be able to see us from the balcony, we'll be right in front of the hotel. But that's it! No roaming around. It's either here or there."

"Okay," said Becca, eyes down. There was a small crash in the bathroom, the sound of hard plastic on tile.

"We'll be back between seven and seven-thirty to clean up for dinner. So we'll see you then and leave for dinner about quarter to eight."

"Okay."

Gary turned to go. Pamela hesitated. "Got your key?" she asked, knowing that Fred would let them in if they lost it.

"Yeah, over there." Motioning to the bureau.

"I packed two towels in your suitcase. Bring them if you come."

"Okay."

"It's a beautiful day. You should be out."

"Uh-huh."

A torrent of water flowed into the bathroom sink.

"All right. See you later, I guess."

"I guess."

"She never did this before," complained Pam as they set up on the beach. "She always came with us."

"It's all right. Let her have some space."

"Meg always wanted to join in. If Meg were here..."

"Things change. She's growing up."

It wasn't just the growing up. It was that girl, Carly. But Pam left it alone and allowed Gary to rub sunscreen into her back, even though the danger of a burn was nonexistent at this hour. It was all part of the therapy, skin on skin, blending smells of salt air and tanning oil, the rhythm of the surf, voices muffled, immersed. They leaned back into their beach chairs, side by side, elbows on armrests. Pinkies hooked, unhooked, fingertips explored warm skin on forearms, backs of hands. A few hours of this could make you forget where you were, who you were, could suggest the idiocy of obligation and responsibility.

Good enough that the twins remained somewhere on the fringes of Pamela's peripheral vision, if and when she opened her eyes. What a blessing that they got on so well together, tossing the football halfway up the beach, nearly as far away as the girls, back in their room. The girls! How easily they were forgotten, the need to forget lingering just below consciousness, tinged with guilt.

Maybe Gary's experience was different. He'd remained himself, apart from the children, and could accept their individuality. She glanced sideways through half-closed eyes, contemplating his secret. Maybe he was better at covering it up. Didn't he feel the same kind of torment over their daughter? The fear of mistake, the need to control and protect, the opposite urge to disengage, the burden of responsibility, the hurt of rejection, the futility of breaking through. Overwhelming love. He felt all these things, didn't he? His face was placid, relaxed, eyes fluttering shut, heavy jaw tugging his mouth slightly open. She didn't need to ask. Didn't want to discuss it! Just to forget—such bliss, an empty mind!

She settled deep into the canvas chair and pushed impressions into the sand with her toes while her eyes skimmed the edge of the world, a fuzzy gray membrane between ocean and sky at the horizon. Everything between here and there was clouded with thousands of miles of emotion pulling her farther and farther out to a place where she couldn't keep afloat, where she might just drop off the end of the world if she didn't resist and pull some of it back home to a safer place where she could ride the roll, the push and pull, the groping and withdrawal. Closeness and distance, the surf rushing in and receding.

Something cold on her feet. From inside the surging ocean, a voice was speaking.

"Pammy."

Her arms were folded under a towel draped over her chest and shoulders, extending to her knees. A cool breeze prickled goose bumps into her skin.

"Pam."

Sand stung the bare skin of her calves.

"Ow! Get away!"

"Boys! Cut it out! Pamela."

She opened her eyes. Foam licked her toes.

"It's seven-thirty. We have to go."

"Oh!" She sat upright. "Where's Becca?"

"Still in the room. Let's get back."

Still groggy, she sank back into the chair, not willing to give up her private, internal beach just yet. More sleep was needed, a gentle dissipation into the sea mist. When at last she rose, the boys were halfway back to the Villa, Gary at attention with his chair folded under one arm. She folded the towel, collapsed the chair, and asked, "Did they come down while I was asleep?"

"Nope, still back in the room." A touch of annoyance, maybe worry.

Back inside, they stopped first at the threshold to the girls' room. A TV could be heard, but there was no response to Pamela's knock. She tried the door. It was locked. "Becca?" She called more than once. "Just like her to leave the TV on. Maybe they went to the pool."

"That was against the rules," declared Gary.

"We'll go check the pool!" screeched Steven.

"No, you don't," said Pam. "You all go take your showers and I'll check the pool."

But she knew, well before arriving, that she wouldn't find them there. Something told her in the hush of the corridor and the silence behind closed doors. Certainly there were people in the Villa; she'd seen the cars in the lot. Outside in the back, shadow engulfed the patio with its small square of blue water and that cement urn displaying a dead coleus. The dolphin fountain still spouted a thin stream into the shallow end where she'd waded and splashed with her babies in years past. Empty.

Lingering, she put her fingertips in the water. Warm. *See, it's warm. Don't be afraid!*

In the next minute, unaware how she arrived, she was back upstairs in the third-floor hallway. Magically, there they stood, bedecked in their best teenager-style eveningwear, cotton mini-dresses and platform sandals. Holding Coke cans. Standing next to Pamela's door.

"Where *were* you?" demanded Becca.

"Looking for you. No one answered when we knocked." She focused on their hands. "You'll spoil your appetite—"

"We've been waiting for you *forever*. We're *starving*."

From behind the falling sheet, Carly single-eyed Pamela through black-mascaraed lashes. Becca's eyes had also sprouted black twigs, and her lips were the silvery gray hue of an asphyxiation victim.

"Sorry. We fell asleep on the beach. But we aren't too late, are we?"

"You're always falling asleep."

"Well, okay, we'll be ready in a minute."

In the suite, Gary was nearly cleaned up and the boys had accomplished their obligatory thirty-second rinse off. Pamela quickly changed without taking a shower.

Out in the hallway, Steven took one look at Becca and screamed, "*Yowza,* it's Spider Woman!" before running ahead. Matthew caught up with him, and the boys kept their lead while the girls lagged behind during the ten-minute trek into town. Gary glanced back and whispered into Pamela's ear, "How can they walk in those things?" From behind, their guest grumbled: "Why can't we take the car?"

At Giovanni's, everyone ordered the usual heap of spaghetti and garlic bread. Becca spoke up for a silent, indecisive Carly and ordered for her. Every McClennon had taken several heaping forkfuls before Carly managed to pull up a few strands from her plate. The tip of her loose sheet of hair hung dangerously close to her mouth, but she slid the fork just underneath it, biting off the strands and letting the rest fall to her plate. She chewed slowly, swallowed, dropped her fork and announced, "Noodles make you fat."

Becca gulped down the wad in her mouth and waited a full minute before taking another bite while Carly examined, then nibbled, a buttery piece of garlic bread. Apparently Carly's dietary beliefs didn't condemn grease, thought Pamela, reminded once again of the odors in the Defner home. But her judgments vanished when Carly gave one of her surprising smiles and said, "This is good." Before the meal was through, she'd eaten two full pieces of the bread, tidbit by tidbit.

* * *

The next morning, even with a comfortable time for sleeping in, Pam, Gary, and the boys had eaten breakfast and were ready for the beach by 10:30. Lunch was packed with the hopes of enjoying the fine weather before thundershowers loomed, predicted for late afternoon. Set to go, Pam went next door to rouse the girls. There was no answer after several raps. Gary came into the hallway to coax her back.

"Leave them be," he suggested.

"They could sleep through anything. The hotel could be on fire and they wouldn't know."

"But it isn't."

"They must have been up all night."

"What did you expect? We'll just go, and they can come or not."

"But we can't leave without telling them."

"Mom?" A muffled voice from inside.

"Becca? Open up, please."

"We want to sleep."

"Okay," said Gary. "Just come down to the beach when you're up."

"Okay."

And so they left, and once out on the beach, it was again easy to forget. They had a few good hours, but by two o'clock, the sky had started to cloud and people around them were packing up. The surf rushed in. The tide was high, at the end of its gradual, inevitable return. Pamela felt a presence behind her, more of an intuition. She turned around in her chair to see Becca standing a few yards back, silently contemplating the ocean. Alone.

"My goodness, Becca! How long have you been standing there?"

Gary turned around too.

"Not too long." She was barefoot, wearing a tank top and shorts, no towel, nothing else. Her eyes were red and smudged black with yesterday's mascara.

"Where's Carly?"

Becca looked down at her feet and said, "She didn't want to come."

"Here." Pamela grabbed a fresh towel and motioned. "Come sit." She spread the towel next to her chair. "Come on, honey." Here was her daughter, returning to her.

Becca hesitated before sitting. Pam leaned over the side of the chair and draped an arm around her daughter's shoulder while glancing back the other way, hoping to share a knowing look with Gary. She was startled to find a stern look on his face, his eyes straight out to sea, avoiding them. Well, she would just ignore him too.

"Have a nice sleep?" she asked lightly, but somehow it rang of accusation.

Becca's lower lip started to quiver. "She didn't want to come, and now there's no sun left."

"Yup, looks like a storm, sooner than they predicted. But let's stay out here 'til the last minute, okay? Until the thunder starts! It's so beautiful, isn't it?"

"We'd better get back." Gary's voice cut through, harsh.

"I don't see any reason—"

"We're not leaving Carly in the room alone. We're responsible for her."

All of a sudden responsible! "Well, if we can leave two fourteen-year-olds alone together cooking up mischief, we can certainly leave one of them alone, and Becca came out to enjoy the beach."

"We're not at home. This is a strange place to her—"

"Strange? The Villa Del Mar?"

"You know what I mean! We shouldn't leave that girl alone in a hotel room." Instantly their avoidance U-turned into a head-on collision, eyes caught in a look of anger and astonishment. They stared into each other, opposites of their usual selves.

Pamela was the first to give in. That girl. Maybe acceptable to leave someone else alone in the room, but not *that* girl. "Well, sure, of course, we'll go back," she whispered.

Gary softened too. "No need for all of us to go."

"Of course we'll all go."

"I'll go up alone. You stay here with the kids and enjoy—"

"Dad—"

"That's ridiculous. The clouds are about to burst anyway."

"Mom—"

"Don't let me spoil your beach time. I'll go."

"Dad, she's not—"

"Not what?" Gary turned to stare at Becca.

"She's not, well maybe, she might not really be in the room right now."

"Not in the room? Where is she?"

"Just maybe. I really don't know. She might be back by now."

"By *now*? Where did she go?"

Pamela couldn't stand this. She jumped to her feet and called out, loud and raspy into the wind: "Steve! Matt! Come on! We're going!" Down the line of surf, the boys chased another retreating wave and dropped to their knees, digging furiously for sand crabs. "Boys! Come on!" Pamela waved her arms without effect while the boys laughed and poked at squiggling life in their hands.

"Pamela! Sit down a minute!"

She remained standing and turned around with hands on hips, looking at Gary, at Becca, at Gary. "So, where is she? Down at the pool?"

"I don't think so."

"Where then?"

"She said it was so boring with my parents all the time, and how could I stand to be around you nagging me every minute, and she just had to take a little break and get away, you know…"

"No! I don't know! Where did she go?"

"Just, she just said she was going into town—"

"Into *town*!" Pamela spun around to face the ocean. She shook her head, clapped her hands over her ears. "I don't *believe* this! I'm not hearing this! How could you just let her wander off?"

"Jeez, Mom! It's just into town! It's no big deal!"

"Don't get so riled up, everyone." Gary, rational and calm again. He stood. "We'll just pack up and go look for her. She couldn't have gone far. Becca just got here a minute ago."

"But Daddy." Her voice quavered. "She left, like, a long time ago."

"Oh!" Pam stomped a foot and folded her arms across her chest, refusing to look at them. Both of them.

"When?" Gary.

"Like early, like just before you knocked on the door, and I've been waiting for her..."

"My God, why didn't you tell us?" The lie was replayed: *We want to sleep.* Pam looked back in time for a clue. She'd been listening to the radio while making their sandwiches, but even so, why hadn't she heard anything through those thin walls? Voices, a closing door? Was she so absorbed in her picnic making? A picnic for God's sake!

"She said she was coming right back, and I told her to, and, oh Daddy, she's been acting so weird this whole trip! All I said was I wanted to go to the beach today, and she just got all weird and said like, 'with your parents?' It was so *disrespectful* I didn't even want to be around her. Why did I even invite her anyway? She ruined everything!"

Heaving, wrenching sobs, the end-of-the-world kind. *So disrespectful!* Pamela's chest filled with pride, and a tear came to her eye in a surge of mother love—but too late! Gary had won out. Father and daughter stood as one, the sobbing Becca wrapped in Gary's arms as he stroked the long, soft hair down her back. Despite her lost chance, Pamela reached out and touched Becca's crown. "I'm so sorry, Becca. It wasn't your fault." She let her hand fall away. "I'll get the boys."

An angry sky spoke with a distant rumble, telling them it would soon be dangerous under this black roof. Whitecaps crested, sand swirled and flew, wind lashed strands of hair across eyes. Running up the line of surf, Pamela felt a single drop on her cheek, a splash of water so big she nearly mistook its source. She gathered up the boys, and they all fled to the Villa, chased by thunder. They were just inside when the sky opened up and the heavens descended.

Becca checked her room, no Carly. They decided to split up, Gary and Becca in the minivan to town, Pamela staying behind with the twins. Carly will return any minute, they said out loud before parting.

Minutes later, cooped up inside and unable to act, Pam was overwhelmed by the falsity of hope. Becca and Gary would get a good drenching is all. The noise was unbearable, a source of childish excitement in the boys, who stood at the window, whooping it up with every boom and flash. She wondered if Gary had remembered his cell phone. She called it and received no answer, but how could he hear anything under the din?

Half an hour later, the lightning diminished but the deluge continued, nearly as loud. The boys lost interest in the storm and turned on the TV, volume turned high to cover the downpour. Deafening. Wouldn't it be funny if Carly had just walked in next door, unheard? "I'm going to the girls' room," she told them. "Don't you dare move from here!"

Pamela stood in the hallway, remembering she didn't have a key. She raised her hand to knock—how many times had she knocked on this door?—before noticing that it stood open a crack. "Carly?" she called softly, pressing fingertips gently on wood. The door swung open on a room littered with clothing, shoes, magazines, CDs, and beauty notions, every square inch of floor covered, the abandoned scene of clandestine activity and conversation. And dark, always so dark in here, especially with the storm.

Becca had left the balcony door open behind closed curtains, now bloating up under a mighty, gusting wind. Pamela went to that opening, stepping on things along the way and not caring about the crunch of plastic underfoot. Swiping at the billowing curtains, she caught them wet in two arms as her canvas shoes soaked up the water from soggy carpet. A stray fissure of lightning and crash of thunder. She pinned the curtains in the crook of an arm and managed a two-handed pull of the sliding glass door, shutting it with a satisfying vacuum seal and a sudden limp surrender of the heavy, wet material. She was drenched. Canned laughter came up from the TV next door.

She chose the twin bed that appeared to be Becca's and pushed her daughter's things aside. Sitting with elbows on knees, chin resting in hands, she surveyed the mess, searching for evidence—of what? In a far corner lay Carly's ungainly suitcase, open and spewing its unnecessary contents. At the foot of the bed were Becca's small bag and backpack. Near the bathroom door lay Carly's cosmetic box, unzipped and half empty. The duffel and the canvas bag seemed to be gone.

Maybe underneath the mess? She could search, but no, she wouldn't. Becca would have said something if Carly had left with a packed duffel bag. She would have told them, wouldn't she? Still, maybe a search was in order, just for the peace of mind. But a weight bore down on her, making it impossible to move.

Extracting her cell phone from pants pocket, Pam saw the time and fought back tears. 3:58. Carly had been gone most of the day, and that woman should be called. It was time to call. But what if she called and Carly walked through the door a minute later? Pam could wait just a bit longer before calling a person like that, a woman who appeared to have given up, who didn't even care to say goodbye. A woman who'd raised a girl like that. Pam would wait. After all, what could be said? How could anything help?

The laughter was gone. There was no sound in fact. The rain had stopped, and light filtered in through cracks in the curtains. It was quiet enough to hear…nothing at all.

She bolted out to the hallway and into the suite, but there they were, sitting on the floor, television off, amazingly quiet, obedient, radiant children, models of good manners. "Your turn, Matt," said Steven. A roll of the dice and a click of the metal racecar five spaces to Park Place. "Hi, Mom! She come back yet?" And instead of Steven's face, Pamela saw that girl's face opening into one of her toothy, surprising smiles.

The vision sent Pam on a straight line to the bedside table where she fumbled with her little leather book, thumbed the tab for "D" and opened it to "Defner." How could a mother not love that face, not wish every possible best thing, even for *that* girl—a struggling, confused, beautiful girl who only needed to be loved, a girl who could cause such worry and fright? And who else would know how to help but the girl's own mother? Pam burned with shame as she punched in the numbers.

There was no time to plan what to say. Voicemail for "the Defner residence" clicked on. "Sandy" came to mind under the influence of the beach, but really it was Stacey, and still Pamela was afraid to go out on a limb. She pushed down her beating heart and said, "Hello. This is Pamela McClennon. Um, please give us a call when you get in. Just give us a call as soon as you can. Thanks so much." She'd barely pressed "END" when her cell phone rang, sending her heart back up into her throat.

"She back yet?" asked Gary.

"No, not yet."

"We'll keep looking. Maybe you'd better call—"

"Yes, we should, and I did. I did just now."

Two hours later, Gary and Becca returned, still damp, although the rain had ended some time ago. They'd traipsed through town getting drenched, asking at the pharmacy, the movie theater, the donut shop, the grocery store, every restaurant and hot dog stand. It wasn't a big town, but they'd doubled and tripled back, even gone into outlying residential neighborhoods, following up on leads. She'd been spotted here and there, clearly it was her, a teenager with four piercings in one ear carrying a medium-sized duffel bag. Yes, a duffel, but how could Becca have known? She'd been so angry that she'd gone out to sulk on the balcony deck when Carly left.

The police were discussed. Gary and Becca had searched more thoroughly than the police would have, but when was it proper to report a missing person? Twenty-four hours seemed likely and it had been only eight, but wasn't this a different case, and what exactly made it different? An intuition that the child would run? "Did she ever speak of running away? Did she, Becca?" Met with a shrug and downcast eyes, and a "No," and then "Did she ever, Becca?" and a "No! Never!" The interrogation caused another round of sobbing, Becca suffering more than the rest of them combined. After all, she'd been the one to invite that troublesome enigma. With the approval of her father, Pam might add.

The only ones not seriously concerned were Steve and Matt, now fallen off their good-behavior mode. Peanut butter sandwiches had gone only so far and they were crying for dinner, clawing to get out. Pizza in the room wouldn't do. "Stop asking, we simply can't leave," said Pam. "We're not going anywhere. We stay until she returns."

"She's not coming back!" yelled Matt.

"Shush!"

"I'll stay," said Gary. "You go. Take the kids to dinner."

"I can't eat a thing."

"Me either," said Becca.

"Go on anyway, you need a break from this place," he said, opening the refrigerator. "I'll try the Defners again and we'll decide about the police…"

"You go!" she said. "You're hungry, I can tell." Gary was always hungry, come what may. "We can't eat. We'll stay, won't we Becca?" Pamela wrapped an arm around her daughter and pulled her close. The girl slumped down to become a child again, pressing her face into mother's shoulder while mother pressed a cheek onto daughter's soft crown, not wanting to look at her husband and wishing for him to take his sons and be gone. *You* go to dinner, she thought, because a mother's intuition should *never* be reasoned away, and a young daughter must be protected from her own immature judgments. Protection was never wrong. Never wrong.

But then the door opened, and Carly walked in.

Pamela looked up over Becca's head. Becca turned to look. Gary looked. The boys looked.

"I heard all of you in here." Carly glanced around the room, one face to the next. "Am I too late?"

Silence. In the doorway stood Carly, a stranger to them, duffel slung over one shoulder, maybe not such a huge duffel, not an overnight kind of duffel, but a very large bag for someone who needed a large number of possessions along for the day. She smiled brazenly, showing all those teeth one wouldn't think a mouth could hold. "I mean, what is it? Is it past dinner? Like, last night you ate later."

Tears sprang into Pamela's eyes, relief mixed with outrage—such outrageous behavior! The line was drawn, the McClennons, dumbfounded, in one camp, the sole Defner in the other, worlds apart, wanting to understand but not wishing to be the other, not for a second. The gleam in Carly's eyes, a tiny, self-satisfied gloat, slowly transformed into a frantic cast, a searching look filled with fear and insecurity, a silent scream for attention, approval, inclusion.

"Yes, we're ready for dinner. We've been waiting for you…a long time."

"But I told Becca I was going into town. You look all

worried or something."

In her hand, Pam's cell phone rang. Everyone froze. Pam glanced at the screen, stepped away from Becca, and answered the call.

"Hi. This is Shelley Defner." *Shelley.* "You called?"

"Yes," said Pam.

"We were out to a matinee." *We.* Yes, a Mr. Defner, a marriage, a home. Out to the movies, just like Pam and Gary would be if the kids were away with friends. "Is everything all right?"

She sounded worried, and how could she not be? Pamela remembered every word of the message she'd left, the clues, the break in her voice.

"We, uh…" She couldn't say all of it. Another time she would relate everything, hide nothing, because the mother must know. But not just yet, not in front of Carly. She would hold onto this daughter of Shelley's. Hold her fast and away from harm and return her home, as quickly as she could. "We were just thinking of coming back earlier than we planned. Maybe tomorrow. The weather's been bad. Very bad."

She looked up at Gary, caught his eye and held it while Mrs. Defner, Shelley, said something into the phone about her plans for tomorrow. *I'm sorry*, Pam's eyes said while his returned, *no, I am*, because that was their way in most things whenever the ground beneath them rumbled—to rush toward one another, open and changing, ready to settle once the tremor ceased.

☾ *Everything We Do*

IN 2021, LEONORE PONDROSE, well loved by her husband Philbert and daughters Thalia and Suzette, dies peacefully in her sleep at the age of eighty-five. Phil is eighty-nine and the girls are fifty-six and fifty-eight, respectively.

Without going into a lot of names, suffice it to say that Leonore also leaves behind two sons-in-law and six adult grandchildren, a few of whom are on the brink of starting families of their own. These ten family members take advantage of a special bereavement-rate airfare and fly into New York to attend the funeral, Thalia and her family from Houston, Suzette and her family from Chicago.

Back in the '80s, a complicated set of circumstances involving college and career and fiancés caused Thally and Suze to drift away from the East Coast and become ensconced in their lives thousands of miles away from Leonore and Philbert. But they are good daughters and they love their parents and they've always visited—or tried to visit—at least once a year. Now that they've returned after the death of their mother, they each stay a decent fourteen days with their grieving father. Sons-in-law and grandchildren are not quite so attached, and they book flights back home within a day or two after the funeral.

For fifty-five of her eighty-five years, Leonore had a law practice specializing in wills, trusts, and estates. Phil is also a lawyer and now a retired judge. Given this set of circumstances, Leonore's financial affairs upon her death are very well in hand. Everything passes to Phil, and a trust is established for his living expenses. The girls are co-trustees but have the option of appointing a financial manager in their stead.

Phil's papers are also very well in order. Upon his death, the fruits of the combined life efforts of Mr. and Mrs. Pondrose will be distributed in equal parts to Thally and Suze, or to their descendants should they predecease their father.

For two weeks, Suzette and Thalia sleep in their girlhood bedrooms, surrounded by the furniture they picked out as teens. Insomnia rules, and they spend many a late night together in one bedroom or the other, talking into the wee hours.

On the second night after the funeral, they've brought a copy of the will and testamentary trust into Thally's bedroom. Powers of attorney, in their names, are attached. The midnight oil burns.

Thally quotes aloud from a particularly dense bit of legalese and declares, "We can't possibly handle this." Neither daughter has followed the footsteps of their parents into the esteemed profession of the law.

"Speak for yourself," replies Suze, the one with a

business degree. She gave up her career at a trading firm when her kids were small. Now back at work, she's had to settle for the tedious job of income tax preparation.

"Speaking for myself, I don't have a minute to breathe in the day." Thally has cause to complain. Her youngest, a special needs child, is now twenty and still lives at home. Further to this, if one were to catch Thally in a particular mood on book group night (every third Wednesday of the month), she might be heard to complain of her "special needs" husband as well. Although Thally has a degree in social work, she has never had the opportunity to use it in a professional setting outside the home.

"Maybe there's not so much to do." Suzette is thinking of Daddy's office with its file cabinets full of alphabetized folders—a pinnacle of organization within the family home and an extension of the career of the retired judge. A computer too, but mostly paper, quaint and slowly efficacious. It is the judge's habit to shuffle into the office every morning at about nine o'clock, lean into the desktop while lowering himself defensively into the leather chair, and apply himself to the correspondence, bills, and family accounts for a good two to three hours. But he hasn't set foot in that room since the morning of the night that Leonore died.

"Right now, I don't think…" They are in tacit agreement that their daddy needs help.

"I can do most of it," offers Suze, not foreseeing her state of mind a year from now, when she will rue the day and become slightly resentful.

They fall into silence. These discussions of practical

details are a convenient but fragile cover for greater things within.

A big splotch of water lands on the residuary estate clause in the document on Thally's lap. "Lenny and Phil!" she exclaims in a quavering voice. "What a sweet couple!"

"So perfect for one another!" agrees Suze.

"They took care of each other, didn't they?"

"And now what?"

"We're leaving. He'll be alone."

"We have to stay a while longer."

"Jeff is already going crazy. I have to get back."

"But who's going to…?"

"Oh, what will Daddy *do*?"

"You saw him today. He didn't want to get out of bed."

"We can't leave him."

They are both crying now, at opposite ends of the twin bed. Thally scoots close and buries her face in her older sister's fluffy terrycloth shoulder of calming baby blue. An arm pulls Thally in, and they clutch and sniffle and hiccup like this for another five minutes.

A thought zings through them simultaneously, and they raise their heads, each finding the red rimmed, gold-brown eyes of the other. In the same breath, they exclaim: "Greta!"

Thally launches directly into "a Greta," acting both parts.

"Mr. Pondrose, are you comfortable?"

"Yes, perfectly so!"

"Would you like me to fluff the pillow?"

"Oh, I always love the way you fluff, please do!"

"And is the temperature of the tea to your liking?"

"Greta, you know how to make my chamomile tea just so!"

Suzette is now in stitches, with tears of loss streaming down her cheeks.

Leonore was generally a reserved, serious kind of person, but every once in a while, particularly when she'd had more than one glass of wine at dinner, she could let loose and make everyone laugh. She had a night like this in the summer of 1985 when the girls were home from college, Suze between bachelor's degree and grad school, Thally between sophomore and junior years. In their absence, the house had been so deathly empty despite the elder Pondroses' love of Mahler symphonies, especially the Resurrection, played at high volume on the home entertainment system.

The girls' brief homecomings were a pure delight for Leonore and Philbert during these college years, when their daughters were no longer girls but girls enough to infuse the air with that special kind of jazzed energy and spark and idealism only the young possess. Grown but not quite adult, gone but not yet permanently away. Suze the pretty and smart one and Thally the prettier and almost as smart one, or this is how the girls, not quite women, thought of themselves with some bit of inaccuracy. Leonore and Philbert knew—and had the evidence to prove—that both of their daughters were exceptionally gifted, beautiful, and intelligent in vastly different ways.

"I declare this before the entire family!" Mommy's

cheeks were pink from the wine. "When I'm gone, my husband should marry again! I give him my permission and blessing!" Only moments before, she'd declared a lack of interest in acquiring a new (old) husband if Phil should be the first to go.

"Never!" boomed Daddy. "You're my one and only love."

"I'm not saying you have to *love* her." She looked at her daughters one at a time. "He'll need someone to take care of him, don't you think?"

"Definitely for sure," said Suze.

"But he *can't* have another wife," Thally pouted. "I won't let him."

"Don't worry, Thalia. I'm not dying 'til I'm ninety-two, so Daddy will be ninety-six. At that age, the new wife won't really be a wife, if you know what I mean."

"This is ludicrous!" exclaimed the judge. "Married at ninety-six!"

"Now, Phil. A younger woman is all right. Find someone who's hard working, and make sure you don't squander the family assets. Get her to sign a pre-nup."

"Ludicrous!"

"Everything we do is for *you*, girls," said Leonore, turning a pointed look at Thalia while squeezing the hand of the girl nearest at table, Suzette. "Don't let the new woman get a penny!"

"You can't force me into this!" Philbert banged the table. "I will *not* get married again!" He stood and crossed his arms, snorting like an angry horse.

Suze giggled.

"Darn right, Daddy!" Thally cheered him on.

Suze said, "Don't worry, Mommy, we'll take care of him."

"Sit down, darling. I know what you need." And Leonore got up, placed her hands on Philbert's shoulders, kissed him lightly on the cheek, and gently pushed him back into his chair at the head of the table. "There, there." She reached over, cut a morsel off his lamb chop, and guided it into his mouth with the fork in her right hand while the left caressed the nape of his neck. "Chew thoroughly now!"

"I think we can do all that, can't we baby sis?"

"We're not letting him marry anyone!" said Thally gleefully.

Leonore picked up the napkin and dabbed at her husband's mouth. He was thoroughly enjoying the attention. He swallowed and said, "I'm not marrying anyone," a bit softer than before. "And I won't allow the girls to take care of me. They have their own lives to live."

"All right, darling. You tell us. Have another bite?" She took up the knife again.

"Yes, please. But if you aren't my second wife, who *are* you?"

She cut off another morsel. "My goodness, things are getting a little fuzzy now, aren't they? Don't you remember me? I'm your home health aide. Here, take another bite. That's a good boy." He opened up. "Just call me Greta."

And from that day on, Greta took up invisible residence in the Pondrose household, now and again choosing to enter the body of Lenny or Suze or Thally or

Phil. Greta was on call 24-7, and if any one of them happened to be down or ill or in need of special attention, she would miraculously appear, ready to soothe and feed and pamper and offer love.

In 2028, Philbert dies peacefully in his sleep at the age of ninety-six. He dies at home because he has never left it, although he began sleeping in the ground floor guest-room three years ago when the stairs were finally too much for him.

The blood descendants of Leonore and Philbert are now thirteen in number. Thalia is a grandmother of two, and Suzette a grandmother of three. For the funeral, Thalia and Suzette and their husbands and a few, but not all, of the remaining thirteen fly into New York. In a day or two, all of them, except Philbert's daughters, fly home.

The sisters, now sixty-three and sixty-five, take up a brief residence in their girlhood bedrooms. Their love for these rooms, this magisterial old home, is magnified tenfold from within the prism of their new status as orphans. Immersed in memories, the girls are over-whelmed by the steady rich goodness and perfection of their upbringing in this house, where the walls still breathe and hush and scold and laugh in the voices of Mommy and Daddy. This house is a physical mani-festation of the Pondrose family, a treasure-filled memorial to the man and woman who built a life here for their two little girls.

In the aftermath of the funeral, their days in the family home are tense and strained and throat-choking, more so than they might otherwise be. Greta is sleeping in the upstairs master bedroom—the bedroom of the departed. The love children of Lenny and Phil have asked her, kindly, to go, but she will not. Her presence does not seem right, now that Daddy is gone.

They are surprised even at themselves. They are forced to look back and can see, without difficulty, the foreshadowing. Everything has always been out in the open and with their knowledge, if not their blessing. What did they expect?

But their intense need obliterates acceptance of these predictable consequences. In this moment, the only thing they should be required to endure is the death of their father. They feel this acutely. Very unfairly, the circumstances do not allow them, simply, to grieve. Unpleasant surprises yet await them, things of which they are still unaware but sense with the knowledge of dread.

After several days, they must return to their own lives, to cope with their loss within the arms of the families they have created. The surprises will be communicated to them by strangers, from a distance. The sisters will make their decision together with the resolve to present a united front. At first, Thally is willing to roll over, but Suzette is not. In the end, Suzette prevails and they decide to act, but they haven't yet discovered what their driving motivation might be, or whether it is the same or different for each of them.

Almost a year after Daddy is laid to rest, the day comes when they sit in the front pew, feeling the smooth slide of wood under their thighs as they watch Greta, stepping up to the confessional. She is a woman of about forty, cushiony and maternal in look, nothing at all like the tall, angular figure of their mother. Only a Pondrose would know how unlike their real mother it was when she first conjured Greta on that evening in 1985. Leonore was nurturing to her core but never obsequious. She loved them infinitely within a moral framework of high expectation for self-sufficiency and personal responsibility.

Of course, the real Greta is known by a different name, but she has proven her talents when it comes to making chamomile tea and plumping pillows.

"State your name for the record."

"Philomena Cutler."

Hand on Bible, she takes the oath, this Philomena Cutler. Thally leans into her sister and hisses, "Ludicrous!" mimicking Daddy and putting a smile on Suze's lips. Seven years ago, on the day they hired Daddy's Greta, the girls had childish fun with names behind her back. A real Greta would have been an anagram of "great," but this one is a Phil for Phil, and a Cutler besides, bringing to mind Mommy's adroit handling of that lamb chop. The name was scary, but they couldn't pass up Philomena (she would *not* allow them to call her "Phil") because they knew a good one when they saw her.

Just yesterday, on the eve of Philomena's testimony, Thally and Suze were talking, trying to make sense of the past. They remembered the very, very tough time for Daddy in the months after Mommy was newly gone. For a while, they maintained a constant communication with him by telephone, and Suzette helped with his financial affairs. Six months later, they both flew back to New York "to gang up" on him—as he put it—insisting on hiring help for him. They knew better than to suggest that he move out. It would kill him.

Don't worry about me, he kept saying in that masterful voice, rich and low. In their minds, the judge had always spoken from the bench and always would.

But we do worry about you all alone in this big house.

My God, girls, how can you worry? You haven't lived here for thirty-five years!

The edge surprised them. It was a new Daddy, wrapped in his continuing grief. The girls had left him long ago, and now, so had Mommy.

These thoughts float beneath consciousness as they watch their attorney examine Philomena. She renders a detailed history of her employment. She has no immediate family of her own and is able to work long hours. At first, she juggled Mr. Pondrose with her other cases, working for him three half days a week. In a year's time, it became five half days, in another year, five full days, and in the last four years of his life, she lived in. She did the shopping and cooking and laundry and driving to medical appointments and procedures. There were plumbers or repairmen to call when something went wrong in the house, landscapers to supervise. There was the accounting to Suzette, who released the funds for living expenses and doctor bills and paid Philomena's wage, granting her yearly raises.

Philomena does so much for me.

There was the effort to maintain the professional calendar of a retired judge, the occasional bar association dinner or ceremonial function at the court. There was a dwindling social life with close family friends who, one by one, died off. There were the funerals to attend.

I'd like to give her something special.

For exercise, the judge maintained his daily walks in the garden and along the sculpted paths of the Pondrose grounds, at first on Philomena's arm, then shuffling on the walker. In the last year, walks were impossible, but the judge liked to take his fresh air in the wheelchair. Ramps were installed. The process of getting him into the wheelchair and out of the house took at least an hour.

Of course you should, Daddy.

There was needed help in the bathroom, increasing over the years, a catheter when Mr. Pondrose suffered a UTI, and finally, the diaper-like briefs to change. There were occasional trips to the emergency room, not many, one of them particularly frightening, resolved with a pacemaker. In the end, there was the frequent turning of the skeletal form to avoid bedsores.

Just let us know.

There was the extra housecleaning, shopping, cooking, and preparation for visits from Thalia and Suzette and their children and grandchildren. Mr. Pondrose—she never called him by his first name—frequently spoke of his daughters and grandchildren and great grandchildren with affection.

Before this day, Thalia and Suzette have been in the presence of Philomena dozens of times. But today is the first day they really see her.

This morning, at the start of the court proceedings, Thalia's stomach was clenched in knots and acid reflux cinched her throat. Now, as she listens to the witness, the knots loosen and her mouth becomes sweet tasting again.

At the start of the proceedings this morning, Suzette was in the throes of red-eyed, fist-clenching anger. As Philomena speaks, Suze is mesmerized by the fuzzy aura emanating from the woman's plump, dark cheeks. A warm bath rinses Suzette's bloodshot eyes and relaxes her fists.

Philbert's Greta is, after all, their Greta.

Philomena's voice is even toned and melodic, her posture erect, hands resting in her lap atop a little clutch purse. She is unobtrusively self-assured. She possesses a depth of genuine feeling and keeps a handkerchief available for those occasional moments when a teardrop escapes the corner of an eye. She is unassailable.

After two hours of this, their attorney has come to the crucial part of the examination, the reason they all find themselves in this courtroom today. Surely now, Thalia's acid stomach and Suzette's rage will resurface.

"Calling your attention to June 25, 2027, a Friday, were you working that day?"

"Yes, most certainly."

"Do you recall a visit to the house by an attorney, a Mr. Robert Grantham, and his assistant, Delia Jackson?"

"I do."

"Had you arranged that appointment for Mr. Pondrose?"

"I did not."

"Are you aware how these people came to visit?"

"I don't know exactly. I would assume Mr. Pondrose called Mr. Grantham. There were times he spent alone in his office."

"By the way, how would you describe Mr. Pondrose's mental state on the day of the visit?"

"How do you mean, 'mental state'?"

"If you had asked him, say, what year it was, would he know the answer?"

"Certainly he would."

"If you asked him to give the names of his children and grandchildren, could he do that?"

"Without question."

"If you asked him to list his assets and their approximate value, could he do that?"

Philomena pauses and seems to contemplate.

"Could he do that?" the lawyer repeats.

"I have no doubt that he could. Mr. Pondrose was sharp as a tack until the day he died. I only hesitate because I, personally, never had any conversations with him about his assets or their value."

Thally and Suze are thinking the same thing. Philomena's testimony on this point really doesn't matter. The first witness this morning was Mr. Grantham, who attested to Daddy's complete awareness and knowledge and clarity. At the age of ninety-five. Amazingly, Daddy had even obtained a recent appraisal. On that day, June 25, 2027, he produced it when Mr. Grantham pressed him on his knowledge. Not that Mr. Grantham doubted him, but he was duty bound as an attorney and fiduciary to make sure Daddy was in his right mind and his wishes would be honored. To make sure.

"Getting back to the visitors, Mr. Grantham and Ms. Jackson, tell us what happened when they arrived."

"They asked to see Mr. Pondrose. I left them at the door and checked with him first to get his okay. I showed them in and they all sat together in the living room at first, as I recall. I went to the kitchen to prepare coffee for them, and when I returned, they'd all left. From their voices, I could tell they had gone into the office. The door was closed. I knocked and was bid to enter. I set up the coffee for them and left, closing the door behind me."

"How long did they stay in the office?"

"A good hour I'd say."

"Did you enter the office again during that time?"

"No."

"Did you come to learn what went on in that office?"

"Not for some time, no."

"But at some point you did?"

She pauses again for several seconds. She clears her throat gently and brings the handkerchief to a corner of her eye.

"Yes, I did. After his death... I learned everything then, after he was gone."

At five o'clock, the proceedings adjourn. More testimony will be heard tomorrow in this never-ending will contest. Philomena is excused, for now, and she is the first to leave. Everyone rises, and the presiding judge takes leave of the courtroom. The attorneys pack their briefcases and go. Suzette and Thalia, exhausted, remain seated for a moment. Finally, they are the last to retrace their steps down the middle aisle and out the swinging doors.

Outside, the corridor is empty and quiet. They click a

few echoing steps and come to a halt. To their right is the elevator. To their left, a slant of late afternoon sun stripes the floor through the thick slats of venetian blinds on a tall window. A wooden bench is placed opposite the window, and she sits there, straight-backed and serene, waiting for them.

Instinctively, the matching gold-brown eyes of the sisters go to her. Their attorney has advised them not to speak to Philomena, but there she sits, waiting for them. There is no debate about this.

When they've come close, Philomena stands to face them with the little clutch purse held tight against her round abdomen. In the way of all decent people who want to love and be loved, these three women cannot help the pleasant smiles that grow on their faces. But there is a trembling underneath.

"You must be wondering...," she starts. Thalia and Suzette say nothing to fill the awkward break as their little smiles tremble on their faces.

Is this about money and greed? The Pondrose daughters and their families are not impoverished, nor are they wealthy.

Is this about their father's betrayal? Philbert's daughters have never doubted his love for them.

Is this about justice? Perhaps it is just to bequeath a three-million-dollar home to a single woman who gave her childbearing years to an old man, caring for him more intimately than his daughters ever would in their lifetimes. Perhaps it is just to leave the remaining estate of less than a million to the two daughters and their families, the thirteen blood descendants.

"I thought you might have wondered if I ever considered renouncing his gift."

Is this about their father's betrayal of their mother?

Suzette tries to speak but cannot. Her mind screams *yes.*

Philomena's eyes, a very deep chocolate brown, fill with tears. This time, she does not make an effort to find the handkerchief. "Well, I *have* thought of it. Such a large gift."

Thalia tries to speak and manages this: "You never knew our mother. Never knew them together! Everything—" She chokes on the word. *Everything we do is for you...*

"No, I didn't know her. But I knew your father."

The silence, five seconds of it, is deep and long.

"And I loved him."

They know this.

"And I've thought and thought about it. But I cannot renounce his gift."

They know this as well.

"Because it *is* what he wanted." The tears involuntarily spill.

There is nothing left to say, until tomorrow. The trembling little smiles on the faces of the three women grow larger as a means of communicating a farewell. The sisters remain frozen, exchanging stunned murmurings, as Daddy's Greta takes the long corridor alone. They wait until she enters the elevator, alone, until she's well on her way to their childhood home, alone, before they take their first steps toward their destination, a pleasantly sterile hotel suite, five blocks from the courthouse.

☾ Lucky

A SINGLE DROP hung suspended from Jenny's lower lip, stretching, hovering. In a daydream, Marion gazed at the dangling spit, glistening in a ray of light from the kitchen window. *Soft, shiny hair in sunlight. So pretty.*

Jenny's head bobbed forward, the drop fell. Already her shirt was soaked in areas, making black patches on the navy cotton material, smeared with white spots of farina. Marion, by now, had given up on bibs. They did little good.

Jenny's head lurched upright again and tilted slightly to the side. The movement seemed involuntary but was purposeful, filled with the effort of a discus thrower. "Muh." Saliva and unswallowed farina pooled inside her slack lower lip. She was asking for more.

Marion lost the sunlight. She pushed the plastic baby spoon into stiffening cereal, now cold for the past twenty minutes. Jenny's eyes grew earnest, her tongue sticking to the roof of her mouth and pulling free: "Toe-t," in thick "t" sounds. Jenny wanted the toast, not cereal. Marion understood, reminded of her tendency to favor the softer foods at mealtime, a habit she'd developed long ago.

There'd been a time, in the beginning, when harder things like toast were scary. But that was then, and they'd come a long way. Jenny was almost five. Everything was still a risk, while nothing ever seemed to come of it. Now, only the remnants of Marion's habits remained while the fear part of it was gone, replaced with a question, *What if?*

"I miss my little Jenny! But it's so hard to get away. Maybe this Saturday. You know how your father is."

It was a Tuesday. Marion, phone to ear, nodded her head, eyeing Jenny across the room. In fifteen minutes, she'd made it up onto the couch, and now her stick-thin legs were splayed out behind in a diamond like a frog's, jerking inward one at a time toward the goal of a crawl position, arms batting at the couch back. Eventually, through effort and pure will, she would pull herself up higher. The exercise did her muscles good, and although a fall from the couch might hurt, it couldn't do any serious damage. Marion watched from a distance.

"Yeah, I know."

"Helpless as an infant. Retirement does that to a man. And the mood swings! He loves to talk about *me*, but I tell you, menopause is nothing compared to that."

In the middle of the sentence, Marion heard the extension lifted. "Don't listen to your mother. She likes to complain."

"Hi, Dad."

"*Who's* the complainer? Not a pleasant word out of your mouth since the day you retired."

"Why don't you bring Jenny over here? I'll make sure Astrid watches the baby. Go do something for yourself."

"George. She doesn't need to drag the girl over here. Do you know how hard it is to strap her in that car seat? You haven't tried. I said, *I'll* go over on Saturday."

"Saturday. Mark your calendar, Mari."

"Maybe, if you want, Dad, maybe you can come over."

"You know me, honey. I'm not the helpless blob your mother says, but I'm no sitter either. Never was any good at babysitting. No, you bring her over here. I've got a few projects to take care of at home..."

"Projects!"

"...a few things to do here. Your mother can watch the baby and *I'll* watch your mother. It worked out fine last time."

Jenny, on her knees, swung an arm above the top of the couch and hit the wall hard, sending her backward into the couch cushions, halfway over the edge. *It's too late—the baby's too far gone. No one will know.* Marion's chest moved forward an inch—the old habit—while the rest of her remained stationary.

"I'll be over on Saturday, dear. Plan on doing a little shopping or something for an hour or two, and when you come back, we'll *talk*."

A soft "thud." Jenny had gone over the edge in a slow roll. On her tummy, she snapped her head up to issue a report: crooked baby teeth in a broad, beaming smile that pushed out the hollows of her bony cheeks.

Jenny's hair was soft and thick and honey colored, its roots so deep and needy they might have sucked all that sweetness and life from her limbs. She sat on the floor, rubber legs bent and squeezed beneath her, head bobbing and mouth grinning from the feel of her mother's firm stroke. Sitting above on the couch, Marion held Jenny upright in a vise between her knees as she brushed the velvety mass, formed a ponytail and banded it, adding a ribbon. Her best effort, still it was messy, Jenny's slack neck defeating perfection.

Marion steadied Jenny's forehead while holding a hand mirror in front. "See? See what a nice ponytail?"

"Pruh-ty," said Jenny with her thick "t," a smack of tongue against palate. Sunlight entered the room through the window, stabbing the mirror and Marion's eyes. *Sunshine, a pink ribbon, ponytail bobbing, a girl skipping. Pretty, so pretty.*

"Yes, you *are* pretty. Such a pretty girl."

Marion checked her watch. Early morning hallway traffic would be gone by now. "Let's go for a walk," she announced, releasing Jenny's forehead and opening the vise. The girl sagged forward from the waist and jerked upright again, bouncing repeatedly on her knees, arms flailing. "Wah-k, wah-k!" she chanted with a throaty, smacking "k" like a Bushman's click.

Half an hour later, they were in the hallway outside their second-floor apartment, Marion pressing the elevator button. Most people on their floor used the stairs, but Marion had to avoid straining her back, now that her daughter was getting bigger. Jenny's thirty-eight pounds still fit in a toddler-sized stroller, arms dangling at the sides, head drooped forward, intermittently bobbing upright, the seat belt doing little to keep her from slipping.

They waited, two, three, four minutes. Marion filled the time by checking right and left for neighbors, stooping to absorb Jenny's drool with a handkerchief, pulling her up in the seat, adjusting the waistband of her pants to cover the edge of the diaper. No elevator. "This thing's broken again, Jen. Hey, that's a rhyme!"

Jenny gave a happy bounce in response to her mother's trained, upbeat voice.

"Guess you get to practice on the stairs."

Marion pushed the stroller to the stairway door, turned the knob, and backed into the stairwell, pulling the stroller in. The metal door clanged shut, echoing up and down the well, one floor below, seven floors above. "Here you go, Jenny." She unlatched the seat belt, lifted the girl out, and set her on the concrete landing in a crawl position ready for a backward descent, feet hanging over the edge of the top stair. Jenny threw her head up, holding it long enough to meet her mother's eyes and deliver a slow blink with thick, honey scoops of eyelashes. No surprise, no confusion, no fear. She'd done this before, often with success.

"Go ahead, Jenny. I'll be right behind you." Marion folded the stroller as she sidled past her daughter and walked down to the halfway landing, twelve stairs below. Jenny started backward, pushing one knee over the edge and down to the next stair, settling into the new position with a jolt. Her second knee went back over the edge and down as she kept her arms stretched forward on the top stair with hands balled up knuckley. A jolt. Jenny squealed with her accomplishment, the echo filling the stairwell, then she squealed again, liking the sound.

Marion propped the stroller in a corner and waited, looking up the stairs, down the stairs. Jenny moved one knee at a time, hands following, down the second stair, then the third stair, but the fourth, fifth, and sixth came all at once, all of a sudden, in a slide and a drag of arms and clutching hands, head bumping on a concrete edge. She came to an abrupt stop and screamed but didn't cry. *It's too late. No one will ever know.* Marion stayed put, her chest moving forward an inch. Jenny wasn't hurt. But later, there'd be a nice purple lump on her forehead.

Marion heard the metal door on the first-floor landing, giving her the impetus to move. She took six stairs two at a time up to Jenny and laid a hand on her back. A moment later, an overweight, middle-aged man puffed up behind them and stopped on the halfway landing where Marion had been standing.

"Hi, there," said the neighbor. Marion had seen the man many times but had never asked his name.

"Hello," said Marion over her shoulder, hand still on Jenny.

"You all right there?"

"Sure, just fine."

"Going down the steps now? The little girl?"

"We're managing."

The man started up toward them.

"Can you get by?" asked Marion.

"Oh, don't worry about me!" His cushioned backside hugged the railing, double chin pushed into chest. Despite the man's girth, a foot of clearance remained as he passed them while not caring to hide his look at Jenny. "Blast the elevator! I'm up three more floors." He wheezed. "I'm calling the super the minute I get in."

As soon as the man was around the corner and out of sight, Marion returned to the halfway landing. Jenny renewed her efforts. Marion waited, listening to the man's heavy breathing and plodding footsteps. Jenny achieved the next stair and squealed, sending reverberations up the well. In the aftermath of the echo: sudden silence above them. Marion remained still, listening.

Seconds later, as Jenny made her way down to the next stair, the labored breathing resumed, along with the heavy footsteps all the way up to the fourth floor.

By early afternoon they were in a quiet suburb on the street with a row of single-story homes, blue, pink, yellow, and green. Small enough to think of them as cottages, all matching. The white one in the middle of the block was his.

Marion parked her rusty hatchback at the end of the block and extricated Jenny from her seat. They could have stayed in their own neighborhood, sparing the time and expense of a forty-minute drive. But after such an effort on the stairs, the task of putting Jenny in her car seat and driving seemed blessedly easy. Nothing thought out, everything automatic. It had been this way many times, especially on sunny days, the light blinding.

Pushing the stroller, looking down through dark glasses, Marion couldn't see Jenny's face, only the top of her head. Normal. From this position, she could ignore the rest, the fringes of body beyond the head. But the sparrow's claws dangled from either side. Marion bent to tuck them in under Jenny's thighs, out of view. There. In bending close, Marion's nose had brushed the soft, fragrant cushion of Jenny's crown. *Brilliant, a ray on honey-brown. Skipping, ponytail bobbing, small hand reaching up for Mommy's...*

"Duh-day," the d's much like the t's. Jenny bounced and strained against her seat belt. "Duh-day!"

"I don't know, Jen. He's probably at work today. He used to get Wednesdays off, but I don't know anymore." It *is* Wednesday? she asked herself. The days were like this, one and the same.

She pushed the stroller slowly up the sidewalk toward the house. "If he's there, maybe he'll invite us in. Wouldn't that be nice?" Jenny bounced and her arms popped out over the sides.

As they got closer, Marion noticed the woman squatting at the side of the front walkway, spade in hand, a flat of petunias on the ground next to her. "Wouldn't that be nice?" To plant flowers in your own front yard on a sunny day. *No, sweetheart, don't pick them! We want them to grow tall and strong like you.*

The wife rose and stood in profile, making it evident—the rounded belly under a man's oversized shirt. Marion halted for a moment, feeling betrayed all over again. He hadn't said or written a word about a new baby. But her shock was brief, and she took the next step forward, wearing her mask of gaiety.

Looking down, admiring her work in the flowerbed, the wife didn't see Jenny and Marion until they were in front of the neighboring house. She looked up and dropped the tool, hesitated, took a step toward her front door, turned back and froze, holding her ground. *Her* ground, after all.

Marion didn't flinch, maintaining her steady pace until she came to the front walkway where it met the sidewalk. She stopped, no more than twenty feet from the woman. Jenny bounced. Marion looked at the wife and smiled, as cordial and distant as a friendly stranger. "Beautiful day. I like your flowers."

The wife looked at her and said nothing at first, her eyes narrowing. Finally, "You think I haven't seen you?"

"Seen me?"

"I look out my own window and there you are." Her lips trembled. Moist puffy lips, younger than Marion's, and the hair was full and clean, gathered hastily in back. Funny. A ponytail just like Jenny's, and almost the same color too.

Unable to do anything more, Marion smiled. Jenny bounced. "Duh-day!"

"You get your money every month. We can't live in anything better than *this*." She flung her arm behind her, toward the house. "What more do you want?"

Marion's smile froze.

"Just leave us alone. Go walk somewhere else. Take her for a walk somewhere else." On "her," the wife glanced at Jenny briefly, for the first time.

Marion bent forward over the top of the stroller and found Jenny's wet smile below the swollen purple spot on her forehead. The smiles, so many of them and so bright, often made her forget. Not now. Marion lifted her eyes to the woman's and the words just popped out: "Did you have your amnio yet?"

The full lips pursed and narrowed into hard worms.

"I'm not even thirty."

Their eyes locked while Marion fought against the surprise of her own words. Having the amnio would have changed nothing. What a stupid, stupid thing to ask, something *he* would have said. Marion was acting just as stupid, as if an amnio had anything to do with this, as if those crazy, mixed-up things he said after Jenny's birth made any sense. "You've been like this from the beginning, Marion. Thirty-six and wouldn't even get an amnio because you'd keep the baby anyway, no matter what. You have some kind of sick attraction to this martyr thing. You want to give up your whole life. And what do you get out of it? They have places, you know, but you'd keep the baby even if it had two heads."

"It." Always an it, even after Jenny was born.

The current wife knew of her husband's amnio thoughts, Marion could tell from her look. The eyes told. Hoping for a surge of power, Marion held her gaze steady for a while but finally lost the battle and had to retreat. Pivoting the stroller on its rear wheels, she turned to go the way they'd come, not looking back, feeling the heat of the woman's eyes.

Near the car, they saw another woman walking hand-in-hand with a preschooler, younger than Jenny but bigger. "What a beautiful day!" said the mother as she approached, looking at Marion, then at Jenny.

"Yes, isn't it." Marion's hands shook, but the water in her eyes stayed welled up behind her sunglasses, waiting for the woman to pass before it rolled down her cheeks.

Behind her, Marion heard, "Mommy, that girl! She

was funny—"

"Hush! It's not polite."

Picture books were strewn all over the floor when Marion went to check. She had left Jenny in the bedroom they shared while taking an hour for herself on the living room couch. Marion didn't mind the books. She kept them on a low shelf to give Jenny exercise.

"Want me to read to you?"

Jenny looked up, her eyes sunken. Reading to Jenny almost always made the girl happy, but there'd been few smiles that day.

"Come on." Marion knelt and reached for her daughter, who sat frog-legged before an open, tattered copy of "Benjamin Bunny." Jenny applied a pincer-hold to the book and resisted, making her slight weight leaden. Marion easily unglued her from the floor but had trouble hoisting her up onto the bed, struggling against an unpredictable, squirming mass of life. Yelps of dis-pleasure. But Jenny finally succumbed. Marion propped her on pillows and settled in beside her with the book she'd been clutching.

While Marion read, Jenny lay in a dispirited heap, not looking at the pages or mimicking the words in her usual way. Halfway through the story, Jenny's spindly arm sprang up like an automatic tollgate and swiped at the book, batting it from her mother's hand.

"Jenny!"

"Luh-cky!" The hard, throaty "k."

"But I just told you the lucky story." Lately, Jenny had been asking for it more. She was older now, getting outside and seeing other children more often.

"Luh-cky!"

"Okay, Jen. Okay." She laid the book on the bedside table, paused a moment, and began. "One day, the day you were born, I knew you were coming so your daddy took me to the hospital. We were so happy—I was so happy you were on the way. But when we got there the nurses and doctors at the hospital were worried about you. They did a stress test—"

"Strussss." Spray from Jenny's mouth.

"And they said, 'We have to get the baby out in a hurry. We have to do an operation.' So they numbed my body." *Hold still for the spinal.* "But I was awake."

"See?" More spray.

"Right, Jen. They put up a sheet so I couldn't see the operation, but I could see you when you came out." *Please, let me see her.*

"Kuh-yute!"

"You were so cute, Jenny. What a cute little baby. But they wouldn't let me see you right away." *Let me see her. Please.* "The doctor and the nurse were still worried about you." *Get the oxygen.* "I couldn't see everything. They were over at a table trying to save you and they were whispering; I could hardly hear them because they were whispering, trying not to worry me." *No, it's too late. No one will ever know.*

"At first the doctor thought it was too late." *She's too far gone. No one will ever know.* "But the nurse didn't agree with the doctor and she ran for the oxygen and a respirator so you could breathe. Later, they told me what happened."

"Um-bickle!"

"The umbilical cord was wrapped around you so tight you couldn't breathe. They couldn't get you out fast enough. If it was a minute longer, you would have died." *No one will ever know.*

"Wah-k."

"That's why you can't walk like other kids. Your brain was hurt when you didn't get enough oxygen." *We don't know the full extent of the damage.* "And it's hard for you to talk. Your muscles are weaker. But it could have been much worse. You could have died—"

"Luh-cky!"

"You're a lucky, lucky girl. You're so lucky to be alive."

"Luh-cky!" Arms flailing, she said the word again and again until its sound convinced her of its truth, pushing a smile into her face.

Marion got up from the bed and stood with arms crossed. Jenny rocked from side to side, arms zigzagging through the air, legs kicking, repeating the word over and over, gaining speed in a spastic frenzy of movement. Marion took three steps toward the door, stopped, turned back, sat on the edge of the bed, stood and sat again, arms crossed. Jenny beat the air and rocked, making a mess of the bedspread and pillows, slipping down from her propped position, a pillow falling over her face. "Luh-cky!" The pillow muffled the sound, "luh-cky," muffled the sound, muffled it. *What if? No one will ever know.* Marion leaned over, felt the softness of the pillow, the squirming body underneath, leaned and pressed, muffling it, muffling it, legs kicking harder and harder, muffling it until it was gone.

She lay beside the prone body and cried. So lovely in sleep. She always looked so lovely. A normal-looking, thin child. Not just normal, but really very pretty, the long eyelashes resting gently on translucent skin.

As a baby, she'd been easy to love because all babies were helpless. But days and months passed, and the helplessness remained, her progress so slight it escaped perception. Days and nights were strung together in a chain of sameness, the days unreal, the nights wakeful with nightmares and Jenny's crying, the days a nightmare of disbelief spent in daydream. The few nights of blissful escape in dream were marred by morbid interruption. Sunny mornings and Jenny's smile defied evidence of her difference, but memory of the doctor's words brought it back, a daily and nightly reminder that an act taking a few seconds had defined a life.

Somehow, anger had crept in. Exactly when, Marion couldn't remember.

She cried, knowing the girl couldn't hear. "Jen, will you ever forgive me?" But the only forgiveness she needed was her own. Jenny had forgiven her almost immediately. Or perhaps she just didn't know, had thought it was all a game.

Afterward, when Marion had lifted the pillow, Jenny lay quiet as stone with her eyes closed. Marion kissed her warm forehead, causing Jenny to open her eyes. Still bright. A smile burst onto her face, splashed with Marion's tears. Pretending. It had been a game after all, or did she know?

"O-kay, muh-mee?" An arm sprang upward toward Marion's face, a gesture of comfort. She wanted to know that her mommy was all right, but Marion ignored it, playing her own game of pretend.

"Are you okay? Was I playing rough? I'm sorry if I hurt you. I love you, Jenny. I'm so happy you're here with me."

"Luh-cky." Now, she was twice lucky. Did Jenny understand? If she did, the word 'lucky' meant so much more. It meant forgiveness too.

Searching for a clue, Marion looked deeply into Jenny's eyes.

They seemed to contain infinite substance—or emptiness. Someone else might find Jenny's eyes vacant. But Marion had to believe in the depth and wealth she saw there, had to ignore Jenny's difficulties in communicating to find, underneath, the innate intelligence. Her belief was based on more than faith. Jenny seemed to understand so much. And Marion, to stay alive, had to keep believing. After all, she might never have anyone else in her life close enough to understand her.

Now, night fallen, in the small light thrown from the hallway through the open door, Jenny's hair shone thick and soft on the pillow, a living part of her. *Sunshine, honey-brown ponytail, delicate features, intelligent eyes. Jenny.* Lying beside her, Marion pulled her daughter close and grew calm from the rough sound of her breathing.

On Saturday morning, Marion fed and bathed and brushed and changed Jenny into crisp clothes. A dab of perfume behind her ears. A blue hair twist in her ponytail.

Astrid arrived just after ten, bearing a wrapped and ribboned gift. She greeted her grandchild with loud cheer before turning to Marion. "I got her a book. I hope you don't mind."

"Not at all."

"I know how you like to read to her."

"You can read to her too, Mom. It's her favorite thing."

"Oh, I don't know." Astrid was looking at Jenny with a plastic smile. "We'll see. I don't know how much she gets out of it."

"She follows the words and tries to say them—"

"This book has great pictures anyway. She's eaten?"

"Yes, you don't need to feed her."

"You know how I wish I could. I'll just never be as good as you."

"Experience."

"All those little gagging noises are so alarming. I'll never get used to them."

Marion kissed Jenny and walked out the door to cram a long list of errands into two short hours. Her mother wouldn't last much longer. Still, it was something, and Marion didn't feel the anger today. She'd made a point of asking herself about it and confirming its absence.

Later, when she returned, her mother would likely start the usual conversation. Had Marion reconsidered that nice "home" for Jenny? A regular babysitter, at least? A job? Extra income beyond child support payments and government disability checks? A life?

Marion would listen, keeping quiet about her guilt,

offering her usual rebuttal: the economic impossibility and Jenny's overwhelming need. She'd heard Mom's advice so many times before, she'd become numb to it. But now it was easier to pick out the valid parts and embrace them; time for herself and even a part-time job would be possible this fall, when Jenny started a special ed kindergarten.

They would have this talk, the usual one, and Marion wouldn't feel the anger. She wouldn't cringe when her mother said, "You deny yourself everything. What *are* you getting out of this?" She would only smile at the thought of Mom hovering over Dad in his retirement, and maybe she would reply, "What did you get out of raising me, anyway?"

She was prepared for all this when she returned and walked in the door, grocery bags in hand. "How is everyone?"

Astrid was in the hallway, looking into the bedroom through the open doorway. "Just fine!" she said over her shoulder. "Jenny is such a great little crawler now! All the way in here and, oh, Marion! I meant to clean this up before you got here. Such a mess!"

Marion set down her bags and walked past her mother into the bedroom, where Jenny sat in her usual position on the floor, open books all around. "Don't worry about it, Mom." Marion went up to Jenny. "Did you have fun with Grandma?" A big wet smile. "What's this? Your new book?" In front of Jenny was a large book opened to a page with glossy color photographs of animals and paragraphs in small print.

"Maybe I shouldn't have let her," said Astrid,

stepping into the room. "She already ripped a page, and all those wet spots…"

Jenny had drooled copiously on the open page. Soon, the new book would look like all the others. "That's okay. I'm glad you read it to her."

"Oh, no! We didn't get around to *reading* it. I knew she'd like those animal pictures, and we had such a *wonderful* time tearing off the wrapping paper, didn't we, Jenny? She loves that colorful paper and all those ripping sounds."

Marion crouched and scanned the page. Just like Mom, she thought. With no faith in Jenny's understanding, Astrid had chosen the book without regard for the text, which was far too difficult for a preschooler, more appropriate for a preteen. The open page had pictures of minks and ferrets with descriptions of their habitat, feeding patterns and mating rituals. Marion would wait until Astrid had left, then put the book away for future use. She stood and went back to stand near her mother while Jenny swung at the open page with a curled fist.

"Get a few things done?" asked Astrid.

"Yes, thanks."

"I'll try to get here more often, but you know Marion, you really should do some more thinking about that home I told you about…"

"Fuhr—"

"…or at least a regular sitter."

"Fuhr-et."

Astrid glanced at Jenny. "Yes, honey. Furry animal." Back to Marion with a whisper: "She tries *so* hard, doesn't she?"

Jenny batted the page. "Fuhr-et."

The second time, Marion heard it. She turned from her mother, went to Jenny and knelt beside her. "What's that one?" she pointed.

"Ming-kuh." The deep, throaty "k."

"Jen, you're reading!" Marion picked up Jenny at the waist and settled on the floor cross-legged with the child in her lap.

"Reading? I don't think…" Astrid cast a disapproving look at Marion.

"I've never said a word to you about minks and ferrets, have I, Jen?" The girl wiggled with excitement, her face bursting into a smile.

Astrid grabbed a tissue from a box next to the bed. "Oh my. Here, sweetheart." She crouched woodenly and dabbed at the drool spilling from the side of Jenny's smile but lost her balance and tumbled onto the floor. Laughing, she looked up into her granddaughter's beaming face. "You know, she really is quite pretty when she smiles."

Marion, eyes gleaming, lowered her face into Jen's velvety crown, nestling deeply in the rich honey softness, the warmth and sweet fragrance encasing her daughter's world, still unknown. She closed her eyes and fell into the swirling colors of mystery and possibility.

☾ *Nothing Intentional*

A WAY OUT with dignity had been Pressler's urgent need for some time. Solutions evaded him. Doing or not doing, trying or not trying, living or not living, each and every opposite was no opposite at all but one and the same thing leading to a single result, an absolute nothing or a trap, whichever way one looked at it.

At the office, Rachel wouldn't stop with her passive-aggressive avoidance. Pressler interpreted her behavior this way, even as the intellectual side of his brain reported that she cared too little about him to be accused of passive-aggressiveness. Whenever she failed to acknowledge him, it wasn't a deliberate behavior springing from conscious, or even subconscious, will. A plan. A design. A statement: "I hate you." None of that. Just nothing, an unpremeditated, "I don't care." Pressler would have to accept it, but he just couldn't. He wanted to read something into it.

Office meetings, everyone filed into the conference room. A small firm, ten attorneys, three women, seven men. When Max Bushnel walked by, he would say, "Morning Robert." If Valerie Glick brushed up against him, unintentionally of course, she might say, "Excuse me." Might even say, "Robert." But when Rachel Morehouse walked into the room, she might happen to come close or she might not, but either way it was the natural route, nothing intentional. If she looked at him it was because her eyes happened to be there, not because she wanted to look at him, and if she didn't look at him it was because she had no need to, not because she was making a statement, "I am not looking at you." In either case, she would say nothing to him.

Not as if she'd planned to say nothing, or even as if he were invisible to her, but rather that he did exist and she just didn't care, really and truly didn't care. All emotion with regard to him had been fully spent months ago, that fateful day when he'd done the unthinkable and she'd turned to him and said: "You're such an ass, Robert. You're so completely out of bounds you're blind to it."

He couldn't erase his memory of those words and her face at the moment she'd said them. It galled him. Rachel should be completely irrelevant to him, for he surely possessed everything a man could need or want. He reaffirmed this every time he joined with his beautiful wife Marcie, pounding the happiness into his brain with each thrust to the beat of that song in his head, a familiar refrain, something about discovery and abandon.

Recently—a reaction to his little problem?—they'd begun to pretend at it once again. At least he felt he was pretending even if Marcie was not. It was impossible to shake the oppressive completeness of every day of their lives together, every tranquil morning over coffee, every discussion about the kids, every kiss on the cheek goodbye, everything said and not said. Most of it was good, yes, a good life on the whole, right there in the bed with them, rolling around in a semi-dark cocoon on a Sunday afternoon, suggesting regrets. He loved this woman, the mother of his three grown children, loved every atom of her existence, but under the sheets he had to look away in his imagination to avoid that sickening feeling of bedding a sister or a cousin. Afterward, physically satisfied, he'd fall away feeling disconnected and lost.

Among other new behaviors, Pressler had taken to reading the want ads every morning. He wanted—didn't get—what? He didn't know. He was a decent man with an enviable financial picture, home, and family life. Some might question the moral underpinnings of his professional life, but he'd learned to internalize the loftier ideals behind his practice which involved, essentially, representing crooks, the respectable kind who lived in the world of ostensible legitimacy, rife with tax loopholes and creative accounting. After all, our Constitution guaranteed a defense to everyone, and who better to represent that ilk than this intelligent, articulate, healthy, moderately muscled fifty-five-year-old male? A modern man of the nineties, on the cusp of the millennium. His mental health might be open to debate if one were to ask Rachel. At the present, however, she would likely respond with a vacant gaze of questionable amusement, since she no longer cared to have an opinion on any subject relating to him.

Over his morning coffee, that lilt in her musing voice

played in the back of his mind as he cobbled a new identity for himself from newspaper pages of job listings, personals, real estate, and used cars for sale: Mid-level manager of a Fortune 500 company (with exciting opportunities for advancement), and his girlfriend—an sbf attractive 30s fond of music and dancing—take a ride in his vintage mint condition '73 Corvette to his prime beachfront condo, where they sip cocktails and listen to all the greatest hits.

What an odd advertisement that one, "All the Greatest Hits," with an address but no phone number. The bold lettering stuck in his mind, and from that day forward, the act of opening the classified section would lower the arm of the turntable onto a popular record from his senior year in high school, 1961. The tune pounded incessantly in his temples, the remembered phrases only a few, a timeless refrain about searching and not finding.

Marcie had cooked her umpteenth-millionth pot roast the night of the "you're an ass" comment from Rachel. Her pot roasts were excellent, just excellent. Now that the children had gone off to college, she always selected the smallest cut at the market, but even so, there'd be days of leftovers which she attractively included in new and imaginative dishes for the next few meals, or froze and sprung on him, unexpected, a week later.

Pressler had come home drained that night, as he had every night for the past six weeks during the trial of *United States versus Welcher*, but this night he was at his worst, even though they'd won the case. He and Rachel had won.

Ordinarily this would have added a few, fleeting moments of elation at the very least, maybe an entire evening of self-satisfaction and a buzz from two or three celebratory martinis. Twelve people had affirmed the value of his existence out loud in a courtroom, justifying his continued practice in his chosen area of the law with the anticipation of future wins to come.

But that night held no elation, the alcohol not a buzz but a drowning, for he'd lost very big just moments after the jurors were excused to resume their disrupted and sorely missed lives.

"You look spent, Robert," said Marcie, ever insightful, but not so insightful as to know of his dirty transgression only two hours earlier. He managed to meet her eyes briefly, his attempt at evaluation. No, she didn't know, and how could she? Her eyes were bright and open as always, intelligent and perceptive. Still, she couldn't read his mind. But she knew him well, and sooner or later she would figure things out even if he didn't tell her. Outward appearances, so practiced that they seemed real, only went so far.

She was aware of his win, he'd told her that much on the phone before coming home, and so the "you look spent" comment resounded with hidden significance, a question, a concern. Maybe not a suspicion. Not just yet.

"I *am* tired," he said. "But tell me about *your* day." Just out of his mouth, and already he heard the mistake in it, the signpost, the clue she would pick up, the beginning of her discovery. He was shamed by these thoughts with their smack of guilt over clandestine activities, something he'd never had cause to feel before.

But Marcie didn't let on. She proceeded to narrate the details of the case she was transcribing, as if it were only natural for Pressler to back out of the spotlight which was his due on the evening of a big win. Today's testimony came from the mother of the unfortunate toddler-plaintiff who had been under the crane when it fell. Even as Marcie described the gruesome scene, Pressler was slumped in a nauseous cloud over Rachel.

What an insult to his wife! An exceptionally smart woman, Marcie likely would have been the better lawyer in the family if she hadn't quit law school when their first baby arrived, later finding her way back into the courtroom as a stenographer. He'd always sought her opinion on his cases. Now, suddenly, it struck him that he'd broken this pattern. He hadn't included her this time. Rachel had been the one to fill that role—a shocking realization fraught with sneaky implications. His intellectual connection with Marcie was more than satisfying, and yet, he'd sought that connection elsewhere this time.

Unlike his usual clients accused of "clean" crimes— tax evasion, insider trading, embezzlement—this client had been charged with a crime far more sinister, making Pressler's win that much more surprising. Byron Welcher, an executive in the fashion industry, was accused of racketeering based on payments received from one of his corporate customers. The funds were traced back to accounts filled with illegal cash profits from gambling, usury, and prostitution. The paper trail pointed to conspiracy, but the entire case rested on *mens rea*. Did

Welcher know the source of the payments? Did he collaborate in the illegal enterprise of his ostensible customer? Of course not, he told his lawyers. It looked bad for him, sure, but he was innocent. Nothing intentional.

To beat the charges, Welcher's outward appearance had to clothe the inner man with morality, and so, for the courtroom, he changed his usual flamboyant style and dressed in tasteful, conservative suits. His features were square and regular, he bore himself well with erect posture, but his hair was greasy. Actually greasy, like a caricature of gangster sleaziness. His smile was odious and false.

Pressler alone wouldn't have been able to sell a man like this to the jury, and he took extra care in choosing the associate to second-seat the case: Morehouse, with her unique blend of sexiness, amiability, and intelligence. If Ms. Morehouse wanted to walk up to the witness box and show her legs to this Mr. Welcher, if she wanted to place her hand, ever so briefly, on top of his where it rested on the railing, if she wanted to hold his gaze and smile whenever he made a seemingly offhand but well-rehearsed and refined witticism, then Mr. Welcher and his newly-acquired (with practice) wholesome smile was trustworthy. An innocent lamb incapable of shady thoughts or intentions.

This, Pressler's first case with Morehouse, would be his last.

A dignified way out was a necessity for a man like Pressler, for otherwise, his life would come to nothing. If he didn't love Marcie (and Amy, Russ, and Gretchen, his children), things might have been different. But that was the nut of the contradiction, the impossibility of it all, this seeming veneer of respectability and family love of which he'd so completely convinced himself—actually didn't need to convince himself because it was true—juxtaposed against a single day of shame. He'd glimpsed himself a fallen man, something no one else (but Rachel) had seen. He felt such utter humiliation, believed himself to be internally broken at what might seem, on the outside, like nothing at all, when really, only the intentions mattered.

Just what his intention had been he couldn't fully admit, but certainly it was something wrong, and he alone was to blame. Another contradiction resided there, something he later told that man in suite 55, number 101: unlike his clients, those borderline, quasi-criminals, the arguably unfairly-set-upon-by-zealous-young-prosecutors-eyeing-political-prizes kinds of clients, Pressler himself had always led an upstanding, impeccable professional and personal life. The trial tactics he used were not only legal but ethical, and his treatment of wife and children was open and considerate.

There was no undoing of the past, no living in the present. He needed a way out, an escape. Perusing the classifieds, humming the searching-and-not-finding song while drumming his fingers on the table, he came upon those words again with a shock of recognition, "All the Greatest Hits," in bold. There were songs about girls in red dresses, girls in blue dresses, girls in bikinis, and there was the song that never left his mind these days, the one he strained to erase in an attempt to focus on his daily business and routine, only to find his mind wandering moments later to his second-most-thought-of subject: the escape. A need to do it with dignity. Because how could he go on and on and on with this Rachel problem?

Accidents happened. People fell ill, or misfortune befell them every day of the year. They were hurt, maimed, and killed without any fault of their own. Died with dignity. Why not Pressler? He moaned over the irony of being in the perfect business to explore this solution. He could leave the firm and take on his own clients, seek out a lower breed of defendant, the smart, powerful, violent type who could arrange an elimination and get away with it. Hah! A way to pay the lawyer fee. A little barter, services for services.

He turned the page and spotted another one, a second ad in the same section, "All the Greatest Hits," and an address, number 101 on a street not so very far from his office.

Maybe he should take Rachel with him into this new law practice—the older, experienced attorney taking in the younger, promising one. Would she accept an offer now, after everything, strictly as a matter of business? She would laugh at him outright—some emotion!—from Rachel, an advocate so superior she could make any client look good. She had the talent to choose a vision and twist reality into its shape, mixing every passion, desire, and vice into an orderly, acceptable package, manipulating illusion to draw him in, draw him in, draw him... Everything led to Rachel.

He went over it again, convincing himself he hadn't manufactured the outward signs she'd sent him during all their days and late evenings poring over the paperwork, discussing strategy and legal theory. The possibilities went far beyond anything they were doing in his office or hers, beyond the issues of *United States versus Welcher*, an energy that transcended their two corporal beings and the four walls of their enclosed space. No, he hadn't imagined this! He'd seen it in her eyes, smelled it in her perfume, her receptiveness to the reality of his dream, her commitment to its purpose and inevitability. He knew it every time she said, "Genius, Robert!" and squeezed his hand—maybe more of a touch than a squeeze—with her eyes on his, her red thirty-three-year-old lips open.

Once, even, it had been this: "Did you ever think, Robert, did you ever imagine that you were destined for great things?" Greatness. Yes, maybe twenty-five, thirty years ago. He remembered his dreams of making great law, taking on important cases for the downtrodden and oppressed, arguing weighty causes before the Supreme Court. But after law school, his brief stint with the public defender's office had ended with no great cases (only a slew of street crime) under his belt, the lofty ideals giving way under the weight of financial pressure and a growing family.

Working with Rachel, greatness suddenly seemed possible again. Her confidence in him was the proof that this wasn't about sex. Maybe a little. It was more about a profound connection, a propulsion to higher ground.

Day in and day out, whether the newspaper was spread before him or a deposition transcript or pile of documentary evidence, always, every minute, Rachel was there. He could be examining a witness or talking on the phone or eating the umpteenth-billionth pot roast, and still, his vision remained clouded by all the possibilities that had died with that one stupid encounter and Rachel's categorical dismissal of his entire being in that single, well-aimed, well-deserved comment: "You're such an ass, Robert."

How could he go on?

He'd been down that street many times over the years as he walked from train to office, but the day after seeing the address in the newspaper he took notice of the building for the first time. A nondescript façade, fifteen or twenty stories, about the same height as the neighboring buildings, but the beige brick seemed brighter than all the rest, making of it a gleaming ghost lurching vertiginously overhead as he passed by. The number above the entrance—"101"—was grotesquely larger than any other number on the block. He didn't know what to make of it.

He repeated that route several mornings in a row, finally coming up with a plan one day to return at lunchtime. He would go into that building and he would come out a changed man or he wouldn't come out at all, of that he was convinced. He didn't know what to expect, but it had to be something big and powerful and awful and final—an end to his torment.

Things might have turned out differently, if only he'd shown some restraint. If only he'd looked toward the future and made a wiser plan instead of immediately clawing for something already lost to him, something that was no more than a chimera to begin with.

The jury had just filed out, the defendant given leave to go, a free man. In the minutes these events unfolded, as Rachel gathered her file folders and packed her briefcase, Pressler felt a slowly rising panic, a groping for a slippery, fading possibility, a dream that might never be. When the verdict came in, Rachel had said nothing to him. Smiled maybe, looked pleased maybe, but she no longer included him within the ambit of her focus. There was no more going forward with him. It seemed her energy had turned inward, her connection with him, so solid before, now showed itself as a probable sham, a tool used toward a greater connection and oneness beyond him, completely self-satisfying. She was an island, entire unto herself, an existence to which he'd contributed but was now inconsequential. He was a shell, the juice sucked out, the remains easily discarded.

Like a fool, Pressler made every effort in those moments to win her attention. So suddenly, the days and evenings of intense collaboration had come to a close. Day after day for six weeks he'd sat on her right at counsel table, smelling her clean scent, awkwardly bumping her elbow from time to time, leaning in close to whisper trial strategy, feeling the return of her soft, warm breath in his ear. She was beautiful to be sure, but not as objectively beautiful as Marcie, and now, he knew, not as spiritually beautiful. But it was everything else about her that made him want to go on forever sitting next to her in this way, feeling the presence of her profile at his side.

Welcher had been placed farthest from the jury on her left where he was equally accessible to her, more of a colleague than a client. That was the message to be sent.

She whispered into his ear just like she whispered into Pressler's. And after the verdict, as soon as Welcher had gone and the prosecutor had walked out, tail between his legs with political aspirations shot to hell, Pressler turned to her for an affirmation of their connection. He smiled in a big way, a "hey, aren't we great!" way, his eyes shining into hers, waiting for the thing he'd been dreaming of, a spontaneous burst of affection, an all-encompassing embrace, breasts to chest, with the sweet scent of soft hair in his nose. The emotion that was aflame inside her, what she'd hinted at all these many weeks, could now be released in a socially acceptable environment, a public courtroom where a few court officers and spectators lingered. But instead of showing an irresistible impulse for physical connection, she'd returned his smile with a wry one of her own that said "me" instead of "we."

Like a lost puppy, Pressler followed her out into the hallway, reasserting his presence with babbling and nervous laughter as they walked, filling the air with remarks about the witnesses, the jurors, the judge, briefly cupping her elbow in his palm and brushing the length of her forearm to the back of her hand with his fingertips as he made another nearly profound observation. She remained cold as stone. None of it evoked a response, and so he made that one final, pathetic attempt—if only he'd shown some restraint!

In a quiet corner of the courthouse, he placed a hand on her shoulder, stopped her dead, and stepped in front to face her. His eyes beamed into hers with a longing that was surely there (he saw that now!), his hand moving slowly up from her shoulder to a bare spot of neck, a light touch on her velvety cheek (did his hand shake?). "We're so good together," he said in a deep, sexual voice. "Let's go celebrate; I'll buy you a drink."

He would never be free of the utter contempt in her voice and eyes. He didn't *want* to be free of her emotion. It was the last vestige of their connection, something better than what he had now, the non-passive-aggressive avoidance he couldn't redefine, no matter how hard he tried.

Marcie all but knew, even though she hadn't been able to read his mind. His inability to come clean had only built on the internal frenzy and shame. "Robert," she'd said the night before his visit to 101, "for some time now, you haven't been here."

He was listening, because he always listened to her, tucking his other thoughts in back, to be retrieved and wallowed in when safely beyond detection. He heard her and she was always right but he wouldn't yield. From his own point of view, he'd done an admirable job of keeping things together. As long as the outside was intact, some dignity remained. Intentions could always be denied as long as the shell was sleek. But the effort was showing, especially to Marcie, who saw it in the gradual slump of his shoulders and reddening of his eyes.

"You're doing everything you should. You're functioning. You're going to work. You're coming home. We have dinner. I talk. You talk. But you're not here. It's time for you to come back."

"I've gone nowhere. I'm here with you."

"I don't think you can see what you look like."

"What are you implying?"

"Something is wearing you down."

"Nothing is wrong."

"You're saying it's nothing?"

"I can tell you this. It *will* wear me down if you keep at it!"

And she pursued it no further, not wanting to tip him over the edge. She started talking about the kids, baiting him for involvement, knowing she'd get it from him. (How well she knew him!) He listened, surprised to hear new information, the proof of his recent distance and the brilliance of her strategy to elicit his confession and restoration. Marcie, completely up to date, Robert, far behind, back in a time before Rachel.

A tear came to his eye five minutes into the litany about Amy, their youngest, possibly their brightest. In her freshman year of college, she was homesick but adjusting.

"Little Amy," he said wistfully, reminded he was a father. He was taken out of himself momentarily then plugged right back in, because the father of grown children in college is not really allowed to dream for himself.

Next, Russell. The boy was having some problems with his girlfriend, all recounted by Marcie with meaningful, probing eye contact. *No, this isn't about problems with love*, his eyes returned. *I'm not in love with her. I love you.*

Gretchen, oldest daughter, first year law, was struggling with Contracts and Civil Pro but loved Criminal Law.

"She's going to be a helluva lawyer," said Pressler.

"Like you," said Marcie.

"You're wrong there."

"What *is* this new thing of yours? This self-deprecation? You're a great lawyer. You've proven it a hundred times."

"How? By twisting the system for people?"

"Some of those people deserved to be exonerated. That's what it's about. The people who need help and deserve it. Like the kids. They're gone, but they're still here," she beat her chest, "and they need us. This is what our lives are about."

"The kids."

"Yes, the kids. They're destined for great things." *Did you ever think, Robert, did you ever imagine that you were destined for great things?* No, he couldn't accept this. Expected to give up his dreams and live for theirs, knowing they'll come up against the same roadblock in middle life, their dreams never realized. A timeless refrain. No, a terminal refrain, searching, not finding.

She saw this in his eyes. "I didn't say it exactly right," she said. "Their potential is great and their dreams are big. But it doesn't matter if they don't achieve everything they're dreaming. They're already great, just the way they are."

"Even if they don't achieve…"

"Of course they will," she smiled, "but even if they don't, it's what they intend to do that matters, because it comes out in their behavior. They're good people."

He was silent. He nodded. They're good. All in their intentions.

"And we live in them, Robert. We made them, and we're inside them." Her eyes were searching for a reaction, a "we-created-greatness-together" reaction. Pressler didn't feel it. All he felt was dread.

After the acquittal, Rachel was a bit of a celebrity at the office. A senior partner had watched her brilliant examination of Welcher at the trial and later spread the news at the office. Now, everyone congratulated her while Pressler stood in the shadows, smiling modestly as if the attention was properly her due. Rachel, of course, wouldn't have noticed whether he smiled or not. He was a cipher, his existence necessary only in a doormat kind of way, wiped on to gain entry. One day, very soon, she would be made partner.

Pressler was, in fact, quite happy for her. She would have made partner soon enough anyway, with or without his help. But he saw now what he'd given her that another senior partner never would have: enormous responsibility at Welcher's trial, and a large share of the limelight.

It didn't matter that she knew that he knew that he wouldn't do anything to stand in the way of her promotion, although another man might have. She'd figured him accurately enough. And it didn't matter that she knew that he knew that if he *did* get in the way, she would fabricate (quite believably) the ammunition to counter his attack. He would have no defense, given the way his feelings were worn on his sleeve.

He kept a distance, evaluating from afar, looking at her as if looking at himself, sick with grief. She embodied his past, his energy and idealism, that picture of a young man with his whole life and great things ahead.

The day must come, and it does, and this is it. On the way home, Pressler slouches into the seat on the commuter train, the soft clack-clack of rails underneath. He feels the square edges of the plastic case in his right palm, and the classified section is spread out on his knee under his left hand. He closes his eyes to think of Rachel, her perfume, her red lips whispering in his ear, "you're great, Robert," then a sudden change of voice, "you're an ass, Robert."

The rail car tip-tops hypnotically against its forward thrusting speed, beckoning a release, a flood of memory beating back the darkness under his lids. A flicker of images of Rachel changes quickly to that small flitting man in his room full of the greatest hits, the final stop for Pressler. He thinks back on it now.

Lunchtime, as planned, Pressler found his way to 101, entered the lobby and pushed the button next to Suite 55. A man's voice came over the intercom, "All the greatest hits," just like the advertisement.

"Hello. I'd like to come up."

There was a pause, the crackle of static, and Pressler felt the man considering. Then, without more, no questions asked, the lobby door buzzed open. Up the elevator to the fifth floor, at the end of a long hallway, he found Suite 55.

A knock, no answer, a turn and a push of the unlocked door. The room inside was small, no more than ten feet square, the walls stacked with music, floor to ceiling. A little man sat plumb in the middle, behind a desk. Pressler entered, walking back in time.

There was a wall of CDs, a wall of cassette tapes, a wall of LPs. Pressler reeled and turned. The wall behind him contained 45s on one side of the door and 8-tracks on the other. Each piece fit tightly without a sliver of air between, no labels or markers on the shelves, hundreds of thousands of selections in an unfathomable arrangement.

"What is it you want?" asked the man. He was small, wiry, and pale, a fixture of that windowless room with its smell of dust hanging in the air.

"I'm looking for a song. I don't know the name." Pressler hummed a few bars of the searching-and-not-finding tune, standing dazedly rocking on his heels because there wasn't another chair in the room.

"I have it," said the man, and he shot out from behind the desk to snatch an 8-track from its groove in the wall behind Pressler. "Here you go."

Dumbfounded, he took it, turning it over and over in his hands. There were no markings or labels on the black plastic box. "What do I owe you?"

The man stood only a few feet away at the side of the desk, regarding Pressler with a wry smirk. "The price is negotiable. Go listen to it first and come back. We'll discuss it then." His hands made little fluttery waving motions, sweeping his guest out the door.

So that was that. He'd been dismissed, it was clear. Pressler went away clutching his awkward antique, not realizing his mistake until halfway down the street. How on earth would he be able to play it? He nearly turned back, meaning to ask for an old 8-track player, but his curiosity suddenly turned to anger. What a bother, a useless exercise! He needed to get back to work. Later he would return the tape and maybe give the man a piece of his mind for the trouble he'd caused.

At the end of the day, Pressler returned and made a big production of handing over the tape. "I'm afraid this won't do me any good," he declared, mocking and derisive.

"I didn't think it would," replied the man. "Your intent was pretty obvious."

Pressler's heart jumped to his throat. "Obvious?"

"Yes. But I'm telling you, this isn't my usual line. My business is, how shall I put it, more of a gift service. Most people come here looking for their favorite hit...for a friend. Not for themselves. What do you want from me?" The man sat back in the chair, in no hurry, inviting an explanation.

Without reflection, somehow compelled, Pressler began to talk. His was a long tale. He started at the beginning and didn't end until the end, sparing no details of the events and his inner turmoil.

The man listened intently to every word and waited a good minute afterward to make sure Pressler was, indeed, finished. He gave a nasty smile. "She was right, you know. You're an ass, Robert. She pulled the wool over the eyes of the jury and did the same with you. And you don't see it."

"You're saying this was false, the way she seemed to find something in me? All a sham?"

"I'm just saying you're a fool and I don't care to hear any more of it. You need a shrink, not what I have to offer. I'm selling the hits here. Buy one or get out."

"Yes, buy one. I want to buy one."

"Which one do you have in mind? You said you don't want this one." He banged the aging 8-track on the desk and swiveled around in his chair, a quick half circle, his hand up in the air, motioning to the walls behind him. At once he seemed in a hurry, talking quickly: "I have them all. I never make suggestions. That's up to you. There's only one thing I don't cater to. It's very popular these days, this gratuitous, anonymous violence in all the rap songs. Strangers killing strangers. It's not plausible. I don't consider it a great hit and you won't find it here."

"You can't make a suggestion?" Pressler was lost. He needed someone to tell him what to do, suggest a way out with dignity. Groping for something plausible, he blurted out: "I'm thinking, I've been thinking about one, it's been going through my head, very popular in the '60s, something about a car accident, dead man's curve, no one's fault..."

"People have accidents all the time. They run off cliffs, lose control on rainy nights and hit utility poles. Go ahead and have an accident."

"Everyone would see through it. I'm the careful kind."

"You're asking for someone else to take responsibility."

"I'm looking for dignity."

The man considered this, not for long. "Dignity!" He laughed loudly and said, "You know, Robert, she was only part right. You're not an ass."

"Not...?"

"No. You're a gutless ass. There's no dignity in what

you're intending. People will see through it, no matter what I'm capable of. They'll figure it out—that wife of yours for sure—and they'll see this selfish, whining child, 'poor me, can't get what I want!' But," he stood and pulled a CD from the shelf, "here. Listen to this one, and when you're done, if it's the one you want, come back and we'll talk price."

"It's about an accident?"

"Yes, Robert." He spoke as if to a little child. *Everything's going to be okay now! It wasn't your fault. Just an accident, nothing intentional!*

And Pressler turned to leave, CD in one hand, briefcase in the other.

On the way out the door, he heard a single word said to his back: "Gutless."

At the edge of the lookout, Robert stands empty-handed, crying. He should be home, but he took an exit off the parkway and now finds himself at the high ridge on Overhill Road, a favorite lovers' spot. It's 7:15, still light, no lovers yet. No one in fact. Unseen, he is allowed to indulge himself. He pulls down his necktie, flings his suit jacket into the dust, and makes big gulping sobs while gazing at the sprawling bedroom community below, his home for the past twenty-five years.

He leans against the sturdy rail along the edge, erected last year in response to a citizens' campaign. This place was the scene of an unfortunate accident. A young boy of twenty-one, his life and great things ahead, ran his car over the cliff, hit the rocks below, and burst into a fireball. Some say it was an accident, others say, well, after all, the boy had been jilted only a few days before.

Pressler looks down over the jutting shelf, considers and calculates. Perhaps he can do the same, get his car going fast enough to run it through this barrier and sail into oblivion. *They'll figure it out—that wife of yours for sure.* Or maybe he can stop crying and go home and go to bed and wake up tomorrow and go to work. Call his kids in the evening. *This is what our lives are about.*

But he doesn't move. *Gutless.* His feet are planted in the ground and he sobs with the painful sound of a man who doesn't cry often. In the blur of emotion, he becomes aware of something missing, a remembered sensation of cool, hard plastic in his hand. He looks down and sees that his hand is empty. He blinks, and still it's empty.

Maybe there's a middle ground between life and death. Maybe he's insane. He can't remember what he did with the CD. Perhaps he listened to it on the way up the hill and it's in the car. He walks back to the open door, leans inside and looks in the CD player, on the seat, in his briefcase, pulling five days' worth of classifieds out onto the floor just to confirm what he's beginning to understand. None of it happened, not the man or the little room.

If his mind is that powerful, maybe he can will Rachel out of consciousness, or Marcie for that matter, or himself.

He hears a noise behind him, a crunch of gravel. An engine is switched off, a car door opens and closes. Pressler swipes at his wet cheeks before backing out of the front seat. He turns around to see the car and the man in a business suit standing next to it. A familiar face, an acquaintance from a lifetime of elementary, middle, and high school functions, their kids in the same district. Vague memories of shared pleasantries in school auditoriums and on commuter trains on the way home to pot roasts.

Pressler should get back into his car and drive off. Surely his eyes are red and puffy at the very least, but he's too confused to think of running. *I'm just saying you're a fool and I don't care to hear any more of it.* He doesn't remember the man's name. He will not talk to him, of that much he's sure.

The man turns to him, briefly eyeing the suit jacket in the dirt near the hood of Pressler's car. He smiles in an embarrassed sort of way, but the embarrassment easily could be his own. Here they are, two men at the same stage of life, one of them bent with emotion and the other still suppressing it, both fresh off the commuter train up at a scenic lookout at dinnertime.

"Hello," says the acquaintance, his eyes brushing Pressler's face. He could have said, "You look like hell, Robert," but since the man isn't such a close friend, and since this part isn't a dream (Pressler assures himself), the man doesn't say it even if he's thinking it. Instead, he looks out over the burgeoning suburbs below, gestures, gives a little laugh and says, "What a stink hole." Pressler forces out a laugh for show, at once realizing he doesn't share the man's sentiment. His house is down there. Marcie is down there, in that house.

They stand in silence for a few minutes, parallel lines of view out into the distance. A sort of energy is working itself up inside the man, and Pressler anticipates his attempt at conversation even before it emerges. "How's the family?"

"Fine," says Pressler. "Yours?"

"Just fine," says the man with a little drawl on the "fine," enough to let Pressler know that everything isn't just fine. "You know how it is. Can't face going home to dinner right now." His eyes contain a need to elicit Pressler's agreement.

"Yeah, well, I haven't been up here for a while and thought I'd take a look," is all Pressler admits. He straightens up, squares his shoulders a bit, and the taller he stands, the more the other seems to slouch.

Pressler is feeling less broken the more he works at his shell. He has no interest in this man and doesn't want to hear why he can't face going home to dinner. Who's cheating, the man or his wife? Or are they just worn out from the sight of each other? These kinds of things can't be discerned from the outside and are best left unsaid.

The nameless acquaintance mistakes Pressler's civility for friendliness. He takes another look at the houses below and turns to Pressler quite deliberately. "I was thinking of stopping off for a drink," he says. "Care to join me? We could catch up?" On the last question, his voice cracks, giving him away. Weakness and self-pity.

Their eyes meet, and the man waits for an answer. He seems a bit too hopeful, distastefully so to Pressler, who can see the whole picture now, a slight trembling in the man's lips and the sweat soaked into the shirt collar. *I don't care to hear any more of it.*

In a matter of seconds, Pressler simply knows a few

things without actually thinking them. He knows that he doesn't want to share his troubles with this man or sit in a bar with him, because if he's going to talk to anyone, if he's going to drink with anyone, Marcie is the only person to consider.

"Can't tonight," he says without hesitation. There's no question in his mind. His sudden, unexpected decisiveness gives him a rush. Once he speaks, it's a step toward something and an excuse to take further action. The ease with which he moves feels good to him. "Thanks anyway." He takes the next step and the next, reaches down and picks up his suit jacket. "Maybe another time." Dusts it off.

He will get in his car and go home, such a simple, everyday action, instinctive and nothing remarkable about it. He will do something that's expected of him, something for which he doesn't need to deny responsibility.

With a neighborly wave, he gets into his car, turns on the engine, and backs out of the parking area. Before turning onto the road, he looks up and sees the man still facing him, smaller and forlorn, hands in pockets.

The sun is setting, the atmosphere a diffused orange-pink. He drives mechanically, taking the curves at the speed limit, no more, no less, his body a cog in the machinery of his automobile. The route is programmed. His mind is blank, emotions numbed and thrown far away from him. All the songs are gone from his head, leaving a space so deep and barren that it lies in wait, ready to be filled with something else.

☾ Dust of the Universe

ON A COOL October night, Kip is balled up in the middle of the king-size bed, covers pulled over his head. This is Leila's way of sleeping when she gets in first and waits for him, but the position is not natural to Kip. He is thirty-eight, still hard-muscled from workouts in the gym. Stretched out, his length of six feet, two inches, places his head at the top and his heels at the very bottom of the bed. Now, curled up inside his soft, dark cavern, he tries to feel his bigness and strength. They are lost to him.

The hour is still early, yet he must sleep. Tomorrow will be his first day back at the office. He lies on his left side, making a tight "S." In the quiet under the down comforter, he can hear his own breathing, not much else. The enclosed space gives each breath a bellows-like whooshing sound to complement the whooshing of blood in his veins. He becomes aware of his shallow breathing and endeavors to deepen it, but the changes in rhythm and effort make him doubly aware of his beating heart. Its power reverberates throughout his body.

The effort to keep his mind blank is exhausting but does not lead him into sleep. He opens his eyes. The absence of light is complete under the thick, tightly drawn covers, but there's always something to be seen. He looks into the dark. Thousands of tiny white specks dance about like atoms at boiling point. Intermittently, in the middle of their bright dance, pulsing flows shove them aside, like muddy disgorgements from sewage pipes, rushing rhythmically with every beat of his heart.

In time, his breath and blood warm the air inside his self-made tent. He rolls onto his back and throws the covers off his face, escaping the pitch black with its boiling atomic particles and flowing phantoms of blood. The moonlight casts the room in grainy relief, a surprising amount of natural light. The bedroom is on the second floor and has two large windows, bordered only with decorative swags—Leila's touches. They've always left the windows uncovered because they live in a wooded suburb, very private. Quiet.

He knows he will not be going to sleep. He gets up.

At the window on the front of the house, he stops to look out. Near the mailbox, a glimmer catches his eye, a single gentle swing in a sudden breeze. The realtor came by that morning to post the "For Sale" sign. The outdoor lights are off, but everything can be seen in the moonlight: the driveway, the rock garden, a patch of lawn, the outlines of branches, and in the distance, the porch light of their nearest neighbor. The sky is shot with stars but lacking the moon.

He goes to the back of the house, to the master bath. It has a small bay window with a ledge to rest his elbows upon while gazing out. Low in the sky, the enormous moon bathes the large backyard in a silver shimmer, bright enough to cast shadows from the surrounding trees. The realtor told him to leave the swing set up, it will help to make the sale. He turns. He needs to tell Leila what the realtor said today.

Kip moves back to the bedroom. On the bed is a lump of covers, head invisible. He draws and releases the next breath without noticing it, and the corners of his mouth turn upward. She's climbed in while he was in the bathroom, and now, maybe, he can go to sleep.

"Leila," he whispers when he's pushed up behind her, his head still outside, hers inside. There's not a sound, but the bed is warm. "Are you asleep already?"

Always, Leila has been nearly soundless in the way she sleeps, a kitten without the purr.

"Are you all right, Leila?"

"Fine. Just fine." The voice is barely audible under the covers yet so familiar in the dark. The tone is gentle and sweet, full of contentment. At rest.

But he must know. "You're sure?"

"Yes, don't worry."

"And the kids?"

"I checked on them."

"I'm sorry."

"Don't be sorry."

"I can't sleep."

"You need your rest."

"Tomorrow... How can I...?"

"You'll get through it. They just want to help."

Leila has always believed in the goodness of people, and he tries to be more like her.

He lapses into silence. They both lie on their left

sides but her head is still covered, and he tries to hear her breathing, to gain a complete image of her buried under the covers without lifting them. An edge of the pillow she sleeps on is sticking out and he pushes his face into it, smelling her hair, her skin, drawing up the warmth. Her power should be enough to pull him down into her deep well, a dreamless limbo, an obliteration of consciousness.

Minutes or hours pass. He may have fallen when he senses something behind him, a sound or a movement near the bedroom door. They're in the habit of leaving the door open in case one of the children calls out.

Kip turns onto his back and props himself up on his elbows. The small silhouette in the doorframe belongs to Jonathan, their six-year-old.

"What's doin', buddy?"

The silhouette takes a single step in, then another.

"Come here. Come on!" Kip pats the bed on his right. Leila is on his left.

The small figure is up beside the bed now. A fist rubs an eye. "I can't sleep."

"You've been asleep. Your mom saw you."

"I don't want to sleep."

A choking sound jars the stillness. "Come here, bud." It came from Kip's throat.

He holds the covers up, and the boy climbs into the bed. Kip slides his right arm under the small, bony shoulders and pulls him in tight. They snuggle close.

"Did you see the moon Jon-o?" The boy's room has a window on the backyard.

"It's huge. I touched it."

Kip gently places his lips on top of the head, feeling

the silky softness, smelling the snips and snails. His lips move across his son's hair as he talks. "It seems close enough to touch, but it's thousands of miles away."

"Closer than Zorq?"

"Way closer."

"How far away is Zorq?"

"Oh, at least a million light years."

Jon thinks a while, imagining life on Zorq, the fascinating aliens his father has conjured so many evenings at bedtime.

"I forget, Dad."

"What?"

"Do the Zorquians have cars?"

Kip falters.

"Shh, now Jonathan," says Leila, thinking of Kip.

She always uses their son's full name when she's serious. Kip takes in a deep breath and says, "They don't need cars. They dematerialize and rematerialize at their destination."

"Oh yeah, I remember."

"They just have to think of where they want to go."

"They blink, and when they open their eyes, they're somewhere else."

"Right. Like magic."

"We did that."

"Now, now," says Leila. She rolls over onto her back and exposes her face.

"Well, we did," insists Jon-o.

It was instantaneous, the man said. Others agreed.

Kip turns his head to the left and brings Leila's profile into view. He can feel the length of her right leg along the length of his left leg and his left hand reaches for her right. The fingers are slender and cool, and they intertwine with his and press in restrained urgency. He turns his face up, and the three of them lie on their backs, looking into the invisible ceiling.

Minutes pass. "Why is it so light?" says another voice at the door.

In the frame now is a taller silhouette, the outline of their eight-year-old, Isabelle.

"You can't sleep?" Kip asks.

"You're so dark over there. It's like I'm on the stage again."

Her words take him back to springtime, the recital, her pale pink tights and pure white tutu, her long, dark hair pulled tight and slick into the bun that Leila made. "Come here, sweetheart," he says.

She doesn't move. "Not really the stage," she muses. "It's that other light. The light that came for us!"

"No," says Kip. "Come here if you can't sleep."

"But Daddy. I don't want to sleep."

There it is, that choking sound again, coming from a body not his own. "Come here." He feels it in his throat. "There's plenty of room! Isn't there, Leila?"

"Plenty," she says.

They've done this before and like to joke about it. "This is why we stopped at two—there's no more room in the bed!" On nights like this.

Isabelle is at the bedside.

"Izza lizard," says the boy.

"Jon wonton," says the girl, and they both giggle. Their sweet sounds play together, bubbling like fresh, clear water.

"Here," says Kip, scooping the boy up. "Get between me and Mom. Leila, scoot a little. Here, Izza." Jon's bony knees dig into his chest on the way over, but the rearrangement is accomplished, and Isabelle climbs in beside him on the right, her long hair brushing his face before she lies down. Jon is on his left, and then Leila. Each of Kip's arms is under the pajama-clad shoulders of a child, his left fingers cupping Leila's shoulder.

They, four, stare into the invisible ceiling with no beginning or end. Kip tries to slow his breathing, but the wetness on his cheeks turns into trembling that quickly becomes shaking.

"You're not going to ask us again, are you, Daddy?" says Izza.

"I'm sorry," says Kip. He wants to know about their day. Over and over again.

"I love the summer," says Jon. "I never want summer to end."

"There's nothing to be sorry about." Leila speaks over Jonathan in her comforting voice, because she wants so much for Kip to feel better. If he could feel better he would, just for her, not for himself.

"I don't have to ask you again. Ella told me all about your day." Ella is the mother of Ben and Riley. The friends.

"They were late," says Jon. "We had to wait for them in the parking lot."

"Only a few minutes," says Leila. "Patience does not come easily."

Patience, waiting, stages, change, little people. They

want their day to begin sooner than now, yet they have their whole lives to look forward to. Impatient. Their whole lives ahead.

"I wish you could've come," says Izza. "We had so much fun! I made a sandcastle with Riley."

I wish... "I'm sorry, I had to work."

"Don't be sorry." The comforting.

"The waves were gi-normous!" says the boy, using his favorite new word. "Me and Ben ran in, but Mom called us back."

"On the way home...," the girl begins.

"We just blinked, Dad. That's all."

"Jon was being annoying, Daddy." Her favorite grownup word.

"But you didn't look, you didn't see—"

"They didn't, Kip! They were playing and arguing and laughing in the back. Only me."

"What about the light, Mommy?"

"I just blinked anyway."

"It was a light, wonton."

"But you, Leila."

"Don't worry, darling. I'm sure they didn't see a thing."

"But you—"

"Just for a flash of a second when it jumped the median."

"The rig."

"Jumped and it was too late, but so fast, so fast."

Instantaneous they said.

"Did you...?"

"No, Kip. No pain."

"A blink."

"A light."

Kip's heart is racing again, and his eyes are closed tight against it. He's heard their answers countless times in a blur of endless nights. He wants to know.

He knows.

Now he doesn't.

He's ashamed for asking again because it does nothing to ease his mind. Always the tears come, the choking, the shaking, and afterward, a blank exhaustion that can never be blank enough.

After a time, the night becomes still once more. He closes his eyes to look for the bright, dancing specks of light, the dust of the universe. If he looks hard enough into his closed eyelids he can pass right through the frantic specks and out to the other side.

He keeps trying.

Minutes pass, hours, days, and nights pass.

A voice emerges from the void, steady and deep with truth.

"I miss you." His.

Followed by three others.

"I miss you too, Dad."

"I miss you, Daddy."

"I miss you, Kip, my darling."

Lying on his back, he gathers up the Isabelle pillow and the Jonathan pillow and the Leila pillow and squeezes them tight against his chest and face, breathing his family deeply into his lungs to capture their dwindling particles of skin and hair, sucking in the tear-drenched linens. Maybe he can suffocate.

But then Leila says, "No, Kip," like she always does.

"Why not?"

"Because I love you."

"But you're gone."

"I'm here with you."

This is not the truth. She is not here, but he can go there.

He starts to tell her this again, but she interrupts. "You can't, because you know what I would want." It is the voice she uses when she is very sure, and none of them, not Jonathan, not Isabelle, not even Kip, can contradict.

Her words, theirs, have found him out. He opens his eyes and the dancing specks rush in, condense, and explode.

This is the truth.

He allows for some air, still resisting.

"I can't. Tomorrow, and the next day. How can I?"

"You will," says Leila.

"For you, I will."

"For yourself." She waits a moment to let him know this before adding, in her comforting voice, "Now get some sleep."

And it becomes like any other night in the time when they had nothing but any other nights.

"I love you so much," he says. A new stream of tears is flowing, but his chest is calm.

"Daddy, don't cry! I love you."

"I love you, Dad."

He holds them tighter because the hours grow short, and the light has changed in the way that signals the other side of the dead of night. In the morning, he will have to let them go.

"Goodnight, darling," says Leila.

"Goodnight."

"Goodnight."

"Sleep tight."

☾ Conversation with a Biker

A FEW THINGS worry me even before he takes out the magazine. Big, red-faced and raspy, he squeezes into the narrow aisle seat on my right just minutes before we start to taxi. He smiles at me before I turn to fasten the seatbelt of my just-turned three-year-old, Maddy, who sits in the window seat on my left.

He seems to be stealing looks at us, but I use Maddy as an excuse to avoid direct eye contact. I've managed to see just enough of him to form an instant aversion: the tattoo (a dripping dagger?) on his biceps under a rolled-up T-shirt sleeve, the leather vest, and graying, shoulder-length hair, not very clean.

Bending forward, I grab Maddy's carry-on, a pink Princess Jasmine backpack, and search for her stuffed cat, Snowy. Suddenly, my neighbor's face is nearby at knee level. His aroma, luckily faint, is a mixture of tobacco, alcohol, and sweat. Wheezing and growing redder, he's pulling out his desired reading material, then stuffing his rucksack under the seat in front. I've just found the cat and turn to Maddy with a "Here you go." She gleefully begins a conversation with her pet, who responds with

179

"meows" and purring noises. I'm freed, temporarily, from motherly duties.

My eyes shimmy to the right long enough to notice the man openly leafing through the kind of magazine a discreet pervert would tuck inside a *Field & Stream*. The page I glimpse contains a picture of a young woman—clad metallically in a hubcap-cupped bra and chrome handlebar g-string—straddling a Harley Davidson. The owner of this literature does not dwell on the photograph but takes more interest in the article alongside.

The biker—as I dub him—notices my surreptitious glance and smiles at me with aqua blue eyes and a complexion that goes ruddier, not from embarrassment, but from the exertion. I decide then that he is from California—the place we are headed—rather than New York—the place we are departing.

I nod and quickly pull my eyes away, feeling the butterflies rise in my stomach on the way down the runway. Maddy continues to chatter and purr above the heightening noise of the aircraft while I instinctively reach for her hand. Flying is bad enough even when I have Travis by my side, his arm available to my sweaty palm as he verbally soothes my fears.

I'm thankful for Maddy and her ignorance of the risk that we may not make it up into the heavens. She will spare me from a lonesome death while I masquerade as her protector. And maybe my physical attachment to her will also spare me from the biker's involuntary clutch during our split-second realization of inevitable doom. As the jet noses upward, I reconsider this thought and decide that bikers probably don't seek the comfort of human contact at the moment of death.

Minutes later, safely airborne, I begin to relax. With my head close to Maddy's, we look out the window and I point out the tiny houses, streets, and cars below. "It's a map!" she shrieks, a gratifying indication that she actually remembers the lesson I gave her with a Sesame Street map. Maybe *this* would be something to impress Travis, but he isn't here to see.

Maddy turns her attention back to Snowy. Her relationship with the cat is soaring to new levels, amusing her more than I ever could. But Snowy can't be good for more than ten minutes, and we have five hours ahead of us. I envision the worst—fidgeting, crankiness, tantrums, gymnastics, and the inevitable potty needs of a newly-trained child. And now, a biker to maneuver around besides.

My elation about her recently acquired toileting skills quickly evaporates with the thought that a diaper is good (depending) for a full five hours, while panties require two or more trips to the facilities in the same length of time. Gone is my hoped-for freedom from preoccupation about bodily functions. It's been a difficult, all-consuming task. "That's all you talk about anymore—poops and pee-pee," Travis said one day in a matter-of-fact tone. The statement was close to accurate, but his bluntness and lack of humor bothered me, like so many other things he says. The day I announced the successful completion of training, all he said to me was, "That's great," before sweeping his little girl up in the air and saying, with passion, "Good job, Maddy!" The accomplishment was, after all, entirely hers.

I wonder what he's doing right now and whether he's begun to suspect.

Maddy soon distracts me from these thoughts. She meows and translates: "Snowy wants to color." I pull the coloring book and crayons from the pink backpack and set them up on her tray. Blissfully, she opens the book and places the cat alongside. "Meow! I want to color *this* picture!" I look at my watch. Half an hour gone, and still a perfect child. Soon enough she will make my life miserable, I think, almost wishing for her misbehavior— something to occupy my hands and mind.

Maddy scrawls a wobbly "S" for Snowy at the top of her colored page. Next to it, a squiggly "M" for Madeline. I work with Maddy on her letters, and for her age, she's way ahead of the game. A few nights ago, when Travis got home and saw Maddy's letters on paper, he repeated his favorite phrase: "She's naturally gifted." When this happens, I like to remind him, "We go over her letters every day," and he responds, "Great! You're so patient with her." I receive a smile from him before he starts to talk about his day. At night, he gives me a chaste kiss.

We never argue, rarely raise our voices. When I first suggested I wanted to take Maddy to visit my parents in California, he accepted it without question, not asking to come along. "I know your folks miss you. And they want to see Maddy too." Perhaps he understood that I wanted to go without him. Perhaps he simply didn't want to go. Nothing was said. We assumed he would stay and work. I would go. For a "week."

I packed and packed, not entirely sure of what I was doing. If appearances are any indication of intentions, I was sending the clues. Travis pretended not to notice. Sweating in the July heat under the weight of my huge load, he hoisted our bags into the taxi without comment. Not even a raised eyebrow. Just before the cab lurched forward, he reached in through the open window and touched my shoulder. Our eyes met and locked. "I hope it's a good trip for you," he said. Was there sadness in his face?

The drink cart inches closer. The biker drops his magazine in his lap and fumbles in a rear jeans pocket, pulling out a worn leather wallet. When Maddy sees the flight attendant handing out drinks, she sits up tall and asks me politely, with a "please," for juice. I can't say no to the future adult self in her face. Setting the orange juice on my own tray, I hope to control the amount of liquid she consumes, and thus contains, in her small bladder.

Meanwhile, the biker orders and pays for an imported beer—an odd choice I think. He seems like more of a Budweiser type. He ignores the plastic cup and sips straight out of the bottle, then quietly swallows a burp, patting his mouth delicately with three fingertips.

I'm sensing the thoughts stirring inside the biker's head as I help Maddy with a sip of her juice. He leans forward a little and smiles at us with messy teeth, a gold one near the back of his mouth. "You have such a good little girl."

I'm stunned by his civility and don't respond immediately, wondering if I have a good reason to ignore him. Replaying the sound of his words, I search for a threat but don't find it.

I'm brought back to the time I first met Travis. From

opposite sides of the lobby, we simultaneously stepped into the line at the Carnegie Hall box office, five minutes before curtain. Taking one look at him, I assumed he would claim priority and hold his ground. He dresses and carries himself with the air of a man too important for civility. But I was mistaken. He immediately stepped aside and begged my pardon. Minutes later, so surprising, he sat in the row and seat directly behind me. Throughout the piano concerto, I was continuously aware. At intermission, he leaned forward and...

The biker is still leaning forward a bit, smiling. His words, so careful and courteous, deserve a response. "Thank you," I say, finally. Perhaps only a second or two has passed, the time it takes to see an exquisite memory.

"It's hard for the little ones, all cooped up on the plane."

"You're right about that."

We exchange smiles and our eyes awkwardly disengage. Maddy continues to color until the lunch cart comes by a few minutes later. "Here, let me help with that," offers the biker, holding Maddy's lunch while I clear away her paraphernalia. He reaches in front of me and places the lunch on her tray. "Thank you," I say, and busy myself, helping Maddy find the contents of her kiddy lunch, hidden inside plastic and cardboard containers that double as toys.

The biker helps out again, placing our lunches on our respective trays, then orders another beer and attempts to tip the flight attendant, who graciously declines. He wolfs most of his food, then slows down and becomes talkative between mouthfuls.

"You folks from California?"

"No. I mean, I grew up there, but now we live in New York."

"How 'bout that! I'm a transplant the other way. Left New York damn near forty years ago." He looks up in the air, counting. "Maybe thirty-seven cr thirty-eight. It was '67. Anyway, California was the place to be. Peace and flower power and all that! Went out there on my first bike—just a scooter really, but I thought I was hot shit." He gazes out on a distant past but quickly turns a worried look on me. "Excuse my language, ma'am. You don't think the little one heard?"

I look at Maddy, in her own world, cheerfully humming as she sets up a cardboard unicorn. "No, I don't think so."

"That's good." He gulps down his last bite and chugs some beer. I'm only halfway through my meal, considering whether to finish it. He blows out a mouthful of air, his cheeks puffing up red. "Boy, these non-smoking flights are killers!" He laughs and coughs, then turns to look at me. "Gonna meet the old man out there? In California I mean."

An ulterior motive behind this one? I don't hear it. His tone is conversational. "No," I say, "I mean, we're going to visit my parents."

"You're lucky there. I lost my folks a long time ago. Now I just have a sister back east. That's who I was visiting. I never saw much of my folks after I left home and always regretted it. You're lucky you can go visit. Too late for me now. But back then, I was too hot for the West Coast. Hardly even called my mom. Boy, I did it all.

Hit all the concerts—Hendrix and Joplin. Even joined the Angels. Man, those sons of... Well, I didn't hang long with them. You can have a hell of a time with a bike without all that crap. Sorry, ma'am." With a self-conscious look, he glances at Maddy. "Excuse my mouth. Things just kind of slip out." He looks at me and smiles. I smile back, feeling the sudden acuity of all my senses. I'm locked into him and everything he's saying. He continues. "That was some time. Runnin' free. All that wild and crazy kid stuff. But you probably wouldn't know about that!" He looks at me for a reaction.

"You'd be surprised."

He laughs. "Yeah. Everyone has some kind of past."

"Things we'd like to forget."

"Yeah. But some of us can't shake it. And then things change."

He stops suddenly, without explaining himself. But I know what he means.

In a minute, he continues. "You don't know how lucky you are. Family on both ends! Still have your parents and a little one. Maybe a husband too?"

I nod. "Yes. A husband."

"You don't know how lucky. Such good manners on that little one."

Maddy is still happily humming. The biker seems to have finished for now, and I'm suddenly disappointed, left hanging for more.

I think of the night before we left. Over dinner, Travis launched into a long story about something that happened at work, something of importance to him, I could tell by his tone, his intensity. Now, I try to remember what he said and realize I didn't hear a word. I looked at him the entire time, nodding and uttering a syllable here and there. Luckily no quiz at the end, no request for advice, nothing to put me on the spot or reveal my crime.

Were my responses appropriate? Did he know I hadn't been listening? How many times had he done the same to me? Something underneath has changed with us while the surface remains intact. Restraint and courtesy. What will happen if, one day, the courtesy is gone?

A few minutes later, Maddy decides she has to go—has to go *now*. The lunch trays with partially consumed food and drink still clutter our space. But the biker understands the problem and jumps to our rescue, swiftly helping to stack the trays and holding all three as he stands aside in the aisle. We lift the little tables and sidle past, getting to the lavatory in the nick of time.

Two hours later, Maddy has to go again, and we repeat our getaway around the gracious biker.

Shortly after the second potty run, the plane starts to descend. My stomach jumps into my throat. A few minutes later, the flight attendant announces our imminent arrival at LAX and tells us to put our trays up and our seatbelts on.

"Sorry, Maddy. We have to put these things away." I collect her toys and books, but the neat little backpack is now a mess and won't readmit everything. Maddy, finally, has become fussy. Snowy is most important and should not be squished! "I know, Maddy. I have just the place for her in my bag." I open my own large satchel and find, for the first time, a white envelope inside, addressed "Cynthia." Travis's handwriting. I hastily put Snowy inside, drop the satchel and use my feet to push it under the seat. I open the letter and read it while holding Maddy's hand.

Come back to me. I'll be waiting for you. Let's talk to each other. And listen. Love always, T.

My eyes start to burn and my lips quiver. I bite down hard but it's no use. The tears spill down my cheeks.

Maddy, looking out the window, doesn't seem to notice. She's bouncing up and down as best she can under the seatbelt, exclaiming over the sights. "A dolly swimming pool! Look—another one!"

But my tears don't escape the biker's notice. "You all right?" he asks, genuinely concerned. I nod a "yes," looking down at the letter in my lap. I wipe my cheeks.

A pause. "Nervous about landing?"

I nod again, thankful for the convenient excuse. A tactful biker! He surprises me yet again.

"Don't worry," he says. "Put your hand here and squeeze hard." I raise my eyes enough to see his right hand slap his left forearm where it lays on the armrest we share. "Grab right here if you want to. Don't worry. I won't bite."

I look up and see him smiling, the glint of his gold tooth oddly reassuring. "That's okay," I say. "Thanks anyway. I'll be all right."

"Okay. I understand. Don't worry about a thing. These pilots land planes every day." A pause. He slaps his forearm again. "It's here if you need it."

And I know that, if he reaches out to touch me in

the moment before death, I won't mind at all, and will be thinking only of Travis.

☾ *What I'd Like to Say*

IF HE'D BEEN shipped off to Desert Storm, one of the few to die a hero in the shifting sand, I'd still have the letter he wrote inside a tent on a hot night in a foreign land. I would remember him by his words on that paper and the sad eulogies of his army buddies, his platoon leader.

If he'd been a doctor at a city hospital, stabbed with a syringe by a delirious AIDS patient, I'd still have his medical plaques to hang on my wall, a sympathy card from the head of staff, a stack of glowing obituaries.

If he'd been a computer wizard, a CEO spearheading a new technology, his corporate jetliner downed in the Far East on his way to global expansion, I'd forever have his name at my fingertips, topping the list of every search engine on my PC, a guaranteed cyber immortality.

He could have been any or all those things. That is who he was.

But there came a day, without my noticing it, when he died. He was lost to me some years ago on a date I cannot pinpoint. His death was just as foreign and absurd as any of those imagined, yet more insidious, a fact without proof, leaving no mementos, no evidence of the person he could have been.

One thing he was and always will be: my older brother. Our childhood faces might have stepped out of a glossy magazine advertisement of the '50s picturing a rosy-cheeked four-person nuclear family, the boy (as usual) the older one, with darker hair than his sister's. The boy is the man-to-be, the protector, the one who shields his little sister when other kids taunt.

Some of that happened. I remember.

But most of all he was exciting, different, and a mystery because I was a girl and he was a boy who led a masculine life with other boys. He and his pals were older and smarter and knew so much more than I. Especially *my* brother. He knew everything.

How unbearable then to wake up to the fact that he didn't. On a day I can't remember, a day when my head was turned, he disappeared from view around the bend of an invisible mountain pass. If an event in his life had triggered his departure, I was unaware of it. The clue was buried. He'd crept and inched and edged away without giving me a second thought while I allowed it to happen.

Time has passed and the fog has dissipated, leaving me the lone figure in a harsh sun. Clearly now, I'm the smarter one at life, perhaps always was the smarter one without my knowing it.

There was a day when we last saw each other. This is a fact. That day dawned some seven or eight years ago. I cannot remember the time of year or where we were or what we said or did and it galls me, producing a whirlpool of disjointed images from every stage of life. I chase the pictures, mostly at night. Was it this day or that one or another one completely lost from memory?

On one of my sleepless nights he calls.

He is somewhere in a nameless state in the middle of the country. He sounds lucid, articulate, charming. At first, I think he's back from the dead. Then he slips, only a small slip, a tiny blur, and I know.

"Still...?" I ask.

He makes a snorting sound, his new kind of laughter. His breath is pushed into the receiver. "Hey sis, why so...?" I can almost smell it.

"*This* is the only way you can pick up the phone?"

Another snort. All so funny.

I think about another telephone call some years ago at the first sign of trouble. I delivered a lecture, full of advice. I'd done my research and recited names and numbers and addresses.

Now I remain mute.

He's no longer able to catch my thoughts as he once could. He talks and talks and talks. He's telling me how he thinks of me constantly, he's missed me, worries about me, wishes he could be with me, remembers the old times, the jokes we shared. He wants to send me money when his money comes through, and he plans to visit me and things will be great again.

He's starting to choke up. I hear a gulp and a glass set down too hard on a table. Finally, he asks, "Do you still love me?"

The question is an attack, seeking an opening. I put on my armor and call up the reserves. For such a long time, my head has been full of the things I want to tell him.

I loved you once. I still love my memory of your younger self, the infinite potential bursting from the stretch of your mischievous grin. I loved your big-handed yank at the nape of my neck and your powerful sprint to places yet undiscovered. I loved your full-throated laugh and your joy and your quick wit.

But now you are someone else, someone I will never know. A man who left all of us behind so long ago and cannot find his old self before asking this question. The old self would have known the answer without asking. How can I possibly love this person you've become?

That is what I'd like to say.

Instead I say, "I still love you," dear brother, for deep inside, and a surprise even to myself, a trace of hope remains.

☾ *Stolen Afternoon*

GINGER BELIEVED HER visits to Grandpa were still secret. Mom and Grandpa never seemed to talk, and if they did, Grandpa was likely to forget.

After the first few afternoons, Ginger began to notice how much he forgot and how much he remembered at the same time. It was mind-boggling. One minute he'd be calling her Vesma instead of Ginger, and the next, he'd jump back to his boyhood a million years ago, remembering things like they happened yesterday. He would describe the farm he grew up on and his favorite horse and the Russian tanks rolling across the countryside and bombings and people disappearing in the middle of the night. Half of it was so fantastic she thought he patched it together from that crazy corner in his mind where old people jumble up everything they've ever seen and done.

A blustery day, Friday, the 19th of December, Ginger walked to the county bus stop a quarter of a mile from her high school. She'd just finished her last class before Christmas break, and Mom was still at work.

She didn't want to go home. Since the divorce, and

after Sean's move away to college, the house had become one huge echo. But tomorrow, Mom would start her vacation and get the house ready for Sean's arrival on Sunday, and soon after that, the three of them would suddenly be together again. Things would be nice for a day or two until Mom became restless, wanting to get out and see her new man. She was still hiding him, but Ginger knew.

The bus trip cost two dollars and took half an hour. Ginger didn't need to ask for money—she had forty dollars saved from babysitting. Nobody took public transportation except maids and nannies, people who spoke Spanish, very old people who could still walk, and Ginger, the stick-out teenager. She'd learned the bus schedule and knew how to time it just right, getting to Grandpa's at 3:30, staying until 5:00, and getting home at 5:40, before Mom pulled up.

The bus took twice the time it should have, making a dozen stops on the way. At some stops, the driver pushed a button to lower the side of the bus with a big "hiss," placing the first stair right on the pavement to give the really weak people a fighting chance to get on.

Grandpa had lived in the same house ever since Ginger could remember, probably from before she was born. It was a dirty color of white, smaller than her house, in the middle of a row of similar houses without much room between them. Hugging the yard was a steel fence made of wire twisted into diamond shapes and a gate with a metal lever she lifted to open the latch. It was the type of fence that should have a dog behind it. She heard a few of them barking at houses down the block. When she stepped onto the cement walkway inside, the gate closed itself behind her with a decisive metallic click. In winter, the grass in the front yard was completely brown with patches of dirt interspersed; come spring, the green parts would be mostly weeds anyway.

She knocked, using the metal knocker. There was also a doorbell, but she preferred the knocker. Her own house didn't have one, and she especially loved this feature of Grandpa's house. It was heavy. Sometimes she would lift it as high as it would go and just let it fall, then do it again. Other times she would take it in hand and apply all her might to produce the loudest possible sound. Either way, she was prepared to wait. She always phoned ahead of time so Grandpa knew to expect her (or maybe he had forgotten?) but either way, he needed the time to get to the door.

Finally, she heard the big click as the bolt lock slid away, echoing back into the front hall. The door crept open six inches, and most of Grandpa's face peered out from the darkness like a raccoon in the night. The next moment he said, as he always did, "Well, well!" and opened the door wider. "Come in, come in!" Things were usually said in twos at the beginning.

"Sveiks!" greeted Ginger in the only Latvian she knew.

"My goodness! Sveika!" He chuckled a little. The way he said the word sounded so much better than her version.

The smell of the place always hit her right away, a closed-in odor, the opposite of an open meadow. She'd gotten used to it and liked it because Grandpa was part of it. She followed him in, took a step and came to a halt, stepped again and stopped, adapting to his shuffle. This kind of stuff used to drive her crazy when she was a kid, but now it was almost a relief just to calm down and become really...really...slow. Sometimes, in the breaks between their little bits of conversation, she actually heard the mantelpiece clock ticking in the living room. They never sat in the living room, always the kitchen.

"Some milk?" he offered.

She sat on one of the yellow vinyl chairs that bounced slightly on its aluminum "S" frame. Her grandmother, who died before Ginger was born, must have picked out this furniture.

"Sure." She didn't like milk very much but always managed to drink it. She sat there and let him serve her. He seemed to enjoy it. He took his time getting a glass out of the cabinet, opening the refrigerator, bending back the carton spout, and pouring from the quart container. She looked at his profile as he did the pouring. The corner of his mouth was turned upward, and his nose was bulbous and covered with bumps. When he shuffled over and set the glass on the table, his face moved into the light from the window, close enough for her to see—was that?—dust inside the cracks and folds of his skin.

He looked at her with a secret in his eyes and waited, but she only smiled back. After a moment he spoke. "I have some cookies too! I know you like cookies."

Excited now, he shuffled a little faster back to the counter, picked up the tin, and brought it to the table, pushing it toward her—his invitation to open it. The lid was on tight and he couldn't open it himself. She'd seen him try. He always had the same kind of cookies, an assortment, some with slivers of almonds on top, some with jelly in the middle, some very thin and brown and hard. Nothing like chocolate chip, but she always ate one or two and replaced the top loosely with a corner pushed up. Maybe, when she was gone, he would be able to open it himself and have a few.

He sat down in the yellow chair opposite her. The tiny table had nothing on it but a plastic napkin holder filled with small square paper napkins. He hunched over a bit like he always did, his hands in his lap with the fingers interlaced. She couldn't see his hands under the table, but she knew. "How was school?" he asked.

"Good. Really good because today was the last day before vacation."

"Vacation! My goodness."

"We have two weeks."

"Two weeks! All that time, what are you going to do with it?"

His eyes, with the slack, diagonal lids over the outside edges, were watery and almost whitish looking on the rims of the gray pupils. She just couldn't tell what he remembered right now.

"Sean will be here day after tomorrow. Mom is really excited because he didn't get to come for Thanksgiving. You remember, we were at Uncle Andi's house." She looked at Grandpa and he nodded with shining eyes, but she couldn't tell what was behind them. "And on Christmas Eve, you're coming to our house, right?"

"Yes, certainly. I'm planning on it. Looking forward to it. Sean will be there."

"And Uncle Andi and Aunt Stephanie."

"We shall have a party. A good time."

"Yes, but…"

He waited for her to finish the sentence, looking at her with sagging eyes like an elephant's.

"…we haven't gotten a tree yet."

"Well, you'll get one."

"Mom's been busy."

"You'll get one."

"We're supposed to go tomorrow."

"Tomorrow, yes." Little backward phrases like that, and the sharp "t's," reminded her he was from somewhere else.

"Tomorrow," he repeated. "We'll cut the tree."

"Cut?"

"We'll pick a beautiful one. And the Yule log. We must pull it around the house three times to collect the sorrows and the worries."

"What's a Yule log, Grandpa?"

"The big log we're going to burn in the backyard, after collecting the sorrows, the misfortunes."

"I don't think we can have a fire in the backyard."

"Well, then we'll do it in the fireplace!" He smiled, happy with his suggestion. "And light the candles on the tree."

"I don't think we can do that either."

"That's right, that's right." He shook his head. There was no longer a smile, but he didn't look unhappy.

They sat for a while in silence. Ginger drank her milk, trying not to make loud gulping noises. Between swallows, she heard the clock ticking. She took out a cookie covered with hard, white frosting and bit down, holding her other hand underneath to catch the crumbs. Now she heard the sound of her own teeth chewing inside her head.

"Yes, Gingiņa."

She hadn't said anything, but she'd been thinking a lot of things. She swallowed her mouthful of cookie and spoke. "I like it when you call me that."

"What, Gingiņa? That means my little Ginger."

"In Latvian?"

"Yes, my little Ginger. Like your mama calls you Gingie."

"You were telling me last time about when you had to move, you know, when you had to leave your home in Latvia."

"Oh, yes. A terrible time. So terrible."

He looked down at his hands in his lap, then up and away from her. She was afraid she shouldn't have asked him this. He seemed to be looking out and seeing everything from that time. He was in the middle of it. She wished she hadn't asked.

"I'm sorry," she said.

"Sorry?" He sat up straighter and his eyes were pulled up and open by the raising of his scraggy eyebrows. "Why are you sorry? You aren't German or Russian."

This sounded so funny she almost laughed. He must have seen it in her eyes and a twinkle came into his.

"Yes, it was terrible, but it was so long ago. The Germans and Russians fighting in our backyard. We ran. Everybody did. We grabbed what we could…," he made swiping motions over the tabletop, gathering imaginary things, "…and we piled it all in the wagon, but when we got to the boat, we couldn't take anything with us to Germany. Nothing at all."

"Why couldn't you stay on your farm?"

"Stay with the Russians in our house? We didn't like either of them, but if we had our choice, it was the Germans, not the Russians."

This sounded wrong to Ginger, who had a memory from history class poking around in her mind, but what did her teacher know? Grandpa had been there.

"And you really couldn't bring anything with you? Nothing? What were you going to wear?"

"What we had on, of course! We piled the clothes on our bodies. It was cold anyway. And we each took one small satchel. I had one book I read over and over again for a whole year."

"And nothing else?"

"We put the pictures in our satchels. My mother, my father, my sister, we all had some." His head drooped and he was quiet for a while. She saw the brown spots on his scalp under the brittle strands of white hair.

Without warning, his head bounced up again. "Go get the pictures."

"The pictures?"

"The pictures, yes!"

This was the one thing she was allowed to do for him. The first time, he had taken her to his bedroom to show where he kept the box, but the second time, he suggested she go by herself while he stayed in the kitchen. It became their little ritual. She stood, and the bottom of the chrome "S" scraped along the linoleum. Out the kitchen she went, down the short hallway, past the bathroom, into his bedroom at the end of the hall. The smell of Grandpa's whole house was concentrated in there more powerfully, right around the bed. It was very dark with the rolling shades pulled down, and she flipped the light switch on the wall, sending electricity into a dim, yellow bulb under a dirty frosted-glass ceiling fixture.

The shoebox was on a shelf in his closet, as if it contained shoes. Maybe this was his way of hiding it. She knew the pictures were precious to him, and he kept them in the bedroom so he could look at them at night, in bed. She hadn't asked him this. She just knew, partly because he kept his glasses on the bedside table next to a little lamp. Her mission was to retrieve both the glasses and the shoebox and return to the kitchen.

When she got back, he put on the glasses, a kind that nobody ever used anymore. They had heavy black rims and very thick lenses and his eyes bugged out behind them. He didn't like to wear them all the time, especially when he was walking, because they made him dizzy.

She remembered Mom saying something about it once. She'd gotten a phone call from Uncle Andris, the one who always told her about anything that had to do with Grandpa. Mom finished the phone call, hung up and turned to them, saying, "Pa has fallen." She had forgotten to say "Grandpa" like she usually did whenever she said something about him to Ginger and Sean. A day passed, and everything turned out to be all right. He hadn't broken anything, and after that, he just wouldn't wear the glasses while he was walking. It was better to be fuzzy than to be dizzy with the floor a hundred feet away.

The photos, mostly old, brown or gray, were curled at the edges and of all sizes and shapes, a scrambled hodgepodge in the box. Some were taken in Latvia before and during the war, some in the German DP camp and some in the United States. "You pick first," he said, the corners of his mouth twitching.

"Okay." She took off the top and put her hand in while looking up at the ceiling. Sometimes she could tell by feel which ones were the oldest, the ones she liked the most because they were so mysterious. She settled on a medium-sized one and pulled it out, happy to find an old snapshot she had never seen before. The edges were curled and the image had faded. It was probably from Latvia, not Germany, and depicted a girl sitting on a sturdy, broad-chested horse with very thick, furry hooves. The horse was more prominent than the girl, whose body seemed tiny in comparison, but her country-girl square face beamed out to the world with a well-fed, healthy and happy look, framed by neck-length wavy hair held back on one side with a barrette. If the picture had been in color, her cheeks and lips would have been rosy.

"Who's that?"

"Let me see, let me see."

He took the snapshot from her and examined it at varying distances from his nose. Finally he said, "Vesma, on her horse."

"That's Mom?"

"My sister. And that is her horse."

"Your sister's name is Vesma too?"

"Did I say Vesma? Tekla. That is my sister Tekla.

Yes, it is."

Ginger had heard the name before. She took the picture back from him and examined it, trying to find a resemblance between this girl and Grandpa. She might have been twelve or thirteen. How happy she looked! How wonderful to live on a farm with horses, cows, and pigs! "She came with you too, when you left Latvia?"

"Of course, yes, she did."

"What happened to the horse?"

Grandpa looked away and shrugged his shoulders, enough to say that the horse had not fared well.

"Was your sister in the camp in Germany too?"

"Yes. But then she got married and moved to Canada."

"Oh. Then I never met her."

Grandpa thought for a moment. "You did meet her. Yes. You were very young, a baby. Your mother took you to Canada. But then, there was no opportunity for you to know her. Tekla died very soon after that."

They sat and let this information sink in.

"Your turn!" she said, breaking the silence.

He took the box and rummaged around inside, making a big show of it like he'd entered the drawing for the grand prize, then pulled one out and held it in both hands, resting them on the table. Ginger leaned toward him and looked over the top. She knew this one. It was a very old, studio photograph of the faces and shoulders of a young couple, their images artistically blurred around the edges. The woman's hair was pulled back in a low bun with the sides in a wave tight against her head and covering her ears. Ginger wondered how she could have gotten that wave into it. Her face was sturdy and square, like Tekla's. The man was behind her, taller, with a long face and stern expression. The first time she saw the picture, she guessed it was Grandpa when he was young, but she'd been wrong.

"I know that one!" she said.

"Why? But certainly, yes, you do." He handed it to her.

"Your mother and father."

"Yes."

"What were they like?"

"Well, my mother was a schoolteacher, and my father was a customs agent in the civil service. This was a problem, you see, when the Russians came. People with those kinds of jobs, well, we had some friends. They just disappeared. My father said to us, we have to leave."

"Where do you think your friends went?"

"Siberia. Or killed. The Germans killed certain people and the Russians killed others. We had to leave."

Ginger felt outrage. "How could they just come into your country and kill people? I wish they hadn't done that. I wish you never had to leave."

Grandpa took off his glasses and smiled at her with his real eyes. "But if I hadn't left, we wouldn't be sitting here right now, would we?"

The question opened a flash flood of generations in her mind: the old studio photo of her great-grandparents, Grandpa marrying Grandma in the DP camp and coming to America and having Andris and Vesma, Uncle Andi marrying Aunt Steph and not having any children, Mom and Daddy having her and Sean. Daddy leaving them.

And whose fault was that? Mom had said "nobody's fault" when Ginger asked.

"Here, have another cookie," he said, pushing the tin closer to her. He looked so hopeful she had to take one. It was unfrosted, without nuts, half brown and half white. She pushed the tin back his way. "You have one too."

"I like the ones with jelly." He picked it out, with much rustling of the little papers inside the tin. "I'm glad you didn't take all of them."

She had to smile. He seemed younger then, completely here and not there. The past was past and they were here.

He probably liked the ones with jelly because they were softer. His mouth trembled a little as he took a bite, and the cookie disintegrated, half of it landing on the table. He looked at her with crumbs on his mouth. "Oops," she said, and they laughed. She got up, walked around the table, and scooted the crumbs off the edge, into her palm. She threw the crumbs in the trash and dusted off her hands in the sink. When she returned, he'd finished swallowing and was wiping the crumbs off his mouth with a napkin.

"Thank you. It's your turn," he said.

She sat down and put her hand in the box, quickly pulling out a photograph near the top. The moment she saw it, her heart jumped to her throat. If she'd taken the time to sort through, the texture of the photo paper might have given her a clue about this picture before pulling it out. They had dozens like it at home, now tucked away in a drawer and avoided by her mother. Ginger would never look at them unless she was in a certain kind of mood, happy and feeling especially strong.

"What's that?" asked Grandpa.

"Christmas, when I was little."

"Christmas. How about that! What luck!"

Do you like it?

I love it, love it, love it, Daddy.

What are you going to call it?

I think...

Come here.

I think the name will be...

Come here.

No, I'm thinking.

How about Bunny?

Oh...

Come here.

Okay.

Up you go. There.

"What's in the picture? Let me have a look."

She handed it to Grandpa. He held it in one hand, using the other to put on his glasses again after a couple of fumbling attempts. Now she understood why he kept those big, out-of-date glasses. The ones with thin frames would have been impossible for him to put on. He examined the photograph with bug eyes and a scrunched nose. "I remember. Vesma took this one."

"We have the same one at home."

"Vesma, she would mail the copies to me. Is that you?"

"Yes."

"You are maybe five years old?"

"Six." She remembered every minute of that

Christmas, a month before she turned seven. Her daddy asked if she had a name for her new stuffed animal while he tugged on a pigtail under her ear and stroked the top of her head, putting little kisses into the part on her scalp. There was a smoky smell on his lips and fingers and that other smell on his breath. A glass with his favorite brown liquid sat on the table next to them.

"Yes," said Grandpa. "That is your father. You were always on his lap. And what are you holding?"

"That's Floppy"—the stuffed bunny she still slept with every night. It was soft and white and had long droopy ears with pink insides.

Her eyes started to sting.

Look at those ears. So floppy.

That's Floppy. That's her name, Daddy. Floppy.

What a good name.

Her daddy would always hold her so tight, no matter what.

Grandpa's head seemed stuck, looking down at the long-ago Christmas, the tree lights in the background, Ginger on her daddy's lap, holding Floppy in the picture her mother had sent to him. They lived only fifteen minutes away, but Mom had mailed it to him.

And suddenly it was clear as daylight, the half-conversation she'd overheard only last week—the half of it spoken by her mother. Ginger had been standing outside the bedroom door. It was ajar, and she was about to knock, but she stopped herself, wanting to hear. Mom was lying on her bed talking on the phone with her new man, deliberately using the kind of low voice she reserved for dark secrets. Ginger's ear strained at the crack in the door:

I should visit more often, I know...

...I guess it just became a habit...

...He never liked him, you see. He was angry at me for marrying him...

...Maybe I should have listened...

Everything froze, and Ginger's stomach hurt as she watched Grandpa examining her daddy's picture under his veil of drooping eyelids. She wanted to grab that picture, yank it from his hand! *We wouldn't be sitting here right now, would we?* This is what he'd said to her only a few minutes ago, knowing all the while *he never liked him, you see...* Didn't want him, and maybe never wanted her either! Their stolen afternoons—never missed. Now, this one was surely spoiled.

A burning anger rose inside her, directed at Mom, Grandpa, Daddy, even herself, all of them and no one. The world.

The doorbell rang. It was the loudest doorbell she'd ever heard. Grandpa looked up toward the door-sized opening between the kitchen and the hallway.

"Who could that be now?" he supposed.

"I'll go see," offered Ginger in a quavering voice. She turned around in her chair as she spoke, hiding her tears, and swiped at her face, getting most of it.

"No need," he said. She turned back again and saw him wave his free hand in the air as if to erase the intruder. He picked up the picture of Tekla again, not making a move to get up. She waited while his eyes went from the photo of her daddy in one hand to the photo of his sister in the other and back again, while his grayish skin and elephant eyes just made her feel sadder. What was he thinking, remembering?

He chuckled low. "Your daddy." He was staring at the Christmas picture. "How he loved his little girl!"

A rush of warm feeling replaced the sickness in her stomach and the burning red in her eyes. Suddenly, she wanted to jump up and kiss him and say she was sorry! It would only confuse him, she knew, and she was thinking this when the doorbell rang a second time. He startled and asked, "What was that?"

"Someone's at the door."

"At the door?"

"I'll get it, Grandpa."

She got up, wiped her eyes against a final, wayward tear, and went to the door. Through the peephole she saw Uncle Andi. She froze in a panic at being discovered. There was an impulse to hide, overlaid by a voice of reason, telling her to face him without embarrassment. But before she could open the door, a key was inserted, turning the lock. Of course, he had a key. Her mother also had a key, the one she never used. The door opened a crack and he called in, "Pa! It's me, Andris."

She took the handle and pulled the door toward her.

"Gingie! I didn't know you were here. Is your mom here?" He looked above her head and beyond.

"No, just me."

"Oh." He looked befuddled. "Where's your grandpa?"

"In the kitchen."

They walked in. "Well, well. Andris!" Grandpa seemed very pleased, giving no indication he had expected his son to come calling.

"Hi, Pa. How're you doing?" He walked around the table and kissed his father's forehead, exactly in the place where Gingie had wanted to.

"Good, good! My granddaughter is here on a visit."

"I can see that." Andris smiled. Ginger liked his smile, which came easily and often. He seemed to have inherited the cheerful side of the family, wherever it may have originated. Now that she'd seen the pictures, his face reminded her of the faces of Grandpa's mother and sister, large, square, and healthy, although the rest of him was tall and lank. Her mother's face more closely resembled Grandpa's in a significant way, stern and emotionless except in moments when the internal controls were let down. The hardness would surrender to a warm look or a smile or a light shining from the eyes so absolutely that Ginger always knew it was the very thing she'd been waiting and hoping for.

"So, are you ready to go, Pa?" Andris turned to Ginger. "We can drop you at home and save your mother a trip." Her heart jumped again.

"Going?" Grandpa asked.

"Don't you remember, Pa? We're doing your shopping now instead of tomorrow. Steph and I are visiting her folks over the weekend."

"Oh, my, but that's a lot of trouble. You go on ahead."

"No trouble, Pa. We planned it, remember? I knew the office would be closing early today. It's the holidays. Most people are taking all next week off."

Grandpa shook his head slightly and scrunched his

brow, trying to understand.

Ginger looked up at the wall clock. "Don't worry about me. I'll just take the earlier bus."

"You took the bus here?"

She got up. "It's coming in about ten minutes. I know the whole schedule." She tried to sound casual and sure. "Bye, Grandpa." She reached across the table, touched his hand and gave it a kind of rub and a shake to serve as a substitute for their usual hug. She didn't want him to get up and didn't want her uncle to move from Grandpa's side. "Bye, Uncle Andi." She started for the kitchen door.

"Wait, Gingie, we'll take you! Your mom—"

"You can't! It's my global warming project for school." She walked into the hallway and called the rest over her shoulder. "I have to take ten hours of public transportation!" She opened the front door—"See you on Christmas Eve!"—and closed the door behind her.

☾ A Love-Hate Thing

CHITCHAT WAS NOT Darla's forte, but somehow she was in the mood and her neighbor seemed amenable. A staid business type in a gray pinstripe, the man needed just a little encouragement, and so, the moment the seatbelt sign disappeared with a bong and an announcement, "While in flight, may we suggest...," Darla's mouth became unhinged.

There were little things to talk about, like the weather and the delay and the struggle with carry-on luggage, which led inevitably to her declaration: "Actually, I play English horn with the New York Philharmonic."

"Oh?" he said, eyebrows raised. Nothing else, but his tone and the light in his eye signaled interest, not dismissal. He was impressed and she wasn't surprised. Music and art and theater were hidden deep inside him. She had remarked his interest when, upon boarding the plane, he eyed her obliquely from the window seat as she carefully tucked her cased instrument into the overhead bin, cushioning it with pillows and blankets. Now, sensing a reciprocal need, she was freed completely to embellish as she wished—as he wished. Briefly, she evaluated, choosing her facts.

"We tour Canada for two weeks. Lucky me! I missed the nonstop to Toronto, so I'm taking this connecting flight through Chicago. The rest of the orchestra is practically there by now."

"What a shame!"

"I'm going miles out of the way! I won't be there 'til midnight."

"I'm sure you don't need the extra stress before a concert tour."

"True," she responded, stopping to consider. Perhaps her playing would suffer. "It doesn't help, especially now. It's a big tour for me this time. I'll be playing *The Swan of Tuonela*."

His eyebrows shot up another inch, halfway to his receding hairline. The man knew and appreciated music, a sensitivity that might have eluded any stranger but Darla, now suddenly aware of her own hidden talent, this sixth sense. "The solo?" he asked. "You're playing the English horn solo?"

"Why, yes! I can see that you know the piece."

"So beautiful. Sibelius is one of my favorite composers."

"Yes, and one of mine." A pause. "Yes."

They fell into a moment of silence, enjoying it, simultaneously hearing the melody of the swan, beckoning. But soon the mood changed. Darla sensed an emotional shift in the man, his ruing of something lost, something of consequence. His aspect evoked her anticipation. She was pricked alert, awaiting his words, certain they would hold something of significance for her.

"You know," he said, "I once played the violin with a string quartet."

But of course. "How wonderful! You must have been quite good."

He gave a little embarrassed laugh. "Fairly good, I suppose. But it wasn't, I mean we weren't exactly nationally known. Just a local group. We would play at weddings and grammar schools, things like that."

"But no more?"

"Nope. No." He looked out the window and she glanced at his hands, folded in his lap, left on top of right. A gold band. If not for the imperatives of tact, she might have said out loud what she had guessed: that his violin playing had taken a backseat after marriage. She knew only too well.

"But I'm sure you still play for your own enjoyment."

He turned to her with a sheepish look, as if caught in the commission of a misdemeanor. "Actually, I don't. My violin is in the attic, collecting dust."

"Why don't you play it?"

He laughed again and rolled his eyes. "No time, I guess. I'm always traveling for business."

"Well, I hope you'll rescue that violin from the attic. There's always time for things you love, and I can tell you love music."

"I suppose I do," he said, looking into her eyes for the longest time yet. "I envy you, playing with the best musicians in the world. I never made it there. Now, if I listen to a recording of someone like Isaac Stern, I wonder how I can ever pick up my own instrument again. The attempt would be so...," he looked out the window, "inadequate."

And here was the signal. Almost a plea for help. Darla, not quite consciously understanding this, nevertheless was driven by instinct to go to his need. She sat up, squared her shoulders and leaned toward him. "Ah, but I envy *you*," she said so emphatically that he turned to her in surprise. Savoring the moment, she responded with a lingering gaze. "You have," she explained, "the thing I lost some time ago, when I became a professional musician. The luxury of making music all for yourself, without the need to impress anyone."

He nodded tentatively, his expression turning thoughtful with new possibility.

She continued: "In my business, imperfection may cost a livelihood. But in your case, only the four walls will hear."

He smiled. "And my wife."

"Yes, but she'll love you anyway."

They regarded each other, eyes bright, and her hand tightened its grip on the armrest with her unexpected discovery of his attractiveness. Had she found the reason for this game? In twenty years of marriage, such thoughts had never crossed her mind.

"Yes, I suppose she will," he admitted, showing that he, likewise, had never had such thoughts.

What, after all, was the harm in any of this? Certainly the man had no inkling of the concert schedule in Toronto. Darla would get off the plane and never see her stranger again, left with only a delicious memory: a perfect, intuitive exchange, a symbiotic capsule of give and take. So satisfying, unlike everything else in her life.

Later that night, sitting on the faded pink-ruffle coverlet of her teenage bed, Darla took out her English horn and played *The Swan of Tuonela*, flawed, but still better than she'd ever played it. The concert hall was sold out, a mirage of adoring strangers with just one familiar face in the midst: there, in row L, the man from the airplane was smiling up at her.

After her solo, she carefully laid the instrument to rest and walked down the hall to Mom's room for a final check. The lights blazed and smoke curled up from a cigarette in the crowded ashtray on the bedside table. Mom sat bolt upright, a stick in the pillows, two light pink spots aflame in her sallow cheeks. *Only the four walls will hear.* But Mom had been listening. She smiled and said nothing, not a single pejorative remark, and Darla felt no anger. Quietly, mother and daughter bid each other "good night," not bothering to avert their eyes as they said the words.

Back in her room, Darla slipped into bed and turned out the reading lamp. Head on pillow, she believed she could make out a sound, drifting in from a distant Chicago suburb: the admirable attempt of an ill-practiced violinist stroking his beloved instrument. Yes, but she'll love you anyway. Darla heard the music for a long time, enjoying every successful note and every imperfection as she caressed herself to sleep.

* * *

Upon Darla's return from the Philharmonic tour, Stephen asked her, as he usually did, "How's Mom doing?" Steadily, with the passing of time, this question had begun to annoy her, and after this, her fourth trip to Chicago in as many months, it seemed she'd lost all tolerance for it.

She couldn't fault his behavior or intonation. He displayed, as always, an appropriate amount of husbandly concern. When inquiring, he wouldn't fail to put aside the task at hand before entering into a conversation about Mom. If he'd been looking through the mail, he would put it down. If he'd been at the computer, he would roll his chair back and away. If he'd been watching television, he would turn it off. His eyes sought hers when he inquired, and he kept them there when she answered. His face was open, his brow gently creased. He seemed to be listening. He would utter soothing responses.

All these things about him added up to the quality that had attracted her in the first place, so many years ago. His sensitivity. But now, it grated rather than soothed. His eyes, offering solace, intruded beyond invitation. She turned away. His arms, offering love, threatened to suffocate. She crumpled and retreated.

And this time, with the perfection of her concert-tour memory intact, she refused to enter into another conversation about Mom's ups and downs. It seemed that the conversations themselves had become another obligation. His duty to inquire, her duty to respond. His duty to appear caring, her duty to render the care. "How's Mom doing?" "She started coughing up blood." "Do you want me to come and help next time?" "No need." Obligations, with an endlessness that eroded the sharp edges of what was and what might be.

Not that she had any right to expect more of him. He stayed home with the children when she was away. Although the kids were old enough to stay alone, it was always best for teenagers to have an adult around. Taking the whole family along was out of the question. There would be many more of these trips, and there was money to think of. Mom was taking a long time to die, and just when she seemed to be on her last leg, gasping for breath and unable to walk from bed to toilet, she would magically revive, looking halfway near her old self on Darla's next trip out.

Just back from the most recent trip—a special one—she didn't want to ruin it just yet. There'd been the man, the rehearsals, the concerts. The man. How he'd admired her. How she'd helped him, without really even trying.

"How's Mom doing?" Stephen asked. There, in his eye, she imagined she saw something. An aberrant bit of smugness? His own parents, unlike her widowed mother, were still vibrant and young for their years. They exercised and ate well and had money. Never would they allow themselves to fall into pitifully wretched and dependent lingering illnesses that would break the backs of their children. And when they died, *if* they ever died, his grief would be grave and clean because he loved them so completely, without the need to remind himself of the specific things he loved about them.

She would not enter into another one of these conversations. Offhand, she responded, "Dying of cancer."

Stephen would not go away. He looked at her keenly, as if trying to understand. This once, he was compelled to put in a word for himself. "I'm doing something here, too," he defended. "All of us. Janet, Kyle, and me."

In a way, she understood. They'd all made adjustments, taking over some of her responsibilities. But the significance escaped her. Such piddling little adjustments were mere atoms next to her universe of new burden.

She knew better than to say this out loud. She'd hinted at the thought more than once in recent months, even as she recognized her deviation from reason. Still, her thoughts remained, the underlying feelings inexplicable, constant and never ending.

"Do you want me to come along on the next trip?" he pursued. Always that question. Dutiful but meek, the decision hers.

"No need," said Darla, finding the old words the easiest. "She's my mother after all."

Of course that man, the violin player, wasn't around on her next trip out, and so, Darla's engagement as a soloist with the Philharmonic ceased. But there were other men in airport lobbies, in airplanes, on buses, in pharmacies, each with a unique background and specific needs. Darla was one person to each of them, a new person to herself each time. Identities were donned and discarded without thought. She simply *was* whom she was, not stopping to question her behavior before, during or after, just the way it should be, without deception.

She was a social worker, a pediatrician, a costume designer, a successful novelist. Sometimes she had a name to go along. Hannah Newscomb, Dr. Beryl Fitzhugh. She always chose the man, although she had no awareness of this proclivity, feeling drawn into each situation so naturally that she could deny premeditation. Always she was single, with nothing to give her away. The wedding band magically disappeared for a few days and was picked up again later, on a countertop for example, where she—Darla—might have left it for an hour while scrubbing pots.

More could have happened but it didn't for a while, and always her memories were pure, uncluttered by taboo. Even if she'd wanted more from any of these men, it wouldn't have mattered because her words and actions were always appropriate for the person she was, in that moment.

Mom had been a little hazy. Twelve weeks after the concert tour she demanded, "Play that piece again. 'The Swan' something."

"I didn't bring my English horn this time." She'd brought a camera instead, but always, with Mom, she was just Darla, no one else.

Mom coughed and deposited the product in a tissue, the effort sending her down into the blankets.

"Do you want another pillow?" Not waiting for an answer, Darla lifted her mother's back and stuffed a pillow in among the others, causing a grimace and a bony finger pointing to the jumble of vials at bedside. Darla extracted a pill and fed her, then began to tidy the room until the medicine took.

"Maggie."

Darla turned. "No, Mom, it's Darla." Maggie was her Chicago sister, so deserving of these periodic breaks.

Falling off into a narcotic wash, Mom lapsed into gibberish. Her eyes fluttered to a close.

Darla tiptoed out to the living room and placed a CD in the player—*The Swan of Tuonela*, performed by the New York Philharmonic—raising the volume just enough to allow a soothing wave of music into the bedroom.

Her charge asleep, Darla forgot herself and left the house, taking Mom's car. She drove some distance and walked the rest, headed for the lake. Spring had burst open just that week and the trees were in blossom, the city skyline cutting rectangles in crystal blue.

Crossing the lawn toward lakeside, Darla walked with purpose, her camera strap a safety line hanging from either side of her neck over the shelf of her breast, the camera heavy, bouncing against her abdomen. A relic from college photography class, the apparatus was still impressive enough with its long lens that automatically whirred in and out at the press of a button. She felt the drive of commitment and calling. Her job was a pleasant one that fed her ego and offered reward, yet, like every job, had its downside as well, the tedium, the fight with nerves and perfectionism.

Scanning the scene before her with a professional eye, she spied a man at water's edge and came up close alongside, lifting the camera to indicate her intention. "Excuse me," she said. "I hate to impose, but I wonder if you would move just ten feet to the right."

He complied without comment. He wore tidy sweat clothes and looked rosy, as if he'd just finished exercising, nothing too serious. Easily, he could have jogged away, but he moved only the requested ten feet. She'd sparked his curiosity—she'd chosen the right one. Taking aim at the skyline across the curve of the lake, she snapped photographs in succession, drawing on a natural skill: her eye for color, light and shadow, composition, texture. "Not quite right," she muttered loud enough for the man to hear.

"You're taking a lot of pictures," he said.

The voice was lighthearted, and she looked at him to confirm that intention. His face was open and playful. Almost teasing.

"Yes, I am," she said, pursing her lips against a smile just enough so he'd see it.

"You must be fond of Chicago."

"Well, now that you mention it, I am. I'm quite fond of Chicago. But I have a better reason. I'm on assignment."

"Assignment?"

"For National Geographic."

"Interesting. 'That Wasteland: Chicago.' Certainly a few aborigines live here."

She laughed. "Maybe you haven't seen the magazine lately. We frequently do urban stories."

"I suppose it's part of the geography."

"Yes, a part of the landscape, worthy of study." She turned to the skyline and snapped again, just to see if she still had him. He lingered. When it seemed she was quite done, he spoke again. They fell into conversation and soon found themselves on a park bench.

The man revealed a few inconsequential details about himself and asked many questions about her calling. She told stories of her choice assignments: trips to Ghana,

Peru, and Estonia. He was intrigued and curious and charming with a delightful laugh, a dimple in one cheek, a boyish tendency to play and tease.

But, as their conversation progressed and her stories developed in color and detail, he displayed a creeping disquietude beneath the affability. Nothing alarming. A subtle, nagging discontent, the universal kind that most people try to hide from strangers. And she knew it was coming—the point that always came in these conversations.

"I've always wanted to travel the way you do," he said. "To see exotic places. I had that opportunity—once. I was offered a job that required travel. But I turned it down. I gave up my chance to see the world and took something close to home instead. Now I'm so entrenched here I can't very well change careers."

"Why did you decline the job?" she asked quietly, reverently, because she knew he would have a good answer.

"It was eight years ago. At the time, my father was very ill. We'd never been very close, but he needed help, and I guess you'd say I felt an obligation to spend the last available time with him. He hung on for two years and we learned a lot about each other during that time."

"Then it was worth it."

He turned to her, the twinkle returning to his eye. "If you forget the pain along the way. Not all of it the physical kind."

"But it's an admirable thing, what you did. Unselfish."

"I suppose so. I hope it was the right thing. But it's

almost selfish to pat myself on the back, isn't it? Families are just supposed to do these things."

She looked away, working at her memory.

"Still," he continued, not seeming to notice, "I'm left wondering at my lost opportunities."

"I understand what you're saying," she said, still looking out across the lake. "Of course, I was attracted to travel also, and that's how I got into this business. May I tell you a secret?" She looked at him for permission. Receiving it in his eyes, she went on. "I don't enjoy travel in the least, the actual traveling and even the actual being there. Almost always—and you may not believe this…" She looked at him guiltily.

"Try me."

"I envy your rooted existence. I almost always prefer sitting at home, looking at the pictures in the Geographic over actually being there." She fiddled with the camera, resting in her lap.

"Strange," he said in his playful, uncritical way, but his mind was working, she could see.

"Not so strange when you realize the value of fantasy. So often fantasy is just plain better than reality." She paused and looked into his eyes, finding the dreams there. "Maybe," she said, "we should just enjoy our fantasies for what they are, without making them into lost opportunities."

He shook his head and laughed. "You," he said. "*You* are something else." And he reached to the area between her breast and abdomen and pulled the camera strap with his index finger, like plucking a cello string.

She liked this man so much, that when he asked her

to join him for dinner, she almost agreed. But she declined the invitation, not because of forgotten obligation. She had none. Her assignment was complete. She declined only because her constant travels to exotic lands did not leave her free to give herself over to any man, and she feared, with this one, the temptation would be too great.

Walking away after a gracious goodbye, she moved without thought, slowly changing inside. The camera bounced against her abdomen, becoming a useless weight by the time she returned to the car. She tossed it onto the front passenger seat and drove, not knowing where, yet heading in the right direction. The man's words about his father came back to her, and she remembered, and she knew why she'd parted from him.

When she got back, Mom was awake, sitting up and reading a magazine. Darla walked in with a fresh pitcher of ice water and scooped at the plastic jumble to make room for it. Mom was perky and talkative, a mood that often started out fine and led elsewhere. A mood that Darla dreaded.

"Maggie always sets the water closer." Mom motioned, but her voice was pleasant. Darla looked. The lines of pain in her face had relaxed for now, and her blue eyes were hard, clear, and bright as ice. "This okay?" asked Darla, shifting a few things.

Mom nodded and lowered the magazine to her lap. "You still teaching?"

"Yes. I have five or six students." Down from about ten, she could have said. Now, with all the traveling.

"Next time bring your horn. You play it better than

that record."

"Okay. I will."

Mom looked down at the magazine again, her mouth twisting into a funny smile. "It's all just a love-hate thing anyway."

Darla looked at her, suspecting the meaning but wanting to steer clear. "What have you been reading?"

"Trashy love and sex articles. Pure junk food for the brain. Doesn't matter anyway. There's nothing inside me now except black goo."

"Mom." Darla shook her head.

"Well it's the truth, and you know it. There's nothing left to do for me." She started hacking and kept at it for a minute, the two pink circles staining her cheeks. Darla sat on the edge of the bed, dispensing tissues like a production line worker.

When the coughing subsided, Mom gasped, "But that's the catch. This love-hate thing. One minute you hate life so much the devil can have it. The next, you love it so much you can't let it go." She started coughing again. "Mostly," she sputtered, "the devil can have it."

"Don't talk that way."

"Just waiting to die."

"Mom!"

"I guess you didn't count on any of this twenty years ago, when you ran off to New York with Stephen."

"Think of what? Kids grow up and leave home, that's all. My kids are almost there."

"One day Kyle and Janet will be having the same negotiations."

"Negotiating what?"

"Like you and Maggie. Who does what. Don't think I'm fooled why you're here. It's for Maggie, not for me. No ma'am, not for me."

"That isn't true," said Darla, but she stood and turned to the wall, biting her lip. Her eyes burned. "All just a love-hate thing," she heard at her back.

Later that night when their emotions had settled, Darla tiptoed back. The air was fetid with decay. Eyes closed, Mom lay still as a photograph. Darla froze at the door, searching for movement. She waited a minute or two, standing tense, her heart beating fast and high up in her throat. When they came, her steps were quicker than she'd imagined, bringing her to bedside within the moment between heartbeats. She dropped to the mattress and Mom turned her head, eyelids fluttering. "Maggie," she said.

"It's Darla."

"Oh." Her eyes opened. "Darla." Her eyes closed. "Don't go. Stay here, Darla. Stay here, Darla. Don't go, don't…"

"I'm here, Mom." Darla arranged the covers. They needed changing, but she didn't want to disturb her mother. Fighting the urge to turn away, she leaned forward, pushing against air that resisted her descent with negative magnetic force. She pushed and leaned until her face was close, hovering above the pale forehead. Another inch. Her lips touched and stayed, pressing gently but unmistakably against brittle skin. Mom's eyes fluttered open. "Darla, Sweet Pea."

"I love you, Mom."

Back in her teenage bed, lights out, Darla thought of

the man by the lake and accepted his invitation for dinner. He sat across from her, a red rose in a single-bud vase on the white linen tablecloth between them, the pungent aroma of cabernet, a Bach fugue in the air, candlelight, warm fingertips, lips moving without sound, the words not important, no regrets, no lost opportunities, no tomorrow.

Maggie called sooner than usual, only two weeks after Darla had returned home. With a certainty that the end was near, Darla prepared for her final trip.

For this, she needed control more than anything. From the back of her bedroom closet she pulled a conservative gray suit, something appropriate for a day in court. On the top shelf of the coat closet she found a black leather briefcase, smooth and blemish free from disuse. Stephen was at the office, the children at school, no one around to bring her back from these preparations. The pantyhose, the low black pumps, the oxford shirt. Light, tasteful makeup.

Starting for the door, she glanced out a window and paused. The weather, a fluky mid-spring slush storm, would cause problems. She changed into boots and tucked the pumps into her carry-on. In the cab on the way to the airport, she pulled a legal pad from her briefcase and jotted notes, reviewing her case. She wanted to impress her adversaries, the Chicago lawyers, with her expertise and her composure under pressure.

As the cab approached the terminal, she hoped for the best. A delay or cancellation would be the last thing she needed. Not on this trip. Not this one. Amazingly, the monitor showed her flight to be on time, but as soon as she reached the gate, the announcements started. First, it was a half-hour delay. She scanned the rows of seats in the crowded waiting area. Nothing she wanted: a single seat next to a group of teens, one next to a family with young children, another next to an old man. She spied, in the far corner, a forgotten section of three empty seats next to a window.

She took the middle seat just as another announcement came over the air. Now the flight was delayed an hour. She felt her confidence slipping, her control elusive. She leaned forward, pulled the legal pad out of her briefcase, and bent low again to rummage through the contents in search of a pen. In the background, the din of conversation and faint smell of jet fuel made her dizzy with unreality, and when she sat up again, she was startled to see a man seated on her left. The momentary loss of awareness had shaken her.

He must have noticed. "Hello," he said, tentatively.

"Hello." She looked into his face and averted her eyes, feeling how wrong it would be with this man. She hadn't chosen him. He had chosen her, and that alone deprived her of the control she needed.

"Looks like we'll be sitting here for a while," he started.

"What a nuisance," she said absently, forgetting the yellow pad and pen in her lap.

"Don't let me interrupt you." He eyed her notes.

"Oh, it's nothing. No interruption. I just thought I'd try to make some use of the time, but there's no need, really. I already know my case cold." She waved the pad like a fan and pushed it into her chest, feeling somewhat better. Talking might help after all. A relief from the stress of work and travel and the jitters about her upcoming performance. People would be expecting so much of her.

"Your case? You sound like a lawyer," he said.

"Well, maybe that's good because I *am* a lawyer."

"No offense intended."

"I didn't take any," she said, although his comment only heightened her disquiet. Still hoping to make the best of it, she turned fully toward him.

"Some of my best friends of friends are lawyers," he quipped.

"And some of your worst slight acquaintances."

"Something like that." He smiled and she returned the smile. "My name is Glenn." He stuck out a hand and she took it, briefly.

"Brianne," she returned.

"So, what's your case about?" he asked, eyebrow cocked. There was something prying in his tone, and she detected, under his lopsided smile, a wedge of disbelief. Certain kinds of men acted this way in the presence of a professional woman, threatened instead of respectful. She resented it, feeling again that he was the wrong one. He was not the type to open up and admit to the need that was buried under the accoutrements of maleness.

Nevertheless, she surrendered to an inner compulsion and began to speak freely, becoming completely absorbed, relating in some detail her impending deposition schedule and the facts of her client's case: the injuries from exposure to toxic substances, the culpability of high-level executives within a Chicago-based chemical plant. Glenn listened attentively and was near the tip of acceptance, but not quite there, when she sensed, then glimpsed, a hovering male figure behind her. She looked over her shoulder, caught her breath, and turned away.

The newcomer took the seat on her right. She gave another fleeting look, their eyes met, and she knew at that moment, without any doubt, that her first instinct had been the correct one. Everything about Glenn was wrong because now, so unexpectedly and belatedly, the right man had arrived.

A confusion of voices spoke in her head, children playing in the aisle, her own children, Brianne, Mom, Maggie, and Darla, the airline announcers, babies crying, Stephen, disgruntled passengers. Unbearably, they fought for her attention in that capsular moment of shock between ostensible normalcy and certain aberration, until a single, insistent voice broke through. It was Glenn's. Still skeptical, he was asking, "What evidence do you have against these executives? What makes you think they knew about the danger?" He waited, expecting her to explain, but she couldn't. Quickly, she gathered her briefcase and carry-on bag, made an excuse, apologized, and stumbled to her feet.

She spent the remainder of the delay in the restroom, one ear out for announcements of her flight as she shuffled between stall and mirror, horrified and attracted by the sight she beheld: the image of her, Darla—decidedly herself now—wearing that suit. The suit was nice enough but something she'd thrown in the back of her closet years ago because it was simply ridiculous on her, inimical to her lifestyle and sense of self. She shivered and clutched her sides, cold and hot and nauseous, unable to see a way out.

And just as she feared, there was no escape. An hour later, boarding the plane, she saw him again, several rows ahead in a window seat, gazing out. The aisle seat next to him was vacant. She checked her boarding pass and counted the rows just to be sure, but she knew. The shivering intensified, her fingers numb on the handle of her briefcase, the strap of her carry-on bag cutting deep into the palm of her hand. So heavy, too heavy.

Tears welled in her eyes, and she used all her willpower to call them back. Nearly there, he turned from the window, his eyes reaching out to hers, and with that look, the shivering stopped. The tears spilled.

After she had settled into her seat and blown her nose, he said, "You know, I couldn't help overhearing what you were saying to that man about your case. It sounded interesting. I suppose you could get lost in it, working on a case that interesting."

"Yes, you *can* get lost in it."

He smiled. "Me, I seem to get all the mundane cases in my practice." His eyes remained on her as if he needed insurance against her departure. She saw nothing that was mocking or accusatory or skeptical or betrayed in his look. He was simply curious, in need of an explanation.

She would need to separate herself from it before she could explain. For now, all she said was, "That man thought I sounded like a lawyer."

"You did. And I should know. You must have gotten some of that from me."

They both smiled then for a long time, until he turned to look out the window. She sensed the shift. She recalled the first man, the violin player, on that occasion when, so unexpectedly, her storytelling had sprung into existence. She recalled his turning, his shift in mood, not unlike what she sensed now. His regret and grief over loss, the feeling of no return. Her anticipation.

"I have a small problem. Perhaps you can help me with it," he said. "My wife has been absent for quite some time. Not physically gone that much. Three or four days a month. It's more like she's been distant from me emotionally."

She opened her mouth to speak but couldn't. Her tongue met a familiar resistance. Finally, at this moment, she understood its source.

She shouldn't have to ask for what she needed when she was too weak to decide exactly what that was. She shouldn't have to ask for what she needed when it would only add new selfishness to her store of guilt. He should know what she needed. He should act without asking.

Her expectations and resentment, she suspected now, were unfair. It was her turn to speak. "Maybe..." She stopped.

"Maybe what? I need help here. Any help you can give me would be much appreciated. Any help at all."

"Maybe you're not the one who needs help. Maybe she needs the help."

"She doesn't want help. She never asked for it. She declines my offers."

"Maybe she's not in any condition to ask for it. Asking would make everything worse, would make her feel weaker."

His face fell, stricken with understanding, and all of a sudden, she saw his pain and felt her responsibility for it. "But maybe you're doing something about it, right now," she said. "And maybe she's feeling better already." He looked at her and she crumbled. "Oh, Stephen." Her head went to his shoulder, and his warm hand came up to cover her cheek, offering protection from the world. This time, she accepted.

John and Maggie were at Mom's, their children home with a babysitter. Darla insisted they leave immediately and go home, return to normalcy and a decent family dinner, at least for one more night. Maggie resisted at first, concerned that she hadn't changed the bedding yet, but Darla was unyielding. Maggie and John said their goodbyes before Darla and Stephen entered Mom's room.

"Who's that?" said Mom.

"Stephen," he said. His face was ashen, but she didn't seem to notice.

"Stephen. So glad you came." Her voice was weak, barely audible, and Darla was unsure. Lately, Mom had dropped much of her sarcasm, at least when it came to real feeling.

Stephen helped Mom with a drink of water before turning away and motioning to his wife, leading her out of the bedroom. He closed the door behind them and whispered, "She looks bad. Very, very bad. Why didn't you tell me how serious it was?"

Darla said nothing.

"We've got to take her to the hospital."

"She refuses. You know her. Don't do that to her."

He shook his head, looking as unsure as she had ever seen him. They stood that way for a long time. Finally, Darla took a step toward the door and said, "I have to go in there and clean up." Stephen's hand shot out, catching her arm. "No," he said. "No. This time I will." And she didn't resist, allowing him to do this for her.

Stephen went in, leaving the door half open. She heard his gentle greeting to Mom and the silence in return. Last time, before going to the lake, Darla had left the door half open, in just this way, so Mom could hear the music. Perhaps she'd like some music now.

Darla stepped over to the CD player and stopped dead. Her hand flew to her mouth. Mom had specifically asked her and she'd forgotten! So lost in her own stupidity and selfishness that she'd forgotten!

Paralyzed, tears streaming down her cheeks, she chastised herself, whipping and whipping, trying to find the sense in it. The fantasies and escape, denial and weakness. Yet, she hadn't forgotten everything, so why this? Something so important, so easy to bring along.

Her carry-on bag was already too heavy, she remembered then. So heavy, not enough room for everything... With a flutter of hope, she went to the spot of living room carpet where she'd left it. Falling to the floor, she unlatched the bag and ripped the two sides apart, groping down through the layers until her hand hit something solid. She grasped the secure hardness and right angles of the case, cushioned deep in the clothing, exactly where she'd placed it that morning before leaving home. Darla had placed it there, not Brianne.

Still sitting on the floor, she dried her tears, opened the case and comforted herself with the familiar ritual, assembling her instrument. She stood, and after two very deep, cleansing breaths and a moment of thought, she started to play, tenderly, confidently, *The Swan of Tuonela.*

When she finished, she hugged the instrument to her chest, closed her eyes, and basked in the memory of the sound she had created.

☾ Reckoning

THE LITTLE MAN, as crisp as the fall morning, arrives at Arthur Creaton's office. He's punctual, eight exact, the clock marking a third of the pie.

His name is Thomas Henry or Henry Thomas—first and last impossible to put straight and keep in order. Somehow, this small blip in memory doesn't bug Arthur. It's easy enough to think of him as "Henry," sometimes with a "Mr.," sometimes not.

Henry is gray-business clad, about thirty-two or thirty-three, slight and trim, no more than five-seven, multi-American-racial, closely cropped, unimaginative, staid, but also carefully manufactured, rehearsed, and aware of his presentation. By contrast, Arthur is a WASP of fifty-seven, worn and rumpled, unassuming and ostensibly timid, although he knows more than this about himself. He surpasses Henry's erect stature by at least four inches despite his stooped shoulders under the oxford button-down and a well-worn tweed jacket, his standard ensemble while in the office.

There's been a progression to things. First, in the mail, Arthur received a photocopy of the front page of his 2007 tax return, black-ink stamped "NRP," with Henry's business card attached. A week later, Henry phoned. Arrangements were made. "Have all your bank statements, income and expense records available. Business and personal." Thoroughness was implied. *I will find it, yes, I will.* Finally, the day arrives for the big event, the audit.

On the phone, Henry had avoided that term. It was to be "an examination" as part of the National Research Program. A statistical study of compliance. A random selection of small businesses. Of course, any necessary adjustments to the taxpayer's return would not be left uncorrected.

"Make sure you have all records available. For *both* of your Schedule C's." A vaguely sinister tone.

Henry's exacting voice foreshadowed the outer package arriving today. Tidy and precise. His eyes are a scrim over the suggestion of wheels turning inside, the well-oiled machinery of the many lessons learned in agent school. His mission is to extract proof of his preconceptions, to detect what he judges to be the carefully guarded flaw in the record of the older man, the taxpayer, his target.

Arthur might simply tell him there isn't a flaw to be found, at least not where his tax affairs are concerned. His business, a sole proprietorship, is an insignificant bit of nothing from a federal standpoint, merely enough to keep him alive while he pursues his passion, dreams his dreams, and massages his concept of reality onto the canvas of life. His balance sheet for the business is clean and complete. His honesty is embarrassingly meticulous down to the penny. Such virtue surely beams from the figures on his tax return. How dare this stranger imply otherwise! Yet, these are not the kinds of things one should say to an IRS agent.

Arthur's place of business for the last many years occupies a barren landscape off a lonely stretch of the interstate, and its vivid orange and black sign is visible from it. Easy enough for Henry to spot. On the driveway in, the first building has a glass door looking out onto the world, bearing the black vinyl press-on logo "Store-All." Directly inside is the office, a shell on the clam of Arthur's studio, moist and wiggling behind a door in the back marked "Private." Past this building runs a long drive with four slender, parallel lanes shot straight out from it like the tines of a comb, each with a neat row of connected boxlike sheds.

Orderly and symmetrical and pedestrian as this layout appears, the studio bears witness to the other.

Arthur is behind the counter, looking out the glass door, when Henry, Mr. or not, pulls up in his sage-colored government sedan. Henry gathers his things and takes the walkway briskly, carrying a cardboard, plastic-lidded deli cup and a small laptop case. Cup in left hand, case handle in right. Even then he's plotting his entry, the need to free up his right hand to open the door, and moments later, to feel the skin of the man he's about to deconstruct. In a swift move, clutching the large deli cup in the left hand, he shoves the laptop case firmly under his left arm and squeezes it tight against his ribcage to avoid dropping it. The door is opened efficiently, a whoosh inside, three paces neatly taken, a deliberate grip offered. "Mr. Creaton?" A brief flash of teeth.

Arthur nods and extends a diffident hand. The counter is between them. As they physically disengage, an inch-square piece of paper at the end of a slender string flutters and comes to rest at the side of the deli cup.

"Excuse me," Arthur says. "I'll lock the door." He rounds the end of the counter.

"Yes, of course," Henry responds, stepping aside to avoid further physical contact.

Privacy is ordained, one of Henry's implicit demands. To accommodate, Arthur reluctantly granted him a Monday, the official "closed" day, although Arthur is always around, hidden from view in the back. Monday is *his* day. Paid-up renters are free to come and go to their units at any time, but the office door is locked on Mondays and Arthur enjoys his freedom from the needs of the public during daylight hours.

Now, a Mr. Public of a sort has come to take a precious Monday away. Arthur's blood simmers even as he maintains the studied, blanched exterior of the innocent. He can play along—he will have to.

Without invitation, Henry has made his way to the nook in the office. The small waiting area has four moderately uncomfortable chairs, a low synthetic wood coffee table, a square stand for the Mr. Coffee and Styrofoam cups, a vending machine packed with junk food, and a rack of sales brochures and rental forms. Henry takes a seat, unbuttons his suit jacket, places his teacup on the coffee table, his laptop next to it, and powers up. Arthur notices this with a glance over his shoulder as he locks the door.

Henry's cache of niceties was exhausted with that initial flash of teeth. Now he's down to business in a peculiarly awkward way, bent forward from the waist to reach the low coffee table, elbows resting on knees, and fingers just below them, pattering at the keys. "We'll start with the ten-forty and the first Schedule C, the one for...this." Henry looks up from the screen and slides a withering look around the office.

Arthur is walking back to the counter when he catches the look. Instantly, he forms judgments of his own but holds his tongue. He's learned to remain quiet. Honesty doesn't require more, and self-explanation is useless when the recipient will never really understand. Arthur learned this hard lesson years ago, when his youthful exuberance fell on deaf ears and his colors met blindness and his ideas were received with blank smiles and speechlessness. Gradually, over time, he's been shaped on the outside to resemble anyone else, a creeping crumble into grayness, while he continues to live on the inside, sending out tendrils of hope.

Wishing to maintain a distance, Arthur takes up a place on his stool behind the counter. Except for a phone and computer at the far end, the countertop is empty. Underneath the counter, on a shelf out of Henry's view, Arthur has placed an expanding file folder containing all the documents he might possibly need, assembled in advance. Black figures on paper—the concrete proof to supplant his unacceptable word. The tax year in question is now ancient history, its financial transactions long forgotten, but Arthur's conviction as to the accuracy of his tax return holds steady.

Henry does not remove his eyes from the screen of his laptop as he starts the inquisition. "Your full name is Arthur, middle initial F, Creaton?"

"Yes."

"Date of birth is May 24, 1953?"

"Yes."

"Social security number 826-13-4198?"

"Yes."

Henry pauses to move his unusually small hand, sliding the tip of his slender index finger around the mouse pad of his laptop. The hard tip jabs a click. Arthur's dignity is already wilting under the subtle heat of Henry's test questions, the baseline against which the answers to the really tough questions will be measured. Henry absently picks up the deli cup and slurps through the hole in the top. A messy sound, somewhat out of character. He carefully returns the cup to its exact position on the table.

"Your filing status is single?"

"Yes."

"You claim no exemptions other than yourself?"

"Yes. I mean, no."

"You have no dependents."

"Yes. No family."

"No dependents."

Henry looks up and aims his surprising kiwi-colored irises. In a small moment of truth, Arthur's imagination is awakened. He lives for these moments, but this one disturbs him. That eye color is the only remarkable feature of the little government agent, a fleck of beauty completely wasted on his tasteless and banal task.

Arthur's kaleidoscopic lenses shift and close. He responds to Henry's question with a trancelike nod which becomes, in the next moment, an affirmative shake.

His examiner is absolutely right. There are no dependents. Arthur left home at a young age, never started a family of his own, and has lived alone these forty years. He rarely sees his aging mother and older sister, who live a thousand miles away within blocks of each other. His father always refused to see him, but his mother pretended otherwise. Up until a few years ago, in every conversation, she would say things like this: "Your father says hello." "Your father sends his love." "Your father is asking after you."

Artie is the frozen baby boy, at best grown to age seventeen, wearing his navy blazer with the school insignia. Mom calls him on holidays and birthdays, but his sister, Elise, calls more frequently, their conversations going deeper, especially now that her two children, Arthur's niece and nephew, are fully grown and independent. She lives with her husband in a cavernous house with nothing to want but food for the imagination.

In the early years, Artie quite looked up to Elise. She was one of the few to come close, and she still tries, but he resists, preferring the rare, pleasant surprise of an insightful stranger. If a sister should try, and fail, the disappointment will cut deeper. "I'd so like to see them, Art," she says every now and then on the telephone. She remembers the early, childish works, and now, well, he senses it would be too much for her. He never gets around to arranging a viewing, even today, when distance is a dimension so easily erased yet queerly maintained on the Internet, by virtual tour.

Henry is already on to the next topic, something more important to him. Line 7 of the 1040.

"Income, wages, salaries, tips," says Henry. "You've listed zero."

"Zero, because, of course, you look farther down…"

"Yes, I know, I know. Your two Schedule C's. But wages, salaries, and tips must take into account income from all sources."

"I understand."

"You received no income in 2007 from any source other than the two," he searches for a word, "businesses?"

Arthur shakes his head. *No.*

"I'll just need to confirm."

Their eyes meet again, but this isn't enough. Henry seeks the precision and comfort of documentary evidence.

"I suppose you want…"

"All checking, savings, and money market accounts. I'll start with the first three months of 2007."

Arthur's hands shake as he rummages around under the counter.

"Personal and business, whether in your name or the d/b/a."

Surely this is another test: will Arthur disclose everything or attempt to hide? He well knows that the IRS has a record of every bank account linked to every social security number. He's unnerved by his sweaty fingers and slight tremor, a reaction he didn't anticipate, made worse by his fumbling under the counter. He decides to make an open show of it and hoists the entire expanding file folder up onto the counter. As he riffles through the compartments with eyes cast downward to the task, his ear picks up Henry's loud slurping from the sippy cup.

Arthur finally extracts the statements and looks up to see Henry's affected nonchalance, a half-lidded gaze at his screen while the material of his white business shirt stretches taut against an impatient expansion of chest. Arthur walks around the end of the counter and offers the statements from two banks, M &T for Store-All, Citi for himself.

Henry accepts the offering, drops the stack onto the table, and pulls a small, handheld calculator from his right jacket pocket. "I hate those damn calculators on the computer." He chuckles demurely, as if this is the most exquisite of accountant jokes.

It's now 8:20 by the digital wall clock. A painful hour follows, cut into four segments. Every quarter, Henry asks for the next three months of statements. He examines each batch of thirty pages or so, one page at a time, tracing down line by line with a fingertip, every once in a while reacting. He emits a small grunt, or raises his eyebrows slightly, or slurps audibly from the sippy cup—until it runs dry—followed by an intense computation on the handheld calculator and a computer entry.

Perhaps there's a worksheet of sorts on the screen. Arthur only guesses. He cannot see it. He faces Henry, or rather the top of Henry's thin-cushioned head, which is dipped downward to the screen or the handheld or the papers. The silver-colored cover of the laptop with its backlit apple, marred by a generous bite, stares back. After each little episode of discovery, Henry makes a delicate swerve of the fingertip and jabs a click.

Henry thus absorbed, Arthur periodically rises to stretch his legs and walk about. Standing near the front door, he folds his arms and rocks back and forth, heel to toe, looking down at his brown scuffed Hush Puppies. The left toe bears a noticeable vermillion splotch.

Gazing now through the door, he sees a van pull into the driveway and continue past the office, heading for one of the units in back. If he were to enter his studio and look through the northwest window, he would be able to see the van's course and determine its destination. Beyond that window, the symmetrical lines of units are laid out into the distance on a gentle slope. The last two units of the farthest line are filled with his own life works. Soon he will need a third.

On the other side of the studio, the southeast window faces a small clearing and a wooded area beyond. This is the window Arthur most often faces when he's at work, hugged by the clutter of easels and canvases and paint-spattered walls. The blood red, bile green, and pus yellow of a previous period are now partially overlaid with the sunset orange, aqua blue, and shining white of recent years as Arthur begins to feel his mortality. In the studio, he's completely alone in his universe, not wanting it any other way.

Edging near the fourth quarter of 2007, Arthur is back on the stool when Henry makes a discovery of significance. He sits upright in his chair and exclaims, "What's this?"

Arthur's heart stops.

"A deposit of $20,000 on November 29, 2007. $20,000 even."

"Twenty...?"

"The Citi account," adds Henry. "Your personal savings account."

Arthur is dumbfounded. The amount is completely foreign to him. $20,000! A staggering sum bearing no relation to the rental of a unit or the sale of a painting.

Henry leans forward, picks up the deli cup, then remembers it's empty and sets it down again. "I don't recall this figure. Will it show up on one of your Schedule C's?" His voice betrays mild annoyance.

A bead of sweat runs from the base of Arthur's right armpit down the length of his ribcage, rolling past an intestinal growl. The explanation is on the tip of his tongue but cannot be found. With an electric zing, this feeling of separation and mystification is replaced with something worse—gut recognition. This figure, this twenty thousand, twenty thousand, twenty thousand, is now so blaringly familiar he has no reason to doubt its veracity.

"Yes, I did receive it, but..." He is equally sure it does not appear on his tax return.

"The source?"

That is the question. Emotion rises from the depths of this new doubt about himself, his shame at being unprepared. He tries to rationalize. How could he have prepared for this question when the twenty thousand is not on his tax return? This thought, however, merely seems to confirm a subconscious act of concealment.

"The source," Arthur repeats, buying time. He knows he received this money. It's associated with a strange voice, an unexpected call from an attorney in a distant city, yes, that was it, and a day later, a call from his mother. "He was thinking of you, Artie," in the past tense, finally.

Arthur's cheeks grow hot and his eyes sting. The tears well and threaten to spill because now he remembers this "gift" from his father, the man made of millions who had forsaken him, convinced of Arthur's uselessness to the world of true men. His father's bequest was a business strategy, a token to thwart any possibility of a will contest. *Yes, he was thinking of me.*

Arthur chokes on a sob, angry at himself and supremely embarrassed. "It was an inheritance. From my father. He died in 2007." He swipes at the single drop of water under his eye and clears his voice, ashamed, profoundly disappointed in himself for succumbing to these mind games, acting as though he had something to hide. There was nothing to hide, not from himself, and certainly not from Henry.

The government agent is taken aback by this show of emotion, clearly mistaken as to its cause. Well, maybe not completely, thinks Arthur, doubtful as to his own feelings. Whether an expression of insight or not, Henry says, "I see." And Arthur now sees that the agent's clean edges are tarnished. When did he loosen the knot of his tie at the collar?

Henry rebounds quickly from his momentary empathy and shows a small twinge of disappointment. No big discovery after all. The recipient of a gift or bequest of that size does not pay income tax on it. "Do you have a legal document to back this up?"

"Yes, somewhere."

"I'll need to see it."

"All right. I have to look for it."

"Of course, you can forward it later. I'm sure there will be other documents as well."

"Then, we won't finish today?"

"We never do." Henry moves his eyes back to the screen, looking for what comes next. "Now…"

It's 9:30, and Henry is finally satisfied with line 7.

Coming up on one o'clock, Arthur has twice retreated to the back. Each time, he waited until Henry's nose was buried in paperwork, then opened the "Private" door just enough to duck inside and close it carefully behind him. There's a small washroom in the studio. He never allows his customers to use it. "No facilities," he says if anyone asks.

Henry, however, seems to have a bladder of steel. He has not asked once. In their silent, endless minutes together, Arthur has thought many times about that large cup of tea. The deli container still resides in the spot Henry made for it, undisturbed by any of the myriad documents absently laid alongside.

The agent has risen from his chair only once. At about 9:45, he inserted a power cord into his laptop and connected it to the outlet directly under the Mr. Coffee. Henry, the man, has more modest energy needs. There's been no hint of a lunch break, and Arthur's stomach is growling audibly.

"Utilities?" asks Henry, in a voice grown gentler over the hours. They've become automatons in a jointly crafted ritual. Henry says a word, and Arthur produces the needed documents.

Henry is nearing the end of the first Schedule C. All the income and expenses of Store-All have been checked, and utilities are last on the list. The modest profit— Arthur's livelihood—has been accounted for. Finally, there is nothing else about Store-All to confirm.

Eight a.m. to one p.m. may be the longest period Arthur has spent in the same room with a single person in a very, very long time. Subtle discoveries have blossomed incrementally:

At about ten o'clock, Arthur noticed a slender gold band on the ring finger of Henry's caramel-colored left hand.

At a quarter past ten, a cell phone in Henry's jacket pocket musically sounded with a popular rap-like mantra, albeit on low volume. Henry quickly removed the cell, glanced at the screen, and pressed a button to silence it.

Several times, with a slight grimace, Henry has bent forward absently and inserted his right index finger between his sock and the opening of his black, oxford business shoe. Arthur wonders if the hard leather has caused a painful blister.

At about eleven, while handing over a stack of documents, Arthur was amazed to discover, in Henry's left earlobe, a tiny pinprick of a scar, an abandoned piercing. Perhaps not abandoned but involuntarily forfeited.

And for the past hour, Henry has been noticeably

over warm—his forehead has an oily, glistening sheen. He periodically lifts the lapel of his suit jacket to let the air in but refuses to remove it. Arthur supposes that Uncle Sam's rules forbid it.

Time enough for other discoveries as well. The paper ritual, daily schedule, accounting, and planning that go into the storage business—Arthur now admits to himself that he takes pleasure in these activities. Not for the first time, he wonders what his life would have been like without the need to work for a living, if his father had given him a cool several million and a studio bursting with supplies—if he'd had unlimited time for himself. The fantasy is not new, but for the first time he emerges from it without the bitter aftertaste of resentment.

They both know what is coming next. Arthur's second Schedule C. This one shows a loss, the expenses exceeding the income. Entries on the form are few and brief. In 2007, Arthur had two sales, totaling $250. Oils, brushes, and canvases, gallery fees, travel, and correspondence—these expenses have far exceeded the income. But Arthur can account for every penny.

Henry lifts his head from the screen. Their eyes meet and lock in the lengthiest sustained gaze they have yet shared, at least two seconds. Arthur quickly averts his eyes and becomes busy, moving the heavy expanding file folder from the countertop to the shelf underneath.

While so engaged, with his head ducked low, he hears this: "About your second Schedule C." There's a pause through which Arthur makes some noise with the papers in his file. Then the voice sounds again: "Is this your only hobby?"

Arthur is cut to the quick. All the breath goes out of him. For the second time, tears spring into his eyes. Anger and the old humiliation. He looks up, ready to fight or to cave in, he doesn't know which, but he sees— what's this? A most astonishing sight! Henry's face is lit up with a full-toothed smile, friendly and companionable without condescension or any trace of sinister accusation. What on earth does this mean? A backward sort of recognition? A joke meant to convey the opposite? Arthur discerns a nub of understanding in Henry's eyes, those unusual, dreamy irises.

"You mean, my work," Arthur says quietly.

"Reported on this Schedule C, 'profit or loss from a business.' In this case, a loss."

"What do you need to see?"

"Nothing."

"Nothing?"

"Nothing at all. I have it."

This doesn't seem possible.

But then, Arthur understands. Henry already saw the proof—he knew what to look for—when he examined Arthur's personal bank statements and credit card purchases the first time. All expenses are confirmed, and the two deposits, the checks for $100 and $150, are there. But how would he know that the checks were in payment for works of art?

"Don't you need to see...?" Arthur's eyes flit to the studio door.

Henry glances at the door. Is he tempted?

But then, from Henry's pocket, the rapper bursts into the silence. Henry answers this time. "I'll be there in half an hour," he promises the caller. To Arthur he says, "That's it for today," and unplugs the cord from his laptop. "You'll just need to send me those items we discussed."

Arthur watches the drab sedan pull out of the driveway. Henry said he would be back—the NRP regs require the agents to discuss their results with the taxpayers personally.

Arthur forgets how hungry he felt a moment ago. There are two things he must do immediately.

First, he goes to the phone at the end of the counter and dials Elise. Some time ago, she extended an invitation for Thanksgiving, to join her and her husband and children, their mother. He's put it off, and it's time he accepted. Later on, he'll consider whether he wishes to bring a small gift. If so, it will have to be one of his more conventional works.

Second, he enters the studio, sets a new canvas on the easel, and starts to mix his paints. The toughest color will be the kiwi. Flecked with black seeds, this particular kiwi has been enjoyed—a generous bite is the evidence. It floats in a rectangular, gleaming silver backdrop, and in the far distance, another shade of green, the color of money, is fading from view.

In this moment, as he creates in his studio, Arthur doesn't know that, in a few weeks' time, Henry will telephone and say, "This is Tom Henry." Arthur doesn't know that, on the day Henry returns, he will be dressed casually in a stylish leather jacket. Whether it's Mr. Henry or Arthur's perception of him, he will be a different man, relaxed, warm, and jaunty. A large-toothed smile will be pushing out his cheeks, all to convey the genuine relief he feels to be confirming Arthur's meticulous honesty— there will be no adjustments to his 2007 tax return.

In this instant, Arthur does not know that Henry's transformation will be a continuation of the one they started this day, together. He is not yet fully aware of the lines they were drawing, Arthur's toward Henry, Henry's toward Arthur, in the resonance of five hours shared in the same room, on the other side of "Private."

Will he invite him in for a look?

☾ *At the Crypt*

ON THE WAY to the cemetery, we became lost, trying to catch up with the others.

"By the time we get there, Daddy'll be gone."

"Dad's already gone," I told Leslie. "They'll wait for us. We're the daughters. They'll wait, won't they?"

When we arrived at the gate it still seemed possible, but my heart knew otherwise, the higher we climbed. Winding black asphalt, manicured lawns, granite slabs, flags, wilted bouquets, black suits and veils, sprinklers wasted in the noonday sun. The road forked and twisted, every turn ultimately sending us to the top of the hill, to the mausoleum, where the hearse and the cars, cool and empty, had come to rest between white lines. We parked in the next slot and rushed to the open door. Too late, spoke the wind chimes. A whisper of drifting souls, gentle on the breeze.

Breathless, high heels clicking on cement, we crept up behind the others, their backs turned. Too late. The pastor, standing over the flower-laden coffin, delivered his closing words and uttered the final "Amen."

* * *

Three weeks later, a respectable time, I received a white cardboard envelope, the kind specially designed for mailing photographs. The sender's name was identified by initials alone, A.M.O., above the return address, a residence in Santa Monica, California. My name and address, correctly spelled, had been printed with a wet-ink fountain pen in a feminine hand, the letters round and slightly tilted with a suggestion of movement. The only odd touch, the one thing that placed the mailing in a gray area between personal and professional, was the mass-produced sticker squarely affixed over the point of the top flap in back. The bold red letters, "Photographs Enclosed," stood out against the white background.

Curious, I opened the envelope, feeling certain that I should already know its contents. Inside was a lavender sheet of personal stationery folded over and concealing a thin stack of photographs. I slid my hand inside, touched the paper, and immediately remembered what had been pushed to the back of my mind.

The photographs slipped out face down on the kitchen counter, where I left them while reading the letter. "Dearest Helen," it began. The message was warm, expressing good fortune over our meeting and suggesting we keep in touch. Three thousand miles and forty-two years apparently made no difference. "Losing a parent is so difficult. Your composure and beauty were an inspiration to all of us." Reading this, seeing her eyes and hearing her voice, I believed she intended a compliment.

It was then I turned the photographs over. The first

one wasn't difficult, nor was the second. But the third presented a horrifying image. She hadn't done as I'd asked, blindly satisfying her own needs, oblivious to mine.

It may have been too much to expect, asking them to wait a second time that day. We'd already held up the services at the funeral home, arriving late after spending too much time in front of the mirror in our childhood bathroom.

Over the years, Dad never used this bathroom, preserving it intact like an historic landmark but failing to interrupt its decline from the elements. Wallpaper curled and yellowed at the edges, rust circled the rims of fixtures, and the smell of mildew hung in the air. Cosmetic bag in hand, I stepped into this abandoned square of space with its glaring, imperceptible changes, reminded that nothing remains untouched, that time transforms and decays.

It should have been easy, just Leslie and I. Separately, we'd flown across country from our respective homes in different states, leaving husbands and grown children behind. I'd been glad to know they'd all seen Dad in life, only a few months before. If the others had come this time, perhaps they would have focused me outward, away from my inner crawl.

Leslie was the first one ready to go, the opposite of the usual occurrence. She kept me company in the bathroom while I dawdled. Time was abundant and meaningless to me, normally punctual to a fault. In my haze, it seemed that all things should begin and end when we were ready for them to begin or end. Steadfastly, I clung to this illusion of control as I examined and poked at my chignon, fearing it was too severe. Dad would have thought it appropriate, but Leslie's appearance offered such a striking contrast, her hair loose and messy, matching her grief.

When we finally arrived, the parking lot at the funeral home was full. Driving Dad's car, Leslie parked us at the shopping center across the street. Apparently, we learned later, we weren't the only ones to park there. Several people trickled in after us. But I don't recall seeing any of those across-the-street people later at the crypt. Perhaps they also got lost, or perhaps they hadn't intended to come to the cemetery in the first place.

It was my fault, really. If we'd left the house when Leslie was ready, we'd never have fallen in with those across-the-street people.

"He said to turn on Marine, I'm sure of it," I said as Leslie drove right past it.

"But this is the way I got there last time," she said.

We were a bit confused. Only minutes before, milling to organ music in the semi-dark lobby, we'd discussed the plan with the funeral director. The hearse would lead the way, slowly, out of the mortuary lot, and those parked across the street would easily pick up the line at the end. We would proceed—slowly he said—two blocks down Sepulveda to Marine Street, turn left, enter the San Diego Freeway going south, and head down to Palos Verdes. An easy plan.

After that, we said hello and goodbye to a few more people we'd never met before, my eyes still dry. Then we stepped out into the bright sun, walked to the corner, pressed the pedestrian cross button, waited a minute, walked across, got into Dad's car, opened the windows while the air conditioning blew hot, pulled out and circled the lot for the exit, and waited for the red light at Sepulveda with our left-turn blinker on.

How long could all of that have taken? We looked across the street. The funeral home parking lot was silent and empty. Poof. Funeral gone. We looked down Sepulveda. Not a sign of the procession. Perhaps they'd gone another way? It didn't seem possible.

I looked at Leslie, tears rolling down her cheeks. Time had tricked us again into thinking that things would simply begin and end when we were ready for them.

"Now, where did everyone go?" Leslie's eyes searched. Wisely, she'd decided not to wear eye makeup that day. Unlike me, Leslie didn't need proof that she'd cried. I stared out the window, my eyes clear, mascara intact.

The telephone rings. *Helen? It's your Dad calling.* As if he needs to identify himself. Every time now, before I pick up the phone, this is what I hear. Leslie replays entire conversations in her mind, but for me, the content blurs with insignificance. The weather, my kids, his health. Words didn't matter, just the timbre of his voice and the emotions carefully hidden underneath, less artfully hidden after his retirement, the last two years. *Bye-bye now. Love you.*

At the funeral, another life was revealed, one I never knew. In the front row, Leslie and I, Uncle Bill and Aunt Silvia with their son, our cousin Jeff, stood after the services, a short receiving line, shaking one hand after another. A few neighbors, but mostly people who'd worked with Dad, many of them for nearly a half century of Mondays through Fridays.

A man in his mid-seventies, about my father's age: "What a mind! A genius, really. Everyone came to him with their big questions."

A woman my age: "A real gentleman, your father. Thirty years ago, my first day at the office, he said to me," she leaned in closer and lowered the pitch of her voice, "'Let me know if anyone bothers you. I don't put up with that kind of thing!'" She smiled with full, red lips. "He always listened to what I had to say."

Another new face: "It's such a pleasure to meet you and your sister," he said. "Your father was so devoted to you. Always kept pictures of you girls on his desk. He spoke of you often." Yet, he never spoke of this man to me. Or maybe he did, and I never paid attention. Even worse, perhaps I should have asked Dad if he had friends like this. "You could tell how much he loved you girls." Tears in this man's eyes. What did he say his name was? Should I have asked?

After going several blocks and debating the situation, we decided to turn left on Artesia in hopes of finding the San Diego freeway. Neither of us was entirely sure where to find the freeway, but fairly certain that an entrance must be found, since Artesia was a major boulevard likely to have a freeway entrance.

I told Leslie that once we got on the freeway, even if we didn't catch up with the procession, I would remember the directions the funeral director had given us. Leslie, in blubbering certainty, wanted only to go the way she knew, straight down Sepulveda. That would take longer, I argued. And backtracking to Marine, where we knew the freeway entrance, was out of the question. We would lose more time that way. Leslie was in no condition to put up a fight, so she gave in to me.

Once we'd turned onto Artesia, I changed the subject, trying to put our near-argument behind us. "What did you think of that woman?" I asked.

"What woman?"

"Bonnie Oglesby's mother."

"Agnes?"

"Yes."

Leslie grabbed at the wad of damp tissues on her lap and blew her nose. I'd been holding the box, feeding her tissues one by one, hoping not to distract her from the road. By all appearances, I should have been the one to drive. I was the composed and rational one, that chignon-headed person, not a hair out of place. But I felt more comfortable sitting in the passenger seat, letting my older sister act out her distress from behind the wheel as I issued directions, pretending to know better.

"Little Bonnie was always such a kick, wasn't she?" Leslie was smiling through her tears. I smiled too, remembering those silent home movies and the tick-tick-tick of the projector, three little girls jumping in the blow-up pool at the house on Keystone Avenue, Bonnie running wet up to Dad behind the camera until she was no more than a giant, distorted nose. Mom was in the same movie, wearing a Marilyn Monroe bathing suit. Back when we were a family.

"But what about her mother?" I asked.

"What do you mean, *her mother?*" Leslie glanced sideways. "A lovely woman."

I ignored the accusation in her tone and thought of Agnes, one of the few who hadn't been a co-worker. She walked up to me in the receiving line and enclosed my hand in both of hers. Warm, caring hands, like the family physician. "Do you remember me?" she asked. "But of course, you couldn't. My name is Agnes Oglesby, and this is my husband, Jack." The husband at her side quietly nodded and said nothing. "I last saw you when you were six years old! You and Leslie used to play with my daughter Bonnie."

I didn't remember immediately. Her hands closed in tighter around mine, and I was drawn into her eyes, not allowed to escape. She was very attractive, younger than her age, which must have been at least seventy. Her eyes were a sparkling agate-brown, her hair silver but youthful in its consistency and texture. Her smile inspired trust. It was then I remembered her, or more accurately, remembered the feeling of being with her, that pretty and nice mommy next door.

"How is your mother?" she asked, pulling her eyes away from mine briefly to search the room, as if expecting to see my mother standing nearby in a gingham apron, tin of muffins in pot-holdered hand.

I found no need to make excuses for a proper absence, now, thirty years after the divorce. "Mom is doing great, thank you."

"Will you send her my greetings?"

"Yes, I certainly will."

"Perhaps you could give her my address and phone number? It would be so lovely to get back in touch!"

"Well, sure…"

"I have such fond memories of that time on Keystone Avenue! What a wonderful family you had. And your father… Yes, your father!" She seemed momentarily at a loss. "Of course, I haven't seen him now for, what has it been? Forty-some years since your family moved, and then we moved, and then, oh, how the years go by! I was so sad to hear of his death. And what a tragedy! You must be grieving terribly."

Her hands were still on mine. She had felt it to be a tragedy. Or perhaps she'd seen it deep within me. I attempted a smile that came out more as a grimace, my lips trembling. I wondered if the tremor was noticeable. Jack gave his own small nod, and then I became aware of the other people on my right, all lined up, politely waiting their turn. Leslie, on my left, had finished talking with the person ahead of Agnes and had turned toward us.

Agnes removed one of her hands from mine and grasped one of Leslie's, giving her a long, deep look. "Agnes Oglesby," she said to Leslie, who seemed immediately to know her. Agnes stood between the two of us, holding our hands, her arms outstretched on either side like Jesus. "I'm blocking the line here. Maybe we can talk later?" Not a question. *We will not allow these people to stand in our way.* "I have something I want to give you two." She glanced at Leslie and me in turn, gave another warm squeeze, and walked on. Her husband silently heeled.

The building almost wasn't a building at all, designed with

many large open holes in the ceiling to let in the elements, light, air, rain, night. Heavy wooden doors were kept wide open during daylight hours. The floors were cement, the walls made of marble squares, stacked five high, each removable to slide a coffin inside and close it back up again. Soothing music was piped in from nowhere, mixing with the faintest random melody of the wind chimes that mourners had draped on shrubs and trees near the front entrance.

"Your father will get this kind of plaque with his name and the dates," said the mausoleum director, standing next to the proposed crypt, a nameless slab of stone thigh-high, second row from the bottom. He held out a sample plaque, detached, unanchored: "1929 - Joseph M. Quaid - 2001." Not a John Doe. Was he selling us a rejected crypt, the remnant of a failed transaction with the Quaid family? The man wasn't the hushed sort I'd expected, but smiled like a camp counselor, ready to check a new scout into his bunk.

Somewhere, on the way to the elusive freeway entrance, I told Leslie to turn back. Before that point, for the longest while, I denied my mistake, continuing to pretend that time stood still. The traffic was thick around us, a mirage of metal, exhaust fumes, glare, sunglasses, convertible tops, suntans.

"What do you suppose she wants to give us?" I insisted.

"Who knows. Some little memento."

"What kind of memento could she have?"

"Oh, who knows? Some little thing. A snapshot, or a

pressed flower from the garden at Keystone."

"A pressed flower?" Leslie was out of her mind, hallucinating. "How about a rock from the driveway?"

"Or one of our hoppy taws from hopscotch." Leslie was actually starting to smile. "Maybe we left that bald Raggedy Ann doll in the backyard when we moved. Agnes had it all these years."

"She *would* be the type."

"No, I know!" Leslie nearly shouted. "A message from Bonnie in our secret code. Remember that?"

"How do we even know if Bonnie's still alive?"

Leslie shot me a startled look. "Why wouldn't she be alive? She's our age."

"I don't know. So many people seem to be dead."

"Oh, *where* is it?" Leslie blurted. "Daddy will be gone by the time we get there!"

"He's already gone. I'm sorry, Dad." I looked heavenward and down to earth again. "They'll just have to wait for us. It has to be up here somewhere."

"But the freeway isn't this far up on Marine."

"I thought it was a little odd, though."

"It *is* odd. Eight lanes of freeway have disappeared."

"I'm talking about Agnes. This was forty-two years ago. Little kids who played with her daughter. Why would she want to give us something?"

"Because she's a lovely woman, that's why. She's a lovely, *lovely* woman."

I fell silent, fighting the guilt. "She *is* a lovely woman." We had stopped several cars back from a red light, and something caught my eye. In the car next to ours sat a boy and a girl, no more than teenagers, laughing out of control, their mouths wide open. A black car, windows closed, the boy's wrist hanging on the wheel. Their laughter was silent, their radio emitting a steady, pulsing vibration, deep and visceral. I watched them laughing, then talking, then laughing again.

I awoke with a flutter in my chest and a desperate urge to move. "We'd better turn back. You were right, Les. Go back to Sepulveda."

Leslie eyed me sideways and scooped up a bedraggled tissue before I could hand her another. After blowing loudly, the traffic cleared, and she edged into the left turn lane. "Is a U-turn allowed here?"

"I don't know," I said. "I don't know anything anymore." I pulled a tissue out of the box, pressed it to my nose and examined it for the evidence of my grief. Bone dry.

They hadn't waited at all. My small rush of anger was quickly overcome with shame. We tiptoed up, swallowing our quickened breath, afraid to be seen. Inexcusable to be late, but how could anyone be late when there was never an agreed-upon beginning or end?

Their backs were to us, a group smaller by half than the crowd at the funeral home, standing in a cluster near the coffin. They should have waited for the daughters. They should have manufactured their own excuses for us. Hadn't they noticed?

A few people in the back turned around. Sheepish, they attempted to make room, gently pushing us forward in the pack, closer to the coffin. I wanted to scream at them to stop, to turn around again, to ignore us. Only a few words remained, unintelligible, appropriate sorts of things about dust and eternal life, the pastor's mild voice unable to break through my internal din.

Afterward, the rest of them turned and saw us. The pastor was the first to come up and shake our hands. He said nothing about our tardiness. Hadn't he noticed? He smiled and soothed, we thanked. Most of the others, seeing him with us, didn't stop, just nodded kindly and drifted on. They'd all said what they had to say at the funeral home.

Except Agnes. Over the pastor's shoulder, I saw her standing with Jack, very close to the coffin. Her head lowered, she rested her hand on the wood surface and paused long enough to say a prayer before turning around, just as the pastor walked off. Our eyes locked, but I fought her pull and disengaged, walking up to my family instead.

Silvia, looking worn out, was standing with the support of her husband and son, on either side. "What happened to you two? I'm so sorry!" she whispered. I looked into her eyes and saw confusion. My father was her baby brother, the last of her siblings. She wasn't to blame for anything. "We waited for a while, and then they just started. I looked around but you weren't here. I should have said something…"

"No, *I* should have," said Bill.

"No," Leslie shook her head, "it was *our* fault. It wasn't up to you." She steered the conversation toward other things, and we arranged to meet at the house later.

They were barely gone when suddenly Agnes appeared, Jack no longer in sight. In fact, everyone was gone. Leslie seemed on the verge of crumbling again, but Agnes extended her arms to me first, as if I were the one suffering most. Her embrace was entirely too close. I felt her breasts pressing into mine and knew the soft texture of her cheek, the perfume on her neck. Her ponderous handbag, hanging from a forearm, bulged into the small of my back. But I lingered, didn't push away, allowing it. She was our mother, our savior. She would tell us how to grieve.

Leslie received a hug of her own.

"Were you detained?" she asked.

"We got turned around."

"I'm very sorry. Maybe you'd like to have a few moments with your father?" She looked at us individually with those bright, agate eyes, and gestured toward the coffin. I turned toward it. Resting on a waist-high platform, the coffin was a deep mahogany with burnished steel trim around the lid and on the handles for the pall bearers. Yes, there had been pall bearers! But we had missed that. The lid was half covered with a trumpeting flower arrangement in red, white, and yellow. The red assaulted my eyes, all the moisture sucked away.

"Go on," she said. "I'll wait."

Leslie and I looked at each other, guessing at the appropriate ritual. We walked up to the coffin, and I placed my fingertips on its gleaming surface, trying to be alone with Dad. All I felt was the cool varnish and Agnes at my back within the swell of music, the chimes. Leslie kissed her fingers, pressed them to the wood, and closed her eyes. I wondered if Agnes knew I hadn't closed my eyes, if she could see through my back with the kind of intensity I felt in knowing her presence.

We turned around to face her, the coffin behind us.

"Hard to believe," she said in a hushed voice.

Leslie dabbed at her eyes and nose. "Yes," I said for her.

"This must be very difficult for you," said Agnes, looking only at me. She touched my arm. I may have nodded but said nothing.

Agnes quickly brightened. "It's wonderful to see what beautiful women you've become! I'm sure your father was very proud of you. I have something I'd like to give you, a little remembrance of that time." Leslie and I looked at one another while she fished inside her handbag. The snapshot, the flower, the rock? The coded message? Raggedy Ann could fit in that purse. Instead, Agnes pulled out three plastic-covered album pages. "I made these up for you," she said, handing two of them to us, holding onto the third.

I studied the offering. Not one, but four black-and-white snapshots from the '50s, glued under the plastic cover. Children in party hats, at the beach, riding tricycles, wearing Mickey Mouse ears, an odd parent here and there in the background. Each photo labeled by hand with date and event. In the lower right corner, a printed label with the Santa Monica address and telephone number of Agnes and Jack Oglesby. I glanced at Leslie's page. Identical.

Leslie's face lit up with delight. "How nice of you, Agnes! Thank you so much! That's Bonnie?" she pointed.

Agnes nodded.

"I've never seen these. Mom has a few like them, but

they're different."

"Oh, I'm sure she took plenty of pictures with her own camera. We were all such proud parents you know!"

"Well, thank you for making these copies."

I looked at the page Agnes was holding. "This certainly took some effort," I said.

"I made this one for your mother. If you'll give me her address, I could send it to her?"

I held out my hand. "Don't worry, I'd be happy to send it along."

"Of course, that would be best." Agnes relinquished it. "You deserve to have some small reminders of those happy days." She looked past our shoulders, behind us, and asked with a cheerful, everyday voice, "Perhaps you'd like me to take some pictures of you here, with your father?" She nodded toward the coffin and searched the contents of her purse. "I did bring my camera." With a pleased look, she pulled it out.

Disbelief slammed into me. Agnes remained fixed before us, bright and eager, camera in hand. I turned to Leslie for help but saw an expression that couldn't have been unlike my own. She opened her mouth as if to speak; nothing came out.

Agnes looked at us, one then the other. "Think about it a minute," she coaxed. "You never know, maybe someday you'll want a picture."

"Yes, maybe now it's hard to know," said Leslie.

"Exactly," agreed Agnes, turning to me.

"Well, it would be nice to have a picture of just me and Leslie..."

"That's right! The two of you probably don't get to

see each other very often, do you?"

"We make an effort," I said, and jumped into an explanation of logistics and vacation schedules, anything to avoid this unpleasantness. Agnes remained attentive, seeming to forget the camera in her hand, although she did not put it away.

"So wonderful that you have each other! Bonnie will be pleased to hear that I saw you! She lives in Colorado now, you know. She's a clinical psychiatrist and has a son and a daughter. Sandy, she's eighteen, and Matthew, fourteen. Wait a minute." Camera still in her left hand, bag hanging from left forearm, Agnes thrust her right hand into the bag and removed a small, square leather folder. "Here they are." One-handed, she slid a thumb inside the folder and opened it, displaying the contents: a professionally posed and air-brushed photograph of her daughter with the two adolescent children nestled on either side, a close group. "Do you have any children?" She looked at us expectantly, blinking, smiling. She *was* a very lovely woman.

We soon became chatty, anxious to forgive her transgression. I nearly forgot where we were. She asked and we gave her all the details of our lives, our children, their ages, their school careers and hobbies. She insisted on seeing pictures. Leslie had some outdated high school photos in her wallet. I had none.

"What a shame."

"Yes, well, I used to carry pictures of them."

"But no longer?"

"As they get older, you know how it is…"

Agnes stared, blinked, smiled. Placed a warm hand

on my elbow and nodded. "Yes, perhaps you can show me next time we see each other. Let's keep in touch, shall we? You have my address, and now, your mother does too," with a nod toward the two album pages in my hand, "and I'll need your addresses to send these pictures. I know that sometime down the road you'll want them." Without more, she took a few brisk steps to the crypt, where a velvet curtain neatly concealed the emptiness. Propped on the floor beneath it was the marble square, now displaying my father's name, cradled by the dates of his birth and death. Agnes aimed and shot.

I grabbed Leslie's arm and turned away, had to catch my breath. There, down a long wall of crypts, stood three men wearing identical blue jumpsuits. How long had they been there? I smiled, and they smiled back, politely inconvenienced, their purpose as obvious as if they'd been carrying shovels. Meanwhile, Agnes had stepped away from the wall and was centering her viewfinder on the coffin. I tugged at Leslie, and we stepped out of the way a moment before she snapped. These jobs done, Agnes looked up at us and said, "Now, how about the sisters together?"

There was no getting out of it. "The lighting is best over there, Agnes." I pointed to a spot of blank wall a few feet beyond the coffin. No crypts, no plaques. We put our backs to the wall, Leslie, puffy and red eyed, placing an arm around her carefully combed and made-up sister. "All right, you two," said Agnes cheerfully from behind the lens. Apparently dissatisfied, she took a step backward and walked around behind the coffin. Still, she aimed over it, centering the lens on us. "Smile!"

Automatically, I complied with a frozen smile as Agnes, in the final moment, took a step back and tilted the camera slightly downward to include the coffin. I heard the click.

Outside, Jack was pulled up at curbside, sitting behind the wheel, patiently waiting, looking as though he'd done this kind of waiting many, many times before. We said our parting words, including the inevitable sharing of addresses. With final hugs, Agnes got into the car beside her husband and was gone.

I turned to Leslie. All her tears had dried. "What a nice person!" she said.

"Yes, she certainly meant well. Les, can you wait here a minute? I think I left something inside. I'll be right back." My excuse was transparent, but Leslie cooperated nicely. I handed her the two album pages and turned around.

Inside, the mausoleum was cool, airy and light, filled with music and the smell of rotting flowers. The coffin was gone. The men were gone.

I dropped to my knees before my father's stone with its shiny brass plaque, now in place on the wall of squares. *Perhaps you'd like some pictures here, with your father?* But Dad was gone. Images of him and the sound of his voice swirled in my head, making my chest hurt. I'd held it all in and would keep holding it in, fighting the eruption that would surely come, one day.

Agnes had looked deep enough to recognize the emotion, and so, maybe she could be forgiven. But her cold lens, I knew, had failed to record the proof.

☾ *Schizophrenia Indicated*

NOT ENOUGH THAT Lou's death benefits were dis-appointingly small and that Annie was forced to move into the shack (a "cottage" to the real estate lady). On top of it all, Bernie had reappeared, adding a heap of troubles when she was trying to settle into her new life, just the two of them, Annie and Melissa.

No one understood the problem it seemed, everyone giving Annie that funny little look when she told them about it. Even her mother. Especially her mother. Annie's Mom was the expert with granite opinions etched from years of experience, the same experience Annie was going through, left alone before it was natural.

One morning, Mom drove from across town, and they drank coffee in Annie's small kitchen. "Melissa has an imaginary friend?" The eyebrows. The look.

"Yes," said Annie, instantly regretting she'd told.

"The girl is eleven."

"Not yet, Mom. Still ten."

"Almost eleven and she has an imaginary friend. Bernie." Nose and brow wrinkled like smelling turned meat.

"But you remember Bernie. From when she was four. Three and a half or four."

"That was four. Now she's eleven. It's not normal, Annie. It's definitely not normal."

"She's just lost her father."

"It's been a year—"

"Only ten months. Ten and a half."

"—almost a year, and you know, you kids didn't suffer that long. Kids get over these things fast."

Annie understood the unspoken thought, something Mom had said only in gesture and mood when Annie was twelve, after her father died. Grieving had been like spring cleaning, overwhelming and impossible at first, then yielding to a peaceful, bright emptiness once the dirty coveralls and hardhat were whisked away. Annie, too, suspected the same about herself, not wanting to believe it even as she packed away Lou's things, his utility belt with screwdrivers, hammers and nails, storing it all, then acknowledging with a sigh of relief that her new house wouldn't hold the extra boxes. Now, her shack was quiet in the evenings with gentle, feminine sounds.

"But Jane and I had each other. Melissa has no one."

Mom's head turned away and she kept her hands busy with the spoon, sugar bowl, and coffee cup. "Yes, well, what a shame you didn't have more than one child. Now it's too late, of course. But don't let Melissa fill her life with these imaginary friends. It's not normal."

Not normal. Always an opinion about the problem, never a suggestion how to fix it. What did Annie know about these things? Maybe everything would be normal if she pretended as much.

But she couldn't very well ignore Bernie once he became her daughter's faithful companion. Melissa's face, with its pale, sunken cheeks and blotchy freckles, would brighten only when her sliver of a mouth formed that name: "Bernie." There would be a delicate meeting of upper and lower lips around the letter "B," a gentle parting, and a stretch into a dimpled smile with the extended "e-e-e." That smile caused such ripping joy against alarm that Annie wavered between acting and not acting.

Surely, she must do something about Melissa's imagination, but the girl was so happy. Her smiles were the assurance that Annie hadn't made a fatal mistake by moving them back to her hometown in Ohio, fifteen minutes away from Mom, a new school for Melissa. The girl was adjusting, even if it was Bernie who'd helped the settling in. "Bernie was at school today," Melissa told Annie one afternoon.

"Oh?" replied Annie with deliberate nonchalance, unpacking Melissa's school bag. A note about next week's PTA meeting, two sheets of math homework, lunch sack with half-eaten banana. "Did he sit in the desk next to yours?"

"Oh, no." Melissa shook her head. "He never comes inside the school."

"Never?"

"No. Sometimes he's outside. Today he walked home with me part way."

"That's nice, honey. But what happened to Sara? Don't you like to walk home with her?"

"She goes with Patty most of the time now." There

was hurt in Melissa's voice, signifying one of those childhood rejections that loom so large.

"So. Now you have Bernie," said Annie, almost with relief. An old, reliable friend to replace the fickle new one. Instantly she regretted saying it. Encouraging this imagination, an abnormal imagination? But Melissa seemed whole, finally happy after many months of sullenness and withdrawal.

The girl's relationship with Lou had been a jagged graph of exultant highs and crashing disappointments, his death the ultimate low. Her invincible daddy, lowered into the ground. He had loved her fiercely, no question, even with his absences and broken promises. Then came the tragedy, the accident, Melissa still so young—all of it had affected the girl hard, and now, finally she was smiling.

Still, Annie worried that Melissa's way of coping might not be right. She called Dr. Bloom, Melissa's first pediatrician until she was two—a time when they still had health insurance, before Lou moved them out of state. All those doctor visits, three or four times a year, must have created their own insurance policy of sorts, still good for a phone conference at least.

The good doctor returned her call, took a moment to remember her, probably didn't, then listened to her problem. "I wouldn't be alarmed," he advised in a pediatrician tone that simultaneously evoked and quelled panic. "Children have been manufacturing imaginary playmates since the beginning of time. Does the friend have a name?"

"Bernie."

"Bernie." A pause. Annie imagined the look. "And is it an animal friend, or another child?"

"Child. I think."

"You're not sure?"

"I never asked. I just assumed it was a little boy. You see, she had the same friend when she was four. She would talk to him when she was playing by herself."

"Very normal. And she does the same thing now?"

Annie thought. "Not exactly. She tells me a little about him, what he does and so forth. He plays ball with her. They talk. He helped her when she fell off her bike, kissed her scraped knee. That kind of thing."

Dr. Bloom didn't respond.

"That kind of thing. You know," said Annie.

Dr. Bloom was silent for a time that seemed too long, then began to talk very quickly. He was in a hurry, another call maybe, a patient waiting, a sixth sense that Annie was uninsured and trying to take advantage, any one of a number of things that could easily explain the abrupt end to his chattiness, all manufactured from the start for all she knew. He gave her the name and number of another doctor she should consult, then wished her luck.

"Thank you, Doctor," said Annie, thinking she needed it. Luck.

Maybe her luck would have been different had she married Scott. Lately, thoughts like this were popping into her head, now, twelve years later, Annie barely thirty with a child of eleven—no, still ten. While Lou was alive, not once did she think of Scott—well, maybe there'd been a time or two just after her marriage, but not after

Lou had moved them to Idaho. So, why now? Was it just loneliness? A lack of available fantasies?

This neighborhood of dusty, weedy-patched "cottages" held no visible single men. She'd seen only one possibility—no, heavens no, an impossibility—scratching his dark-stubbled chin, a popped-out, fleshy button visible between worn T-shirt and sagging trousers. She'd waved when he came out of his shack across the street. He looked up, pretended not to see, picked up his paper, and went back inside.

The "what if's" cropped up big after that episode, driving her crazy with regret. Things might have turned out better, but no, how could they possibly? How much better off would she be now had she, at eighteen, married a twenty-year-old grocery store bagger, a man with no further ambition? A happy man with soft arms and a wet, gummy smile too big for his face? His love indestructible, sticking like melted taffy, something she couldn't deflect, even with her indecision and ultimate disloyalty.

Annie remembered one conversation.

"You've made a good start," Mom told Scott, forcing encouragement into her voice. Annie sat next to her beau on the plaid couch, her knees glued together. "Bagging. Then you can go on to check-out, and from there, maybe management."

Scott's face stretched to the limits with one of his smiles and he said, "No, I don't want to do check-out or managing."

Mom's eyebrows raised.

"I'm a really good bagger," he explained. "I guess I was born with it in my fingers. I can't just throw that away."

"No, I wouldn't want you to do that."

"We need good baggers. Just think how many times your bananas end up underneath a five-pound economy-size can of coffee. How many times?"

"I don't buy those big cans of coffee, but I see what you're saying."

"Your tomatoes under a gallon jug of milk. A fresh loaf of bread flat as a pancake under your six-pack of soda." Scott shook his head.

Mom shook hers in agreement. "These people. They like to destroy your food. You pay for it and five seconds later it's destroyed." More shaking, then her head snapped rigid. "But Scott, you have your future to think of."

"There's always a future in bagging. Any store, I'm in demand."

"You should go down to the A&P," suggested Annie, quietly. Hands on tight knees, eyes left then right, Scott then Mom.

"I don't go to the A&P."

"I know Mom, but just once, you ought to see it. Everyone tries to get in Scott's line. *Everyone.*"

Annie's mother gave her the look—even then she had it—but quickly concealed it and turned a kind eye on Scott. "I don't go to the A&P, Scott, but I see what you're saying. I *do* see what you're saying."

Mom finally turned against Scott, but when Lou started coming around, she wasn't very fond of him either. Maybe marginally happier about Lou with his self-assured swagger and muscles, his ambition to build up his "construction company," which consisted of Lou bossing a shifting club of undependable buddies, reshingling roofs.

Lou was crazy and loud with a devilish attractiveness, and his unexpected attention thrilled Annie, who never thought she'd snag a handsome man. "Average," she would declare in front of the mirror, pushing back fears of dumpy plainness. Lou showed this average girl some good times in the six months they dated—then came the pregnancy, the quick marriage. Scott, drooping mouth and eyes, was broken-hearted. Lou, square-shouldered and defensive, promised diligence. And as much as Lou liked to party, he proved himself a maniacal worker. When he worked, he worked hard, and he liked to let you know about it. He provided. She didn't go without material things. She went without Lou from time to time, but not without anything else.

Now, sometimes she wondered. What would it have been like over the years, to be lowered gently to the bed like a bag of ripe tomatoes instead of hammered to the plank with a nail gun? What had she missed?

The dreams were an impractical filler of vacant time. With Lou gone, Annie had lost two jobs: the billing and bookkeeping for Lou's roofing business, and the extra cleaning and cooking a man requires. At first, she kept busy. The funeral, the financial matters, packing, moving, sewing new curtains. Now, her days were empty, Melissa at school. Nice at first, but the idleness was beginning to wear her out. So easy not to cook, Melissa happy with microwave pizza, an hour at most to clean the shack.

But the money wouldn't last much longer, even after

cutting down on her rent and other expenses. She supposed her experience with Lou's business was good for something. She could get an office job, ask Mom to babysit, and soon after that, Melissa would be old enough to take care of herself when she came home from school. But Annie didn't want to leave the girl alone with Mom right now. This would be the wrong time.

"I can't give you a definite opinion without seeing the child," said Dr. Place, the one Dr. Bloom had recommended. Annie didn't understand all the initials after her name and couldn't read the Latin in the diplomas on the wall behind her blonde bun, but Dr. Place proved the importance of her credentials in her manner and voice, speaking so carefully and slowly that she beckoned wordless thoughts. "Children often play with imaginary friends," said the doctor, leaning back in her chair, elbows on armrests, fingers interlaced, making a church. "They can be quite secretive about it at times. Almost embarrassed."

"Not Melissa."

"Oh? She doesn't mind if you watch her interacting with her friend?"

"No. I mean, I don't exactly watch her."

"Have you seen her talking to him? Perhaps, overheard something from another room?" The two index fingers popped up, making a steeple.

"No, but she tells me later, after she sees him."

"Later. She tells you later." Dr. Place nodded, then lowered her forehead to the tip of the steeple, resting it there, thinking.

Annie heard the whispery ticking of her wristwatch. "Is that...is it unusual?" she asked, breaking the silence.

The doctor's head popped up again. "Not so unusual, I suppose. She'll likely grow out of it, when she's six or seven. Seven at the latest I would hope." The doctor paused, looked into Annie's crestfallen face. "The child is older than seven," she guessed.

"Yes. Almost eleven."

"Well, then I would recommend professional help. Voices and imaginary people—schizophrenia may be indicated, but you shouldn't worry about something like that until I've evaluated her. There are so many different manifestations of illness, many ranges of normalcy too." The doctor leaned forward toward her desk and began flipping through a large appointment calendar. "It's likely just a coping mechanism. The stress of losing her father." She ran the tip of her index finger down one page, onto the next. "Two sessions a week are recommended. Let's see. Are Tuesdays and Fridays good for you? Say, four o'clock?"

Annie hesitated. Tuesdays and Fridays? Of course. They had nothing else planned. "Yes."

"Good. Then I'll put you down for next week, Tuesday."

"Thank you." Annie stood, ready to leave.

"And before then, it's just wise to double check your insurance." Annie gave the doctor a blank look.

"Often coverage is allowed for crisis intervention," explained the doctor. "Not often for maintenance therapy. I can help you with the classification you need."

"All right. How much do you charge? Just so I can

tell the insurance."

"Two hundred dollars a session."

"Good." Annie bobbed her head as she walked to the door, screaming inside. What could she have been thinking, coming here?

She would call back tomorrow, maybe next week. It was too embarrassing to cancel now.

Hand on the door, Annie heard Dr. Place behind her: "Today's consultation was free, Mrs. Schyller."

Annie looked back and saw the fount of understanding behind the therapist's poker face. "Thank you," she said, and stepped outside to freedom.

Annie and Lou were talking again.

"Spring cleaning. That's what you think of me. Thrown out with the trash."

"No, you don't understand, Lou. I miss you. I always loved you."

"Glad I'm gone. Glad I didn't end up in a wheelchair. Ever think of that?"

"Yes, but—"

"Thankful for that, aren't you? On my head. A clean break. No cripple to take care of. Thanking me in my grave—"

"No!"

"I can tell you've thought of it."

"No, but, yes, but…I don't know. I'm still angry. I told you so many times and you never listened. Beer and roofing. They just don't mix."

"Only one for lunch. The sun was hot on my back. The cold beer. Damn, that's a good feeling!"

"You had more than one."

"One or two. What's it matter?"

"A six-pack, maybe," said a new voice. "A six-pack squashing your sandwich and banana. A liquid lunch because they ruined your food."

"Who asked *you*?" bellowed Lou. "We got rid of you. Had to move to Idaho to do it, but we got rid of you."

"I was only looking out for Annie—"

"Looking out for her? She had a man to look out for her."

"A man who left her."

"A man who loved her. I loved Annie and Melissa. I provided for them, Mr. A&P! You don't know anything about that! You can't come close to that!"

Annie said nothing. Could only listen.

"And what's she left with?" accused Lou's rival. "No husband, a leaking roof. Worried about the bills…"

"You couldn't have done any better."

"Careful is better. I loved Annie. I still love her. I love her. I love you, Annie." Big, drooping mouth, still sad, the words sounding like they used to.

"You love her." Mockery and disdain in Lou's voice.

"When you love someone you're careful. So many things are wasted with carelessness. The eggs, the grapes, a life…"

The voices stopped.

Annie looked past her rose-print, handmade curtains, ignored the crooked seam she had tried in vain to conceal, gazed out the kitchen window to the scruffy lawn, broken sidewalk beyond. One hand on the coffee mug, another to wipe away a single tear.

Schizophrenia indicated.

"He's my absolute best, best friend, Mommy. He's the absolute best."

Bernie again.

"He says I'm beautiful and smart, too." Melissa's plain, brown eyes shone copper.

"When did he tell you those things?"

"Just today, at Linda's house when we were outside jump-roping."

Linda, a new friend. At the first glimmer of Melissa's interest in Linda, Annie encouraged the after-school dates, one already at their own shack, today's several blocks away at Linda's somewhat larger single-story.

"Did Bernie say anything to Linda?"

"Oh, sure, you know, 'hi' and all that. He's very polite. But he only said *I* was beautiful and smart. And coordinated."

"Coordinated?"

"Yeah. And he taught us a new rhyme for jump-roping."

"Where was Linda's mom?"

"In the house. I don't know. Let me show you."

Melissa got out her rope and started jumping, keeping beat with a double jump, ending with single red-hots:

Tangerine, melon, honeydew,
Marshmallow, chocolate, two percent too,
Plastic or paper, double if you please,
Extra-strength single, count the saved trees:
One, two, three, four, five, six, seven…

She made it up to fifty-two at red-hot speed before collapsing on the floor, sending them both into fits of giggles.

"The stores in this neighborhood are rotten. Sometimes I wish I was back near you, Mom." On the phone, Annie clutched the receiver hard. "Have you been to the A&P lately?"

"Why do you keep asking me that?"

"But I haven't asked you that—"

"Always the same question."

"—not for years."

"You know I never go to the A&P. Never."

On the day Melissa planned to bring Bernie home, Annie rummaged in the back of a cabinet for her lipstick and spent extra time in front of the mirror, more than customary for meeting an imaginary friend. Melissa's voice was in her head now. "Bernie doesn't want to come over if it's too early. After school really isn't very early, so I don't know why he said that, but he asked me to ask you if it's too early."

"It's a little early, honey. Well, no, it's not too early. Maybe some people would think it's too early."

"Is it or isn't it? He really wants to know, Mommy!"

Annie had assured Melissa then that it wasn't too early—whatever Bernie meant by that—and she should bring him home after school. A Thursday. Now that Annie thought of it, Melissa's encounters with Bernie were usually on Thursdays, and Annie asked her why.

"It's his day off, Mommy. I told you that!" Melissa hadn't, but Annie wasn't about to point it out. She only smiled.

At 3:00, Annie was waiting out front. Melissa usually got home around 3:05, and today she was on time.

They were talking as they rounded the corner and came into view, a half block away. "Bernie" gently patted Melissa's shoulder, lifted his hand and looked up, catching Annie's eye. Their gaze held for the remaining distance as he and Melissa kept an even, steady pace, not rushing, but not slowing down either. Melissa walked straighter than usual, suppressing an explosive smile inside. Bernie was heavier and softer than Annie remembered, the dull hair on his crown thinning.

Just as they reached Annie, her stubble-chinned neighbor emerged from the house across the street. Annie sensed his presence but didn't look at him. Was he holding garden shears, pretending to trim the hedges? She was concentrating hard on Melissa's imaginary friend, making sure her eyes weren't playing tricks.

When they were close, Melissa introduced them. He stood three feet away, his eyes warm and loving, his mouth bursting into a gummy smile, then shrinking with concern. "Melissa said it was okay. Not too early?"

"No, it's okay."

"You look good."

"So do you."

"And Melissa is you all over again."

"Well, thank you. If I could just get that thin!" She laughed nervously.

Melissa looked back and forth between the adults. They said nothing for a while.

"I'm just confused," said Annie, turning to Melissa. "Honey, did you meet Bernie a long time ago, back in Idaho?"

"I don't know. I think so. I always knew you, didn't I, Bernie?"

"Yes. You always knew me," he said.

Annie wrinkled her brow.

"Even in Idaho they need good baggers," he explained. "And teacher's aides too—"

"Melissa's nursery school?"

"Yeah, well, a little, just a part-time thing, an hour here and there, helping them make block towers, reading stories..."

"But after that?"

"I got worried. Lou, you know, Lou would've..."

"Yeah, Lou would've..."

"So, that was why I pulled back, but I stayed close. I wanted to be close. I wanted—" He checked the excitement in his voice, took a deep breath. "It's been a long time."

"Yes, it has. I'm sorry. I never said I was sorry."

"Don't—"

"Maybe we should just go inside and talk."

"But, Mommy," protested Melissa, removing her jump rope from her school bag. "Let's stay out here. Bernie's going to teach me some more rhymes, aren't you Bernie?"

"Yes, I will."

"A little later, honey," said Annie, shooting a look across the street. Her neighbor glanced up and lifted his garden shears in a gesture of acknowledgment. Maybe

Annie looked better today with her flushed cheeks and pink lips, she didn't know. She returned his half-wave with a half-smile, turned to Scott and Melissa and said, "Let's go inside."

"Later. You promise," insisted Melissa.

"Yes, later."

Annie stumbled on the broken concrete. Scott took her arm and steadied her, then released his hold as they continued along the front walk. "A&P has asked me to do check-out. I'm considering it, as long as I can do my own bagging…" They stepped inside, Annie shutting the door behind them.

The neighbor closed up his shears and retreated into his own shack.

☾ Occupational Hazards

"I WISH YOU were dead!"

Blood spurted from Sandra's fingertip. She swiveled around from the sink to see Tyler's muddy backside flash by in a lightning sprint from the kitchen. "Come back here this instant!" she yelled into the empty space, dropping her assailant—the dog food can she'd been washing for the recycle bin. She examined the weapon, a tiny twisted-up tendril of metal where the lid had been imperfectly removed. Any rust or tetanus bacilli visible? She couldn't remember when she'd last had a shot.

While Sandra considered the depth of the cut, four-year-old Denise shuffled in from the playroom, dolly in tow. She spied the bright red splotches on linoleum, her eyes popping wide. "Mommy! Blood! Are you going to die?"

At least one of my children cares, thought Sandra, sticking the finger in her mouth to suck out invading bacteria. "No, sweetheart," she said around the finger. "Come here, Neecy. Give me a hug. I'll be all right." She stooped and reached out with her free arm. The girl took one look, screamed, and ran, hurtling against the refrigerator like a misguided pinball on her way to the door.

Sandra nearly yelled after her second disappearing child but stopped herself, feeling a drip under her bottom lip. She swiped at it and came up with a red streak the length of her thumb.

The day Tyler wished her dead had been coming for weeks, maybe months—these children with their mysterious behaviors, the causes always unknown. She'd seen it building in the yank of his tangled head against her comb and in his defiant "No" or "Nothing" in response to every question.

Yet, his words and the emotion behind them seemed to come out of nowhere. She'd done nothing to deserve his death wish. Standing at the sink, she'd taken a quick look over her shoulder, saw the tracks on the kitchen floor, and made a polite request—with a "please"—that he remove the muddy high tops. "You don't know anything! I WISH YOU WERE DEAD!" Completely unresponsive (or was it "nonresponsive"?), the term she would use in court when objecting to a witness's answer. Her store of knowledge had inexplicably vanished after Neecy's birth in 1993, the year Sandra took a "break" from her law career to stay home with the kids. Tyler must have sensed as much when he declared that she didn't "know anything."

How could a seven-year-old discern a sore spot and rub salt in it? Children possessed uncanny intuition, an irrational intelligence. Still, an explanation for their behavior always existed, something susceptible of rational cause-effect analysis. An occurrence weeks in the past can give rise to a creeping change without any external signs, until one day: sudden impact.

Hadn't Tyler once been just like Denise? Sandra remembered that wide-eyed, pale-faced shock around age three or four—his first realization that life ends in death. And if everyone died, then Mommy surely would. What a comfort, those adorable, teary-eyed, trembling-mouthed expressions of terror at the imagined loss of mother! A nightmare or the sight of a graveyard from the car window used to be enough to arouse his fear. At some point, all that had ended. Now graveyards were "way cool," presumably including all the mommies who lay dead in them.

Sandra Simmons—formerly Sandra Walsh and now "Mrs. Carl Simmons" to some, "Mommy" to others—was not dead or anywhere close to the grave. She would prove it to them. Especially to Tyler. She would possess a new cheerfulness, a transcendent life force that inspired love and emulation.

It was a Tuesday morning, the day after the death wish, day thirty-seven of the trial, Sandra living in a husbandless twilight zone. She got Tyler off to school after their usual screaming match, afterward resolving all the more to act on her new intentions. She and Tyler were creatures of habit, their bad habits born of rotten morning moods and magnetic friction heightened by his dilatory tactics and her shrewish insistence. The shining light of life would not spontaneously beam upon them. It needed a jump start.

She scanned the exercise class schedule at her fitness

club, nixing every wimpish entry: Aquarobics, Lite and Low, Exertone, Low Impact. Her eyes instinctively avoided, then finally settled on the words that had always struck terror in her soul: Cardio Jam followed by Ab Blast. The instructor, Roxana, was the subject of aerobic legend around the club, and Sandra had timidly glimpsed her through the studio door. This morning, she madly desired the jolt that Rox could deliver.

Neecy, contentedly playing at her dollhouse, was in no mood to go and failed to surrender to her mother's cajoling and bribery. After five minutes of useless effort, Sandra scooped up the hysterical child along with several potential car toys, none of which seemed to be "the one," and clamped the girl mightily between the jaws of her booster seat, receiving several kicks to face and arms in the process.

Bending over her daughter, she jiggled the stubborn metal latch on the seat, trying to snap it shut. "Neecy, you're gonna love this!" she bellowed during a long sucking breath between screams. "You get to play in the nursery at the club! You know how you love it!" A Barney sneaker thwacked Sandra's cheekbone as the metal latch snapped down on her bandaged finger. Neecy recoiled from her mother's sharp grimace of pain. Another explosive wail followed.

Counting to ten, Sandra ran back upstairs from the garage and swiped the shopping list off the refrigerator door. She took a single, deep breath in the luxurious quiet, and with a controlled gait, returned to the car where she smiled sweetly at her securely fastened child.

* * *

Rox, paragon of steely muscle, stood moist, brown, and erect in the locker room. On all sides, white November bodies glistened next to her aberrant bronze glow. Spandex and the natural suction of Roxana's gravitational center had glued a carefully crafted outfit to her skin: shocking-pink sports bra with crisscross straps in back, iridescent pink tights, a black thong cleaving granite buttocks, and symmetrically accordioned slouch socks encased in thick-soled aerobic shoes.

Sandra felt slightly daunted under the sag of her own sweat-soaked, oversized T-shirt, realizing she had never dressed alongside one of the fitness instructors after class. Usually, she would be changed and gone before the instructor and post-class groupies descended from the studio. But this time, Sandra remained hunched over on a bench next to her open gym bag, conversing with a fitness club acquaintance of unknown name while her aching body summoned the energy to disrobe, shower, and change.

Gabbing in the locker room was not her usual thing, but the conversation had just sort of happened in response to an inquiry about her bandaged finger. Her explanation naturally had to include the dog food can, which naturally led to Tyler. Her lamentations received a sympathetic hearing from her nameless acquaintance, a cheerfully chubby woman who was squished into and bulging around the edges of her own Rox-like costume. Their conversation continued while Roxana and clingers chattered nearby.

"It just came out of nowhere," Sandra said, determined to remain oblivious to Roxana's presence. "How can a child have such violent thoughts? He's only seven."

Sandra's acquaintance smiled with compassion. "He's seven and just started that? I think mine were younger. They're ten and twelve now." No more than a dozen feet away, Roxana removed her shoes and began to peel from the top down as she exchanged words with admirers on either side. Sandra glanced at Rox but quickly averted her eyes. "So, they did the same thing?" she asked her sympathetic friend.

"Sure they did. Every minute it was 'drop dead, Mom.' It drove me crazy. That's why they do it, you know. They can tell it drives you crazy. But don't worry; it's only a phase."

Across the room, a momentary lull in the conversation allowed a topless Rox to perk up her ears in Sandra's direction. "Yeah," interjected Rox with a throaty laugh, removing the thong, "I'm still waiting for that phase to end. My boys've been telling me to drop dead ever since they could talk. Believe me, it never stops!" She rolled and tugged, squirming out of the tights. "If you think seven is bad, just wait 'til he's in college." How old was Rox anyway? Sandra discreetly looked for the signs of age. "You know those brothers who killed their parents in cold blood? Just got sentenced to life? Melendez, Menendez, something like that. Just wait 'til you read about *me* one of these days."

Off came the socks and Rox straightened up tall before them, wearing nothing but matching pink lipstick, nail polish, and ponytail band. Not a single white section marred her salon tan. She raised a pistol finger, letting a deep laugh tumble from her throat. "One day—bam!

Dead! I'm just waiting for it. Those Menendez guys'll look like nothing next to *my* boys." Giggles and "Oh, Rox!"es from all sides.

Roxana turned around to pick up her towel on the bench, flashing a small rose tattoo on her left buttock. Flinging towel over shoulder, she sauntered toward the shower room, pausing to study the concern on Sandra's brow, and bent nakedly forward to plant a firm hand on Sandra's shoulder. "I'm just kidding, honey. If he came from you, he *has* to be sweet." She strolled out of the room.

"Don't mind Rox," said the chubby one. "She's just like that. You'll get used to it. Are you coming to her class on Friday?"

"Sure, if I can move by then." Sandra shyly turned her back and pulled the T-shirt over her head. She crossed her arms over her chest to hook fingertips (avoiding the bandaged one) under opposite sides of her sports bra and gave a yank, letting out an involuntary cry.

"You okay?" asked her friend.

Sandra clutched a scapula while clamping the T-shirt to her naked chest with the other hand. "I think I just pulled a muscle taking off my bra."

Another compassionate smile. "I've done that. These damn things are so tight." The woman nervously fingered the bottom edges of her bra, searching for the sliver of an opening as she prepared for her own battle.

Stopped at a red light, Sandra dug in her purse for the shopping list and scooped it out onto the passenger seat along with stray coupons, twist-ties, bobby pins, pens, and pennies. She extracted the list and took a quick look, then glanced in the rearview mirror at her little girl in the back seat. Neecy's mood hadn't improved significantly, and Sandra was bracing herself for the worst in the supermarket. She laughed, remembering.

"Why are you laughing?" Neecy asked indignantly.

"I just remembered something." Nothing could be worse than that, she muttered to herself.

"What? Tell me."

"The time all the apples fell down. Do you remember that?"

"Was I four? Or was I one or was I three?" Neecy inventoried a fist of pudgy fingers, minus turned-in thumb. "Or was I two?"

"You were three, I think. Remember? You picked one from the bottom and the whole pile fell down on the floor."

"The whole pile? What pile?"

"The pile of red apples. At the supermarket. They all fell down, remember?"

"No, what? What happened? Tell me!"

"I *am* telling you. All the apples fell. That's what happened."

"Where? You never tell me anything!"

"Don't you remember? All those apples on the floor?"

"I didn't see any apples! You didn't let me see! I wanna see it!"

Neecy's high-decibel yowl followed. There was only one defense. Sandra opened the ash tray where she kept her supply of spongy earplugs. Keeping one hand on the steering wheel and her eyes on the road, she squished and inserted one, then another. Years of experience had made her fingers deft and sure. There: only a muffled piercing scream.

At the next light she glanced again at the shopping list and summoned the contents of her refrigerator before her mind's eye. Enough milk and fruit left for today, and they could do without mustard and hot dog buns. She vowed never to serve hot dogs again. The spongy bread was gumming up their little abdomens and the salt and fat were constricting and clogging their blood vessels, diminishing the oxygen to that developing curl deep within their brains—the center of reason and civility.

On days like these, the last thirty-seven and likely many more to come, her eyes began their customary darting toward the clock around one in the afternoon and again at seven in the evening. Whenever Carl was on trial, these were the times he was most likely to call, if, that is, he had the time to get away. Lunchtime, over a deli sandwich, dinnertime, over Chinese or Italian take-out. But there were times when he had to skip lunch and dinner to interview a witness or gather trial exhibits or do spur-of-the-moment research on some arcane point that Judge Andrews required immediately.

This day, the phone rang.

"Any more outbursts from Tyler?" he asked.

"No, but things weren't exactly cheery this morning getting ready for school. He fights me on everything."

"Just hang in there."

"Can you spend some time with him this weekend?"

Carl sighed deeply. "I doubt it. I'll have breakfast with you, but that's it. The plaintiff's on the stand, and I'll be crossing soon. God, it's bad too. It just looks so bad, the hole in the side of his head where his ear's supposed to be."

"You better just pay up and come home. His expert made a convincing case for design defect, don't you think?"

"It's not so simple. There were warnings on that table saw. I still think the plaintiff hit the release on the blade. I've got to get it out of him on cross. If he was negligent in some way, we split the damages." She fell silent, Carl's words floating past, Neecy chattering with her dolly in the other room.

"Sandra?"

"I'm here. My mind is just plotting new ways to avoid them. Tyler's in school seven hours a day, and Denise is in preschool three mornings. I put her in the nursery so I can exercise, and then there are play groups and lessons. My whole life is about getting rid of them, don't you think?"

"No. You're enriching their lives."

She laughed. "So, it's better that *I* avoid them, rather than a babysitter."

"No, it's better you're there when they need you. But, listen, if you want a change, you can always work again. Ted and Rob still want you back. You know you're better at this than I am."

"Then we can *both* completely ignore them."

It was Carl's turn to be silent. "I'm sorry," she said. "I just miss you."

"I miss you too. Don't worry. This'll be over before you know it."

She always relished Carl's assurances that the partners still wanted her back at the firm now, after four years, but still shuddered at the thought of returning. All that work, late nights, and then the kids and house. Maybe it wasn't impossible. Carl would help of course, and they would hire a babysitter and maid.

Suddenly she felt tired and run down. Aching muscles from aerobics class didn't help. From the back of a deep cabinet, behind stacks of pans and skillets, she hauled out her juice machine, something she had bought during her last health kick, and found three large, wobbly carrots in the fridge. "Come here, Neecy," she called into the playroom.

The girl shuffled into the kitchen. "When is Daddy coming home?"

"You'll see him on Saturday. He's having breakfast with us."

"Is that tomorrow?"

"Saturday is three more days."

"Goody!!! He'll be home for three days!"

"No sweetheart. We have to wait for three days, *then* we'll see him in the morning." The girl's face fell, tears imminent, but Sandra diverted her attention. "Come, sit over here." She placed the girl in a chair at the kitchen table. "Look what I have here! Today we're going to make some carrot juice. Did you know that carrot juice has a lot of vitamins?"

Denise stared at her with wide, puzzled eyes.

"The vitamins are good for your body. There's

calcium, and vitamin C, and lots of vitamin A. That's good for your eyes." She plugged in the machine and turned it on, pushing the carrot with a plunger down through a hole into the whirling grater. Bright orange liquid began to trickle out into a glass.

Neecy covered her ears and screamed, "Aaaaaaa! Too loud!" Sandra didn't hear; she lifted the plunger, wondering if the carrot had gone all the way in. Something rattled. She lowered her head and peered down into the hole, then jumped back, hand over right eye.

"Mommy, Mommy!" yelled Denise, still competing with the noise.

"Wait! Let me turn this off!" Sandra flipped the switch, unmuffling the full force of her daughter's scream.

"Mommy!"

"It's all right." Tears streamed down Sandra's cheeks. "Something hit me." She spied a nub of carrot with her good eye and picked it up. "This piece of carrot…"

Denise stuck her hand in the glass next to the machine and reached up, aiming dripping fingers at her mother's face.

"Neecy! What are you…?"

"Carrot juice. It's good for your eye."

Friday morning, despite aching muscles, throbbing finger, sore scapula, and purple eyebrow (the carrot nub had not, after all, hit her eye directly), she braved Roxana's class once more, and later, undeterred by her most recent mishap, continued with a fresh vegetable juice regimen, graduating to spinach and kale.

That afternoon, Tyler came home from school and lingered in the yard playing with Ranger, their cocker spaniel. Sandra watched him through the kitchen window. Tyler removed Ranger's long leash and teased him with a stick, holding it out of reach before throwing it to the edge of the yard. Ranger loped off in the wrong direction and sniffed around in the flower bed. Sandra counted to ten. She had no reason to be angry; it was November, no flowers for Ranger to destroy. Without bothering to leash the dog again, Tyler bounded into the house, ignoring his after-school job of walking the dog.

Sandra mentally held back the reprimand—for now. Regaining rapport with her son was more important. "Hi, Tyler! How was school?"

"Okay I guess." He opened the pantry door and examined the contents.

"Anything fun happen at school today?"

"Nothing." He pulled out a box of crackers and thrust a fist inside.

Denise came in and walked over to Tyler, reaching for the cracker box. "Let me have some!" She tugged at the box but seemed to give up, backing off. "Yucky! You smell!"

"Do not!"

"Do too!"

"Wait a minute!" Sandra broke in. "I thought I smelled something. Tyler, lift your foot." The boy absently lifted his foot behind him while munching a cracker. "Now, the other one," Sandra directed. "That's it. Take your shoes off." He complied, toes of one foot pushing off heel of the other, then stuffed his hands with crackers, not looking at her while she spoke. "If you would just do your job after school, Ranger wouldn't poop in the backyard. Now go out and clean up all the dog messes."

Tyler pressed past his sister and headed the opposite direction, toward his room. In the doorway he stopped, glared at his mother, and burst into stage laughter. "You don't know anything! How can I go out when you took my shoes!" He turned and fled.

A seven-year-old, laughing *at* his mother.

In a trance, Sandra picked up Denise, placed her in a chair, and piled half a dozen crackers on the table in front of her. "I'll be right back," she said, picking up the shoes and heading for the basement sink where, over putrid fumes and running water, she let the tears flow while the soles were washed clean.

Saturday morning, and then Sunday morning, for two hours each day, they might have been called a family again had the time not been spent in awkward platitudes and uncertain moods, the children unaware of their own feelings. Sandra discerned an uneasy mixture of anger and longing. Nothing was comfortable, Carl's imminent departure for the office looming. When he left, Neecy clung and cried, Tyler wouldn't say goodbye and sulked in a corner.

In theory he was home, had never left them. Every night he slept with her, his spirit wafting through their bedroom in a nightly hallucination. She needed eight hours of sleep while he seemed to get by on only five or six during the trial, and so, despite her efforts to wait up for him, she always fell asleep with the reading light on, a novel somewhere in the bedclothes. Then, like a prince, he would tiptoe up to the bed and kiss her gently—love's first kiss—and she would awaken just enough to grumble a "hello" and assure herself he wasn't an intruder. In the morning, another dream kiss, and he was gone.

Throughout the day she would sense little things, wondering if they were memories or desires: the scratch of his rough cheek at night, his hand on her breast or thigh as they slept, the smell of his shaving cream in the morning. "Mmm," he might have said one night in her half-sleep. "You smell like fresh beets." Real or imagined? Just that day, beets had been her latest experiment in the juicer. But, by the next morning, she could be sure of just one thing: a new bruise in her ribcage where she had rolled over onto the sharp corner of her hardcover book.

Carl called earlier than usual on the evening of day forty-four. Sandra clamped the cordless phone between shoulder and cheek while she talked, stirring a pot of stew on the stove. "Have you ever thought of me as accident prone?" she asked. "Things just keep happening."

"It's a stressful time."

She looked over her shoulder to make sure the children hadn't entered the kitchen. "We have to do something about Tyler. He has absolutely no respect for me. Ow!"

"What happened?"

"Maybe I should use a potholder. Here we go… What's new at the trial?"

"I think the plaintiff is hiding something. He looked

like he was lying on the stand. It's a long shot, but we subpoenaed the kids."

"The kids!"

"There's nothing else to do. We've talked to everyone: his wife, the neighbors, his mother-in-law. Maybe one of his kids saw something and he's hiding it. Before trial he got a protective order and we couldn't depose them, but now things are different. Andrews is going to allow it. One kid is seven and the other's nine."

"Only seven... We have to do something about Tyler."

"Maybe this weekend I could talk to him."

"There won't be time." She laughed, stirring the stew. "Let's just go ahead with the divorce. Then maybe we'll see more of each other. You know, first the meetings with our lawyers, then the court appearances, and then we'll be handing off the children every weekend. 'Hello, Carl. How has life been treating you?'"

He chuckled, then got serious. "You're starting to worry me. They say there's always a core of truth in every joke."

"I'm just kidding."

"Yeah, but I've heard that joke a few too many times lately."

"No, when have I...?"

"You started with that only a couple of weeks into the trial. Enough already. Cut it out."

She heard something behind her and turned, phone still wedged under chin. Tyler stood no more than three feet away. "Tyler!" She swiveled back quickly, dropping the receiver in the pot of stew.

"Oh no! Tyler! Carl! Can you hear me?" she yelled into the pot. "I love you, Carl! I didn't mean it! I love you!"

When she looked behind her again, Tyler was gone.

For the next couple of days, Sandra made attempts to catch Tyler alone and off guard, at a time when he might open up to her. He sensed what she was up to and sulked under her gaze and forced cheeriness, avoiding her entirely whenever he could.

Then one evening, just as mysteriously as it had started, he came to her. Sandra sat in the living room with her arm around Denise, reading her a story. Tyler shuffled in, timidly. Sandra looked up without saying a word.

"Mom?"

"Yes."

"I have to ask you something."

"What is it, Tyler?" Sandra and Denise both looked at him intently as he stood in the doorway. Even Denise seemed to understand that something important was coming, and she remained quiet, very unlike her usual self.

"Who are we going to live with?" he asked.

"I don't understand. What do you mean?"

"You know, me and Neecy. Are we gonna be with you or Dad?" Sandra's heart flip-flopped. She asked him, even without believing her own tone of voice, "You think we're splitting up? Where did you get that idea?"

"You said it to him, a long time ago on the phone. And you said it again. I heard it."

"Yeah, Mommy," Denise said. "Tyler told me. He did. He heard it."

"That's why he doesn't come home." Tyler stomped his foot and took a swing at the air. "You told him not to! I know you did!"

"No, oh no, kids, I can't believe this! It's all a mistake." Sandra looked at them pleadingly, one then the other. "Come here, Tyler. Come sit with us on the couch. We're not splitting up. Honest, we're not."

Tyler lowered his head, trudged to her side and plopped down. She circled his shoulder with her free arm. "I think you heard some things that you misunderstood. Daddy and I joke around sometimes, but we aren't going to break up. We love each other."

Tyler cast a doubtful, sidelong glance at his mother. "You're sure?"

"Yes, I'm sure. Daddy just has a lot of work right now. Don't you remember last year? He had a trial just like this one, and you went to the courtroom one day to watch. That's what he's doing now. That's why he's away so much. But soon it will be over."

A door slammed, and three heads turned. "Hey, where's that family of mine?" bellowed a male voice.

Denise let out a screech. "Daddy, Daddy! In here!"

Carl jogged into the living room, trench coat unbuttoned, tie askew, and dropped his briefcase before falling into a four-person huddle.

"What happened?" asked Sandra once they had unraveled.

"We settled. It was like we suspected. One of them—the younger one—was there, goofing off, and he hit the blade release. The plaintiff is, you know, responsible for his kids." Sandra and Carl exchanged mildly horrified looks over the children's heads, in silent agreement that nothing more explicit should be said. "There's still a design defect, but they were willing to settle because the plaintiff's negligence was the direct cause."

"Can I see it? Can I see it?" spurted Denise, jumping up and down.

"What, honey?"

"The plaint's necklace! I want to see it."

Carl scooped up his daughter, her arms circling his neck, while he pulled his son close to his side and gazed into Sandra's eyes.

————

Dear Reader

As I write the afterword to this updated edition, I'm celebrating a few book birthdays.

A little more than a decade ago, I gathered up all the stories I had written in the '90s and the '00s and arranged them in three volumes by theme: *Everyone But Us, tales of women, Dust of the Universe, tales of family,* and *Malocclusion, tales of misdemeanor.* Since the publication of these collections in 2012-2013, many readers have let me know how much they've enjoyed my stories.

During the same decade, I've published six novels of legal suspense in the Dana Hargrove series. Each one is a stand-alone, finding Dana at a discrete stage of her family life and career. If you enjoy courtroom drama, legal thrillers, mystery, and police procedurals, these novels may be for you, starting with the first one, *Thursday's List.* The sixth, *Power Blind,* releases in January 2022.

Let me know your impressions of my stories by posting a reader review of any length with your online book retailer. You can also drop me a line through the contact page on my website, vskemanis.com, and I'll respond directly. The contact page also has a link to a free e-book offer.

To keep up with the latest on my books and life, find me on Goodreads, YouTube, BookBub, Facebook, Twitter, and Instagram, and subscribe to the blog on my website.

Thanks for reading!

V.S.K.

January 2022

Opus Nine Books

All works published by Opus Nine Books are dedicated
to the nine members of the family headed by John and
Kate Swackhamer at 3 South Trail, Orinda, California—a
large world under one small roof.